don't think of me

Introduction:

Chu Ying and Xu Jisi had a period of ambiguity.That was five years ago.She had just begun to fall in love, and mistook Xu Jisi's pity for concern. She didn't know that he was the proud man of heaven, and the two of them were completely different.It wasn't until later that Xu Ji missed the appointment and left without saying goodbye.When they met again, Chu Ying didn't want to get entangled, but was forced into the situation step by step.

Xu Jisi, the eldest young master of the Xu family, is well-known in the circle as a flower of the high mountains. He is cold and taciturn and not close to women.No one could have imagined that one day the noble and aloof Young Master Xu would become jealous when he saw a girl talking and laughing with other men.On the phone, the message from Chu Ying clearly stated that she was working overtime.Seeing the two chatting happily, Xu Jisi sent a message to someone.The mobile phone on the desktop lit up, and he saw Chu Ying's smile paused, glanced at the screen, and then turned off the phone as if nothing had happened.His fingers suddenly clenched tightly, but there was no emotion on the man's face. He only lowered his head and warned: Come back soon.

After saying goodbye to friends after the party, Chu Ying arrived home and saw that the house was dark.Unexpectedly, as soon as he stepped through the door, he was hugged by someone.The exclamation was suppressed in the throat, and the familiar cold fragrance hit the nose.Under the cool moonlight, through the floor-to-ceiling mirror, Chu Ying saw the man tightening his arms around her slender waist from behind.That night.Xu Jisi's eyes drooped slightly, his breath sprayed on her neck, and his thin lips bit her shoulder. His expression remained calm and composed, but he brushed his fingers through her sweaty hair, and his lingering voice was hoarse and restrained:Yingying, coax me, eh

Chapter 1 RememberMy heart seemed to be tightly clenched by that gaze from a distance.The autumnal equinox has passed.It has been raining continuously in Lizhou for several days, and the weather is colder than in previous years.The sky was darkened by dark clouds outside the window, and I didn't know when it would rain heavily again. The wind suddenly became louder, the howling wind passed through the cracks in the window, and the papers on the table were shaking.Chu Ying moved her eyes away from the script in front of her and looked outside. There were sycamores and ginkgo trees planted on both sides of the building, and the wind blew the branches and leaves swaying.Suddenly, two or three conspicuous black cars drove past this road one after another. The wheels rolled over the yellow leaves on the ground, sweeping up a few fallen leaves and falling slowly again.Chu Ying's eyes flickered slightly, and the car disappeared.Without thinking much, Chu Ying raised her arm to suppress the flying paper and returned it to the script.Five minutes later, a rush of footsteps got closer and closer.Chu Ying's thoughts, immersed in the plot of the script, were called back by a somewhat panicked cry.YingyingLuo Hui put one hand on Chu Ying's shoulder and rested her hand on the table with a hint of anxiety: Someone from the film crew has arrived in advance.Chu Ying was stunned for a moment and didn't come back to her senses: What?Luo Hui pointed to the script on her desk: Someone from the film crew of "Wild Tangzhi" has come, and it's no surprise that they came for your audition.Chu Ying calmed down for a few seconds, then suddenly realized something and opened her eyes: Didn't it say she would come tomorrow?This book just came into her hands last nightWho knows, don't guess what Party A is thinking, Luo Hui complained, and quickly reminded her of business, Brother Yang has already gone down to pick up someone, let me give you a tip. Be mentally prepared in advance, don't be too nervous.After finishing her words, facing Chu Ying's obviously reluctant expression, Luo Hui paused and sighed: I know, this kind of words sounds light, and you will still be nervous when you should be nervous, but no matter which part of the problem caused them Since we came early, we can't just block people back.Just keep your mind at ease. They know you are a newcomer and I believe they won't make things too difficult for you.

Brother Yang said, you just need to perform normally.Chu Ying calmed down her emotions and nodded under Luo Hui's encouraging eyes. Soon, Luo Hui looked down at her phone again and straightened up: Brother Yang said they had entered the elevator, let's go pick them up together.good.Chu Ying responded while taking the script and following Luo Hui, trying to become more familiar with the plot in these few minutes.However, her heart was beating wildly, almost as if it was about to jump out of her chest, making it difficult for her to read another word.Chu Ying took a deep breath and simply closed the script.The script of "Wild Tang Branch" was sent to her last night. She was about to take a rest after washing when she received a call from Ling Tingyang.She had heard of this drama. It became a hot search topic when it was exposed by Reuters some time ago. The male protagonist is top-notch, and the producer is Xinshi. It can be said that it is a popular drama.In the past, she mostly dubbed for radio dramas or animations. It is rare to get the opportunity to dub for a TV series, let alone such a popular drama.What's even more exaggerated is that the one Ling Tingyang asked her to try was the female lead.Before last night, Chu Ying never thought that such a good thing could happen to her.She has almost never been exposed to TV dramas. The closest she has been to film and television dubbing is when she will be dubbed as the heroine of a ten-episode online drama later this year.The two leading actors in that person in charge of the film. People, just about to say hello to people.The next second, someone slowly walked up from the person she thought was the person in charge, blocking the person in charge's view.Chu Ying raised her eyes and saw the man in front of her, who had silver hair and seemed to be about the same age as her.Then, Ling Tingyang pointed at Yinmao and the older man successively: producer Ji Ran, director Stanley HoChu Ying was stunned for a moment.Unexpectedly, Yinmao would be a producer at such a young age.Silver Hair glanced at her casually and was about to nod to say hello.Just a few seconds after he looked away, he suddenly returned to her face again.The two looked at each other. Ji Ran raised his eyebrows at her and suddenly stretched out his hand to her.Chu Ying blinked, not understanding why he suddenly changed his attitude. But since it was Party A, she still had to give her some face. She quickly extended her hand and said generously:Hello, Chu Ying.Ji Ran hummed and glanced at her vaguely: the name is very nice.Chu Ying smiled and said politely: Thank you for the compliment.After a brief acquaintance, Ling Tingyang led everyone to the recording studio.One thing about Chu Ying is that when she is too nervous, her expression shows no emotion at all.Luo Hui followed the crowd, and seeing her respond with ease and without showing any timidity, she almost thought that Chu Ying had adjusted her mentality, and secretly thought that young people nowadays are getting more and more powerful.Ling Tingyang was negotiating with the people in the front, and Chu Ying deliberately slowed down her pace and distanced herself from them.Then the girls from the film crew got closer. They probably didn't need to make any important decisions, so they followed behind and chatted together.They all wore masks. Chu Ying couldn't see their faces clearly, but she could hear the hushed voices of several of them.The handsome guy in the black coat just now, he looks like the male protagonist of a Korean drama. Why didn't he come up with him?The handsome guy in the black coat reacted, paused, and had a complicated look on his face. Are you talking about Mr. Xu? Please stop that look in your eyes. He is not someone you can just imagine.Mr. XuThat little Mr. Xu from Hejing who just returned to China in the past two years. It is said that he has been working in Lanqin's subsidiary before. Didn't you see that he got off Mr. Ji's car when he returned to the Lizhou headquarters this year?Would I not answer my mother's call? When I got off the car, I saw him standing next to me. I thought he was an employee from another department.The girl on the side rolled her eyes when she heard this: Do you think she has the temperament of an employee? With a face like this, why don't you go to the entertainment industry to be exploited by capitalists? You know we have a good relationship with He Jing. Mr. Xu is Mr. Ji's friend. The two of us grew up together.Hiss, and with this background, no wonder I felt the aura of "Keep strangers out" when he raised his eyes just now. I almost wanted to go up and ask for his contact information.Fortunately, you didn't go. Mr. Xu has a bad temper. If you want to catch up with someone, he won't be happy. You don't even know when he will lose his job.The sound of gossip faintly entered her ears. Chu Ying could only catch a few words. Before she could analyze anything in her mind, a large group of people had already arrived at the door of the recording studio.You go to the recording studio first.Ling Tingyang turned to Chu Ying and said.Chu Ying came back to her senses, nodded, tightened her fingers, opened the door and walked into the recording studio.

The main purpose of the film crew's visit this time was to see the voice quality and level of the actor dubbing the heroine.Ling Tingyang is considered a big boss in the industry. He has profound dubbing skills and has dubbed hundreds of TV series and movies. Up to half of them are male protagonists, and he is the dubbing voice of several top-notch queens.Six years ago, he established Lingting Dubbing Studio.At first, he was the only one in the studio who had a relationship with him. The studio was not standardized. Later, under the advice of his seniors, One of them contributed his voice and the other contributed money, and then they registered the current Lingting Sound Entertainment. The first two characters of Lingting's name are also homophones for "listening", which means the beauty of listening to sounds and the beauty of matching sounds.Up to now, Lingting has become a professional and mature dubbing team and a backbone in the dubbing market. Several film and television giants like to cooperate with them.Ling Tingyang's business ability is obvious to all, not to mention that he is the supporting director this time, so the film crew still has great trust in him. As for the people he recommends, he can basically make a decision directly as long as he doesn't make any big mistakes.But Chu Ying didn't know this.After entering the recording studio, her nervousness spread to her limbs again.Chu Ying put on her headphones, and before the instructions came from the control room, she turned on her phone and found some of the actor's past film and television original sound clips, hoping to learn more about the other party's speaking habits and acting style.In the control room opposite, Ji Ran was sitting on the sofa with his legs crossed, and a few girls next to him were sitting one space away from him.Ling Tingyang and Stanley Ho sat in front of the computer, flipping through the script and discussing something.Ji Ran glanced around and stretched out his hand out of boredom. The woman in a blue and black suit next to him handed over the script. He flipped through a few pages and soon felt sleepy and yawned.After a while, Ling Tingyang and Stanley Ho looked at each other, nodded to each other, confirmed the content, and clicked on the audition clip.Page 13, 414, look at the picture a few times first.Ling Tingyang motioned to Chu Ying on the other side through the glass of the observation window: Don't be nervous, just match the image of Xie Zhao you understand.Chu Ying relaxed her breath, nodded, put her phone aside, turned to page 13, and read the lines while looking at the picture.Ji Ran closed the script again at some point, put his fingers on the armrest boredly, and glanced at the screen. After waiting for only two minutes, he started to feel bored.He raised his wrist and looked at his watch. He took out his mobile phone and opened WeChat to send a message.Mr. Xu, where are you?Even if you call me, you won't be able to get through to anyone.As expected, there was no reaction from the other end.Ji Ran raised his eyebrows and stood up suddenly.Ling Tingyang and Stanley Ho in front both turned their heads and looked at them.Ji Ran raised his hand and loosened his tie: It's a bit boring, I'll go out for a while, you can just keep an eye on it.He was just going through the motions, and it would be the same with or without him here.When Ji Ran walked out of the recording studio, the number was dialed.The phone beeped for a few seconds and was connected.What followed was the cold and slightly deeper voice on the other end.Hello.Ji Ran lowered his voice: Where are you from?Wait for the elevator. It was brief over there.OK, I'll pick you up.Ji Ran took several detours before finding the elevator entrance.A superior and tall figure was already leaning against the wall.The elevator entrance was facing away from the light. The man's long legs were slightly bent and his head was bowed. Half of his face was hidden in the darkness. His eyelashes were lowered. He was holding a mobile phone in one hand, and his long and well-jointed fingers were jumping on the screen.Then, Ji Ran's phone vibrated.The air was silent, and subtle sounds quickly attracted the other party's attention.Xu Jisi paused slightly, put the phone back into his pocket, raised his eyelids lightly, and straightened up at the same time.The corners of his windbreaker swayed slightly with his movements. Xu Jisi put his hands in his pockets, walked up to Ji Ran, raised his chin slightly and said, let's go.Ji Ran felt something was wrong.After much deliberation, I couldn't figure out why.He walked in front and led the way, complaining to Xu Jisi as he walked.I didn't even want to go there. It was stuffy and boring inside. It was really boring.Xu Jisi's voice was cold: Then why don't you bring me here?If you are free today, just do your brother a favor, Ji Ran said in a matter-of-fact tone, otherwise I will have to come alone tomorrow.Do you think you are still fifteen?Ji Ran choked for a moment and complained in a tone of voice: "Isn't this an early death and early birth? I should have run away earlier. I won't be too lazy to come later." It's all my fault that the old man sent people to keep an eye on me. I can't even pretend to be fake. You're more credible when you're by my side.After talking to this point, he was probably feeling irritated. Ji Ran lightly clicked his tongue and said, "Don't talk about these annoying things."Just as he walked to the door of the recording studio, Ji Ran put his hand on the doorknob. Just as he was about to open the door, he suddenly thought of something. He took his hand back and turned around, his expression finally showing a hint of interest.But today is not in vain. I watched the dubbing of the heroine just now. She is so beautiful. It would be a pity not to become an actress.Ji Ran spoke with great interest, and then walked around to Xu Jisi's side, talking to himself.The name is also nice. My name is Chu Ying. When I hear the name, I feel like Chu Chu is lovely.Ji Ran didn't notice that the person next to him, who had always been uninterested and had a dull expression, suddenly stopped and his expression changed slightly the moment he mentioned the name.He also analyzed interestingly:The name Ying is also well-known. It makes people think of "Yingying spring water". Don't tell me, this person gives me the same feeling.After talking for a long time and not hearing any response, Ji Ran suddenly stopped talking and turned around to see what Xu Jisi was doing.I saw the man slowly moving his Adam's apple.I don't know if it's an illusion or not, but the clear voice seems to have a hint of hoarseness:Tell me, what's her name?The moment the words fell.The door to the recording studio was pushed open from the inside.He's a good prospect. I heard from your boss that you only got this book half a day ago, and he secretly asked me to 'look after' it. I'll take care of your current understanding of the plot and characters, so there's no need for me to 'take care' of it. .Stanley Ho, who has always been serious, actually smiled kindly at this moment: I was worried that I would have to spend a lot of time talking and explaining, but I didn't expect that the old man would let me be so relaxed.As the old man spoke, he suddenly remembered something and asked with a smile: Is your voice combined with the actor's original voice? Based on your appearance, it's not impossible to enter the entertainment industry directly. Little girl, are you interested in becoming an actor?Ling Tingyang also laughed: Why would Director blatantly come to my place to poach people?I'm not kidding. Old man, I was born as a voice actor before. I have done everything for decades. I still have some qualifications. The little girl can learn a lot from me.The voices of people talking and laughing rang in my ears.But everything becomes background.Only a soft voice hit my ears.His voice was not loud, and there was humility in his joking reply:Director He is overrated. They say it takes ten years to sharpen a sword. Even in dubbing, I still have a lot of room to learn, so I won't come to complain to you.Xu Jisi stood motionless.His eyes slowly fell on the owner of the voice.at the same time.Chu Ying suddenly raised her eyes as if she noticed someone's gaze.The moment their eyes met.The world seemed to be frozen, and even the sound suddenly stopped.The man was tall and tall, wearing a loose black woolen coat. He stood upright with one hand in his pocket. He didn't say a word, he just stood there, exuding a strong yet distant aura of aloofness.The man's Adam's apple bulged slightly on his cold white neck, and his deep pupils passed through the crowd and glanced into her eyes clearly.The noise around me seemed to be in another world, and the familiar facial features were so far away that they seemed like brief thoughts left over from the encounter in the previous life.Chu Ying couldn't hear anything.It just felt like my heart was tightly clenched by that gaze from a distance.There is no escape, no avoidance.

Chapter 2 RememberJust like the first time we met02The twilight is shallow in the sky.Sunsets always come earlier in autumn.The company is located in the Cultural and Creative Park, with a commercial street outside. The surrounding area is bustling with pedestrians, and even a noodle shop two streets away is packed with guests.There are constant whispers in the noodle shop, and occasionally there is the sound of tables and chairs being moved. From time to time, there are also calls from customers and greetings from the boss.Luo Hui's voice was also among them.Your on-the-spot performance is too strongLuo Hui's eyebrows were beaming, as if she was the one trying out the voice, and her tone was excited, but she still lowered her voice because she was in a public place:The director seems to be very satisfied with you. I even heard him complimenting the people next to you on how beautiful you are and how talented you are.When he raised his eyes while speaking, he saw that Chu Ying was just looking down at her bowl, stirring the noodles as if she was in a fugue.Luo Hui paused and called tentatively into her ear: Yingying, YingyingChu Ying regained consciousness, raised her eyes and saw Luo Hui's worried expression.Yingying, you haven't been in the right state since just now. Are you not feeling well?Chu Ying's fingers curled up slightly under her sleeves, and she quickly curled her lips at her: It's okay, I just didn't react for a while, it felt like a dream.Luo Hui suddenly understood, showed an understanding expression, and nodded:This is true. It is said that it takes three years to find a voice and five years to find a role. People who join our industry start out by recording miscellaneous roles. Most of them have been working in studios for several years without landing a well-known role. I've been on a smooth journey. After three months of running, I found a small role with lines. I also happened to be lucky enough to be spotted by Brother Yang.She fell into reminiscing: I'm a half-match in my major, and I used to do online matching. When Brother Yang said I had talent, I was so excited.Only after you came did I know what the real "God rewards rice" is.Luo Hui changed the subject, with a resentful expression on her face: "You are not a professional, and you have little experience. Three months after you started, Brother Yang asked you to play the second female lead. You don't know how much everyone envies you."You have only been in the industry for two years. Although today is a thrilling day, fortunately, you passed it smoothly and you will be matched with the heroine of the TV series. I am so happy that I am crazy.Chu Ying's dubbing career is indeed going too smoothly.When I was a sophomore, I was dragged by my roommate to sit in on the class of the boy I had a crush on. It happened that Ling Tingyang was invited to give a lecture in the club. After giving some lectures on dubbing techniques, he randomly selected a student to demonstrate. By coincidence, it was Chu. surplus.Chu Ying actually didn't listen much at the time. She just remembered a few key points that Ling Tingyang said and tried to say a line with the emotions she understood.Just that one sentence.She saw Ling Tingyang's eyes light up, and then he signed a contract with the studio inexplicably.It would take an average person several years of hard work to practice or achieve something, but she could do it with ease in two years.What Luo Hui said about God's gift of rice was also Ling Tingyang's exact words.Chu Ying is considered a talented person. Not only is her voice highly recognizable, she also has natural control over her voice. She can switch between two extreme emotions with ease. Even if she needs an instant burst of emotion, she can quickly enter the studio. The role can even be said to be perfectly matched with ease.She has her own unique perception and empathy for each character, and she can always understand the character's emotions and changes just right and shape them naturally. When she dubs, Ling

Tingyang is always very relaxed, and nothing is too common. It requires too much analysis of the drama for her.Just like someone who is born with an absolute sense of pitch, Chu Ying's ability makes her a natural in this profession.Luo Hui sighed and took a sip of noodle soup: But who knows that you really have this capital? The one who can take it.Chu Ying blinked, with a serious expression and a slow voice: Sister Huihui also helped me a lot.She is used to dubbing two-dimensional characters, which is different from dubbing characters in TV series. Especially for anime, the dubbing is always more exaggerated. When she was familiar with the lines in the morning, Luo Hui watched her for a long time and asked her a lot of customary questions. It was difficult for her to realize them in a short time. of.Without Luo Hui's reminder at that time, today's audition would never have gone so smoothly.After hearing what she said, Luo Hui waved her hand: It's only a matter of time before you realize these problems. I am your senior after all, so this little busyness is nothing.She narrowed her eyes and smiled at Chu Ying: "Thank you very much. This meal is yours."Without any hesitation, Chu Ying nodded: What kind of drink would Sister Huihui want?Luo Hui knew she had to make her feel good, so she didn't refuse: Then bring me a Coke.Chu Ying got up in response and came back with the Coke. Luo Hui was holding up her mobile phone to take pictures of the two bowls.Seeing her back from the corner of her eye, Luo Hui clicked send, looked up at her, and complained softly:Don't you know that Brother Yang and the others have a table full of delicacies from all over the world? Look at us, we can only eat this clear soup with little water.Wait, before she finished envying her, Luo Hui suddenly remembered something. You can obviously go with them, why don't you go?The curve of the corners of Chu Ying's lips suddenly froze.Something suddenly came over me.She has been too busy in the past two years, and she has not thought of him for a long, long time.It was so long that she felt as if even her memory had to dust away that person's name and appearance for her.But the fact is that when that figure appeared in her mind without warning, her breath was suffocated.Familiar and unfamiliar faces reappeared in my mind, and the moment they looked at each other seemed to travel back to some autumn.Years have passed, and the youthful face of the young man deep in my memory has long faded, and his facial features have become more mature and profound.She had thought of Xu Jisi countless times in a moment of trance.In the harsh winter days filled with pungent disinfectant, in the quiet late nights when I finish the last test paper, in the rainy nights when the thunder is loud and the fever persists.Sometimes she would suspect that the young man with cold eyebrows was just a dream she had.But at this moment, the dream she thought appeared in front of her unexpectedly.He stood by the door, his loose woolen coat slightly open, revealing the dark turtleneck sweater underneath. He had a tall, tall figure with broad shoulders and a narrow waist, standing tall and tall.Dark eyes, high bridge of nose, neat and smooth jawline.The cold young man from before seemed to reappear in front of him, and gradually overlapped with the noble and noble man in front of him.Xu Jisi stood less than half a meter away from her. After looking at each other for a moment, he looked away calmly.Someone took the initiative to introduce the people in front of him. His eyes met Ling Tingyang, and then fell on her.His eyelashes were slightly lowered, as if he was just listening to something carelessly, making it impossible to see the emotions in his eyes.As cold and distant as when they first met.The moment this realization flashed through, Chu Ying tightened her fingers.The wind blowing through the cracks in the window was as biting as bone-chilling, almost turning into a sharp knife and piercing into the heart. Afterwards, I felt dense pain.She couldn't remember exactly what happened afterwards.I just remember that when I came back to my senses, I heard Ji Ran enthusiastically make a suggestion from one side: Now that it's confirmed, let's go have a nice meal together.He waved his hand: I'm treating youSo the polite words coming and going between you and me rang in my ears again.Chu Ying finally moved her fingers, and suddenly her fingertips felt cold, and even her arms were a little numb.Everyone was laughing and talking, and Ji Ran finally decided on his destination and turned to Xu Jisi for advice.The man raised his eyes with a dull expression and nodded slightly.His gaze inadvertently glanced at her face again.Oxygen is like being swallowed by a monster that doesn't exist.Chu Ying's breathing stopped and she was frozen in place.He didn't stay on her face for half a second, and looked away indifferently as if she didn't recognize her.She felt as if she had fallen from a height of 10,000 feet, and her heart tightened suddenly. She slowly tightened her clothes, her joints turning white from the force.Ji Ran clapped his hands and grinned: OK, let's set off thenFeel sorry.The girl's usually gentle voice seemed to have become dry and sounded suddenly.There was a moment of silence, and everyone's eyes fell on her.Chu Ying's eyelashes trembled slightly, and she quickly glanced at Ling Tingyang and He Hong: I don't feel very well, so I won't go now.It was rare for her to lose her composure, and she walked in a hurry without waiting for anyone to respond.After passing a few people, he walked faster and faster.Almost fled.This word popped into Chu Ying's mind.Luo Hui's gaze in front of her was scorching, and she lowered her voice:In fact, you should go. This opportunity is so rare. There are not many opportunities to communicate directly with Party A, not to mention that it isThe words have not yet fallen.Chu Ying finally withdrew her consciousness, and when she unconsciously exerted force with her fingers, the noodles she had picked up unconsciously broke into two pieces.There are just too many people and I'm not used to it.Chu Ying looked up at her and smiled: It's enough for me to do my job well. I trust Brother Yang for the rest.Luo Hui was interrupted, and for a moment she couldn't find anything wrong with her words. After a long while, she looked at her and sighed.Your idea is correct, the ability to focus is more important.Luo Hui joked: Brother Yang won't starve us anyway.It was quiet for two seconds.The two people sitting in the corner suddenly looked at each other and smiled.

When she returned home at night, it was quiet and lifeless, except for the faint light and shadow cast from outside when she entered.Chu Ying turned on the light with ease. She had long been used to her roommate being away from home for three days.Just when she was about to order dumplings, out of concern for her roommate, she still sent a message to Zhu Ruoxuan.This time, unexpectedly, the reply came quickly, and the other end threw two words coldly, "No need."Chu Ying replied well and put a portion into the pot.Just after eating, Chu Ying received a call from Ling Tingyang, saying that work would officially start tomorrow and asking her to familiarize herself with the script first.Chu Ying went back to her room, opened the script, took notes and recorded and practiced. She listened to it repeatedly and adjusted it. When she came to her senses, it was already approaching ten o'clock.The exhaustion of hindsight swept over me.Chu Ying glanced at the window, where the waning moon hung high and the night was thick. After a few seconds, she still relied on her strong willpower to drag her steps to the bathroom.After taking a shower, Chu Ying dried her hair halfway and wanted to put the clothes she had changed into the washing machine.Unexpectedly, as soon as I opened the door, I smelled a strong smell of alcohol.Chu Ying frowned unconsciously and peeked inside. Dirty clothes were piled up, and she could vaguely see the cigarette that had not been taken out of her pocket.Chu Ying woke up instantly, closed the door immediately, took out her cell phone and called Zhu Ruoxuan.He was hung up on in less than two seconds.Chu Ying took a deep breath and called again.The ringer rang for a minute before the call was finally answered.Noisy music and voices burst out instantly, the collision of glasses and the cheers of men and women hit her eardrums. Chu Ying's temples began to beat incessantly, and she took the phone away.A man's voice shouted at the top of his lungs amid the commotion.Ruoxuan, who is this? I keep calling you.After a while, Zhu Ruoxuan's voice sounded from far away, probably after taking the phone.Hello, Chu YingIt's me. Chu Ying tried her best to maintain her emotions and asked calmly, when will you come back?There was silence on the other end for a moment, and he asked instead: Are you okay?The clothes you put in the washing machine were not washed.Oh, I probably forgot, just leave it for now.Zhu Ruoxuan's voice sounded nonchalant, and Chu Ying endured it:

Where can I wash my clothes?As they were playing, they probably heard that she was here to ask questions. She felt uneasy about having her interest disturbed, and Zhu Ruoxuan's tone gradually became impatient:Will it kill you if you put it in a piece and wash it? I would have forgotten it. The time for you to tell me this has already been finished.The nameless fire shot up in an instant, and Chu Ying spoke one word at a time:When I signed the contract, it was written clearly in white and black, and all actions would not interfere with the other party's life. I mentioned the laundry to you more than once.Are you sick? The rent is equal to both of us. I'm usually not at home. You live alone. What's wrong with me just losing my clothes?Zhu Ruoxuan became more and more irritable, and her tone of voice suddenly rose: If you don't like it, move out.After saying that, he hung up the phone.There was sudden silence in my ears.Tiredness reaches its peak before you know it.All the emotions dissipated instantly.Chu Ying stared at the black screen of her phone for a long time, then slowly turned on the phone, clicked on Zhu Ruoxuan's profile picture, and sent her a message.I will move out as soon as possible and I will pay for this month's utilities.

Chu Ying almost wanted to bury herself in the bed and stop moving.However, she still remembered that she wanted to move away, so she gritted her teeth and got up.Chu Ying is usually simple, and actually doesn't have many things. The main reason is that some of the facilities required for dubbing are cumbersome.After thinking for a long time, she decided to organize these things after she found a house and move out that day.She pulled out her suitcase from under the bed, planning to sort out the summer clothes she wouldn't wear for the time being.Chu Ying has some obsessive-compulsive disorder, and she usually puts her clothes neatly away, so the tidying up went smoothly. She only needed to transfer the clothes directly.After stuffing most of the box into the box, Chu Ying squatted down until her legs were numb. Just as she was thinking about it, she saw a corner of green peeking out from the half-covered clothes on her right side.Her gaze lingered for a moment, Chu Ying reached out hesitantly and pushed away the clothes that were pressed on top of her.This is a book that looks almost new.Hidden in the darkness, Chu Ying could only see the colorful cover. When she got closer and took it out, a piece of yellowed paper fell out.Chu Ying paused and lowered her head to pick it up.A light vanilla smell then penetrated the nose.Chu Ying suddenly froze.The sense of smell is more loyal than memory.The Proust Effect is like Pandora's box at this moment, being easily opened by an invisible hand.As if being bewitched, Chu Ying's eyes focused on the familiar line of handwriting on the paper.The flowing clouds and flowing water are vigorous and free.When the Proust Effect occurs, the sense of smell awakens memories.The photos in my memory seem to be turning page by page with the wind.In the flash of light, Chu Ying seemed to have returned to that intense autumn day five years ago.The young man was wearing a thin shirt, his eyes were slightly lowered, and the light smell of vanilla slowly filled his nose. He dragged his heavy suitcase and passed her.And she fell.

Chapter 3 RememberLike a nightmare with no end in sight03It seems like a dream.The world in the dream is covered with a layer of fog, white, silent and desolate.Suddenly, the fragrance of camphor faintly wafted through the tip of my nose, and even the sticky feeling in the humid air was particularly real.The fog gradually faded away, the eyes gradually became tinted, and the vision gradually became clearer.She saw herself walking out of a slightly rundown clinic with medicine in her hand.The next moment, there was the sound of suitcases rolling by from far to near.There seemed to be a gust of wind blowing around, and then there was a fragrance.She turned around after being stunned, but she only had time to see a figure around the corner.White shirt, blue jeans, the wrist holding the lever is boney and white, and he is wearing a watch.In the blink of an eye, there was only half a black roller left in sight.The sound of the wheels also gradually faded away.The sky soon became dusk again.A clean young man walked out of an old house that had been unoccupied for several years.In front of the blue bricks and black tiles, his figure was out of place, and his face was hidden between light and dark, making it difficult to see clearly.Suddenly, as if aware of his sight, he paused slightly and slowly raised his eyes.She almost subconsciously wanted to dodge.But his legs were uncontrollably frozen in place.Then he was caught off guard and met the young man's clear eyes.Even the sound of the wind has subsided.The next moment, his consciousness suddenly became groggy, and the whole world was spinning.It's like being thrown into the deep sea where you can't see the bottom, all your strength is taken away, and you can only float and sink with the waves.Until I could vaguely hear the sound of rain getting louder in my ears.The loud sound of rain hit the eaves, and then slid down the branches and leaves of the spider plant by the window.Tick tock.The leaf tips tremble slightly.Tick tock. Tick tock. Tick tock.Opening his eyelids, the white hospital bed came into view.Then there was an infusion tube dripping clear liquid.And the old man with a gastric tube inserted in the hospital bed.The old man was wearing a blue and white hospital gown and lying quietly on the hospital bed. She was so thin that the blood vessels on her arms were clearly visible. Her eyes were closed, but her old eyebrows were always wrinkled, and there were black and blue patches under her eyelids.It's raining heavily outside.But she seemed to be able to clearly hear the old man's weak and tired breathing.The girl wanted to raise her hand to smooth the old man's eyebrows, but her whole body was weak and unable to move.The wind-eroded walls outside are covered with dead ivy.This winter seems to be more difficult than previous years.In the blink of an eye, the sound of rain was replaced by the sound of footsteps and conversations coming and going urgently, and the surrounding sounds became noisy.Doctors or nurses kept pushing the bed and medicine trolley past her. She stood in a daze, watching someone not far away grabbing the doctor in surgical clothes and crying heartbrokenly.If the fee is no longer paid, the medication will be discontinued.The nurse's voice rang in her ears, and every word struck her heart, tugging at her almost numb nerves.In two days, she heard that her voice was dry and weak. In two days, could sheThe nurse looked reluctant, showing a hint of distress, and said helplessly: The deadline is here.She nodded stiffly, not knowing that her face was pale and her expression was uglier than crying. The nurse sighed and looked at her several times before leaving to let her make plans.The girl lowered her head and stared at the palm of her hand that she had clenched for many times. She slowly opened it and saw the deep fingerprints on the palm.Her frail figure seemed like she would fall over if the wind blew her.Then he almost trembled and dialed a number.The unanswered beep on the other end of the phone lingered in my ears slowly, as if being pressed.Like a nightmare with no end in sight.Breathing gradually became like drowning in water and it was difficult to breathe.Chu Ying suddenly woke up.Panting, she sat up suddenly and looked around in a daze.The temperatureless sunlight penetrated through the gaps in the dark curtains into the dark corners, and mottled light fell into the eyes.It's not a pale hospital, it's a room she's familiar with.Suddenly there was a pain in the palm of my hand.Chu Ying lowered her head in confusion, and saw that she was clenching the thin sheets tightly, and her nails were still almost digging into her palms.

She hadn't dreamed about this in a long time.Is it because I didn't go to see grandma?Is grandma thinking about her too?While his thoughts were in turmoil, the image of the young man looking at him coldly in the dream flashed through his mind.After a while, another distant glance passed by.Yesterday's reunion was more like a dream.Chu Ying let go of the bed sheets, relaxed her breathing for a while, raised her hands, moved her wrists, and sat on the edge of the bed.Her pajamas were pulled up, and a chill came over her. Chu Ying later realized that her back was almost soaked with cold sweat.Chu Ying looked at the time.It's just past six o'clock.Exhaling slowly, she stepped on her slippers and was about to leave the room and go to the bathroom to take a shower.The smell of low-quality perfume mixed with the smell of tobacco and alcohol spread in the small living room, almost hitting your face.Chu Ying reacted slowly for a moment, and suddenly heard a clanking sound coming from the bathroom, as if something had been knocked over.There was a faint curse, and then someone was seen walking out quickly.The tile floor was cold, and the woman was holding high heels in her hands, resting on her toes painted with dark red nail polish. At the same time, her cell phone was still between her shoulders and face, and she was probably talking to someone on the phone.Okay, you can organize the game next time.She responded in a low voice and walked towards her room without noticing Chu Ying by the door.The pungent smell of wine became clearer and clearer, and Chu Ying's mind, which was still in the nightmare and could not completely escape, suddenly woke up at this moment.Staring at the man's figure, Chu Ying slowly said: Have you just come back or are you going out?The other person seemed to be startled by her, stopped in his tracks, and turned around, revealing a face covered in heavy makeup.Their eyes crossed, and Zhu Ruoxuan froze for a moment, and then she seemed to think of something again, and her tone was cold: You don't need to worry about it.Chu Ying glanced at the high heels in her hand, and then saw a wet stain on her chest. After two seconds, she responded calmly and without emotion: Well, I won't care about it anymore.The atmosphere was silent.The person on the other end of the phone seemed to notice something and asked what was wrong.Zhu Ruoxuan replied expressionlessly that it was nothing and hung up the phone.No one said anything. Zhu Ruoxuan turned around and put her hand on the door handle. It seemed that she didn't understand the meaning of her words and didn't mention anything else. It seemed that she was not the one who asked her to move out last night.Chu Ying stared at her back: Have you read the news?Zhu Ruoxuan moved for a moment, then replied after a moment: I saw it.I'm already looking for an agency and I won't be here for long. You should also find a new roommate in advance.Zhu Ruoxuan was silent for a while, and her response was mixed in with the sound of the doorknob turning, yes.

Whether it was the unbearable mixed smell or the uncomfortable atmosphere, it prompted her to move out as soon as possible. Chu Ying didn't stay at home for a moment, and rushed to the company after taking a shower and washing up as quickly as possible.Although she may soon be living on the street, her work must continue.Today is the first day. After Ling Tingyang auditioned other important roles, he gathered everyone in the conference room and had a thorough chat about the plot and characters.The morning passed quickly.It wasn't until two o'clock in the afternoon that Chu Ying entered the recording studio and started the official dubbing.Fortunately, she got into the mood very quickly and could basically use all the lines she had dubbed. It only took two hours to achieve the process Ling Tingyang expected.Ling Tingyang has always discouraged overtime work. He would let people go as soon as the day's tasks were completed. What he said was that he would see who was still in the company at night and pay for the electricity himself.Okay, that's it for today.Ling Tingyang lightly waved her hand toward the observation window, indicating that she could leave.Just as I was about to take off my headphones, within two seconds, I suddenly remembered something: Wait.Chu Ying looked over here, and a voice came through the earphones: WellThe producer requires direct connection with voice actors. I am now setting up a project group. After joining, you can change your nickname to your first name.The girl blinked lightly, paused, and asked hesitantly: Yes, are all the people who came yesterday in there?Ling Tingyang didn't think much about it: the producer and director, as well as some people who might not have been here yesterday, would be there.Chu Ying said oh, Ling Tingyang didn't notice anything wrong and lowered his head to operate on his mobile phone.Soon, a new group popped up on WeChat.There were about ten people in the group. Chu Ying's eyes quickly scanned a series of names, and her eyes fell on a few nicknames without notes.After a pause, he tapped the upper right corner with his finger.Most of them were familiar faces, and about five or six were obviously people from the production side.There is a portrait with a lotus flower, and Chu Ying guesses it is probably Stanley Ho.Others are useful for kittens, selfies, and landscapes.It didn't seem to fit the style of the person she wanted.She should breathe a sigh of relief, but there seemed to be some more unknown emotions welling up in her heart.Suddenly, she realized what she was paying attention to, her heart suddenly slowed down, and Chu Ying suddenly turned off her phone.The black screen of her mobile phone reflected her somewhat stiff expression.Until Ling Tingyang's voice sounded in his ears again.If you haven't come out yet, are you going to spend the night inside?Chu Ying finally came to her senses and shook her head, trying to throw those distracting thoughts out of her mind.Come out now

The sun sets.After leaving the company under the envious eyes of her colleagues, Chu Ying walked out of the Cultural and Creative Park and suddenly stopped walking.She was supposed to go home, but when she thought that she might meet Zhu Ruoxuan at home, she gave up the idea.She's not good at quarreling, and she doesn't want to quarrel.After thinking about it, Chu Ying decided to just have dinner outside before going home.It just so happened that Wen Zaichen told her a few days ago that he opened a music restaurant near Lychee University. I heard that it was quite popular among students, with a great atmosphere and a variety of dishes.I wanted her to try the dishes and give her opinions before, but she never had the chance to go, so she just happened to go there today to support her.Chu Ying has always had strong mobility, and she reached out to call a car as soon as she made the decision.After getting in the car and reporting the location to the driver, Chu Ying took out her phone and glanced at the time, when she suddenly saw a new friend request sent on WeChat.The avatar is a face hidden in half-light and half-darkness. The most eye-catching thing is a head of silver hair. It has a distinctive personality and its nickname is an R.This is Ji RanChu Ying paused and was about to pretend not to see it, but she saw that he had applied again, this time specifically noting her name.It turned out to be Ji Ran.What did Ji Ran ask her to do?Chu Ying hesitated for a long time, thinking of the dinner party she refused yesterday by pretending to be sick.If I ignore it now, wouldn't it be too obvious?Suddenly, with a short sudden brake, Chu Ying leaned forward, subconsciously supporting the back of the car in front of her.The car stopped, and the driver stuck his head out and cursed: "You don't have eyesight."He turned around and apologized to her: I'm sorry, girl, are you okay?Chu Ying slowed her breathing, shook her head, and then picked up her phone again after sitting firmly.The screen that lights up shows that I don't know when I passed the friend.Two green bubbles occupy the field of view.Hello, I am Ji Ran.It may be a bit presumptuous to add you suddenly, but I just want to make friends with you, and you don't need to worry about the etiquette.While she was stunned, another message popped up.Didn't expect you to pass friends.

How to explain it? In fact, she never thought about it.Chu Ying was silent for a long time and replied hello.There was no reply for a while.Chu Ying's fingers stopped in mid-air, her eyes unconsciously fell on the word friend, and she blinked.Although she had an intuition that he was a more proactive type, but even so, she couldn't really ignore his identity as a producer.After all, she is Party A, and she cannot let others down too much. Chu Ying thought about it for a while and continued typing: OkayAfter sending it, she felt that it seemed too cold, so she added two sentences: Then I will trouble you to take care of me from now on. If there are any shortcomings in the work level, please forgive me and point it out, and I will do my best.Every word is reasonable, but every word seems alienated.A sense of proportion hits you, and there should be no loopholes.Chu Ying read it twice, nodded feeling good about herself, pressed down the car window, and put the phone aside.

I'll ask you to take more care of me from now on.If there are any shortcomings in the work level, please forgive me and point it out, and I will do my best.Ji Ran stared at the most polite lines on the screen, and then looked at the message he sent. He couldn't understand how such a gentle and delicate girl could talk exactly like the stubborn ones in his family.Too slick to be decent.He clearly said that he was just making friends and didn't need to worry about etiquette.What went wrongHe clicked his tongue, and for a moment he didn't know how to continue the conversation. After thinking for a long time, he decided to go straight.Are you free today? It was a pity that you were not here yesterday. I heard from your boss that you are a very talented newcomer. I am very interested in your experience and want to communicate with you. Do you think I can invite you out to eat together? A meal?There was no reply for a long time. Ji Ran scratched his hair irritably and began to doubt himself.He is not a scourge either.Why doesn't Chu Ying refuse to take it hard?At this moment, a clear male voice with a hint of impatience came from behind: Didn't I say I'd be there in ten minutes?Ji Ran glanced at the chat page where there was no reply, exited and clicked on the map to compare the surroundings: Turn left ahead and reach the Young Master. This road is closed to motor vehicles. Just be patient and I won't let you down. .After the words fell, WeChat showed that a message had been received.Ji Ran hurriedly opened it, and the raised corners of his lips froze when he saw the reply.Sorry, but I just had it and thank you for your kindness.The topic became more and more dead, and even the title became you.Ji Ran was completely speechless. He reached out and flipped through the records. In the end, the two of them didn't even talk to each other for ten sentences.Still wondering what he said wrongly, Ji Ran logged out of WeChat with a frown and sighed heavily.Until the man in a gray woolen suit next to him suddenly glanced at her and said in a cold voice: "Look at the road."Ji Ran was reminded by him, and as soon as he turned his head, he suddenly got excited.There happened to be a telephone pole standing directly in front of him.Ji Ran quickly took a few steps to the side, and touched his forehead and patted his chest with lingering fear.Let you chat.Xu Jisi's half-cast eyes raised slightly, half-smiling but not smiling: I've never seen you so active in the company's affairs.Hearing the cynicism in his tone, Ji Ran immediately retorted: I am only doing this because of official business.As if it was rare, Xu Jisi raised his eyelids slightly and raised his tone: "You still have business matters."Why not? It wasn't yesterdayJi Ran even raised his eyebrows when talking about this matter: Didn't the heroine who was dubbing feel unwell yesterday? I added her as a friend today and want to know more about it.I told people that I came here to make friends with her. My original intention was to create a sense of distance, but I didn't expect that this girl is incompetent. Look at it.As Ji Ran spoke, he pulled out the record and placed it in front of him, completely unaware of Xu Jisi's suddenly fixed gaze.Before and after he handed it over, he tsked again as if he had a headache: "It's more impressive than my old man."Xu Jisi's eyes slowly fell on Ji Ran's phone screen.Something seemed to flash across his eyes.It's not even five o'clock. Anyone who eats dinner so early will be 'rejected' by me.As Ji Ran said this, he seemed to be amused by this conclusion, so he took the opportunity to retract his hand and turn off the screen.The phone was suddenly taken away by a hand with distinct joints.Ji Ran sighed and wanted to take the phone back, but Xu Jisi raised his hand without changing his expression and took the phone back.Ji

Ran's movements froze:After staring sideways for a few seconds, he said with a hint of displeasure in his voice: What are you doing?The man's expression was still cold, with one hand in his pocket and the other holding his mobile phone. He didn't look at him, and his eyes fell on the profile picture on the left side of the screen.It was a half-length profile photo of Chu Ying at the beach, revealing her slender neck, snow-like skin, long hair blown by the wind, naturally curved lips, and bright and clean eyes.Xu Jisi stared for a moment, his eyes darkened, but no emotion could be seen.The little face that was a little pale from the shock from yesterday popped up in my mind for no reason.It's in stark contrast to the relaxed look in the avatar.He seemed to pull his lips inconspicuously.After a long while, Xu Jisicai threw the phone back to him and said softly: No normal person will pay attention to you.Ji Ran:No, why can't normal people ignore him?Ji Ran stared and said "Tell me" written all over his face. Xu Jisi glanced at him without explaining, and said in a cold voice: "Don't harm others, little girl."Ji Ran was unhappy: How could I harm others?As he spoke, he turned a corner along the road, and a huge Limai lantern came into view first.The sky gradually darkened, and the surrounding stores all lit up with white and yellow store logos. Only the backside of Limai glowed with a soft light pink in the spring breeze, which was particularly artistic.There are green plants and flowers planted outside the door. It is obviously autumn, but it really looks as vibrant as spring.Ji Ran's attention was diverted and he said, "We're here now."Xu Jisi raised his eyes and looked around. Young men and women kept chatting and laughing at the door. They were probably students from the nearby Lychee University. They seemed quite popular.Ji Ran walked quickly, and while waving to him, he said: Liang Xuqing recommended this to me. He said that a small band was invited to stay here last time. You may have never heard of it, called wilderness. , was on the band's variety show some time ago and became quite popular.Ji Ran didn't have any other skills, but he knew a lot about the entertainment industry.After entering the door, Ji Ran stopped at the service desk to show the reservation, then turned to Xu Jisi and introduced the band members.Xu Jisi's arms were slightly bent, and he was lightly supporting the table. He stood lazily with his slender legs, eyes drooping with no emotion, and he didn't know if he was listening.Then a waiter led them through the almost full crowd and stopped at a location close to the stage, probably a VIP seat.Ji Ran looked around and saw that the environment was indeed clean, the service was in place, and the atmosphere was still online.The waiter pulled out the chairs for them and handed them the menu. In a gentle and sweet voice, he said that there would be a concert at about 5:30, and if you want to order songs, you can scan the QR code.Ji Ran nodded, checked a few items on the menu, and continued the previous topic: The owner of this restaurant has something special.Xu

Jisi had no interest in this. He leaned casually on the armrest, lightly bent his knuckles, picked up a glass of ice water and handed it to the waiter.Ji Ran was scanning the QR code to order a song, and happened to notice it with an exaggerated expression: No, you are here just to drink water.Xu Jisi finally raised his eyelids, slightly twitching the corners of his lips, and said emotionlessly: If you dare to get drunk and crazy today, I will ask your father to take you back.Xu Jisi has always had a venomous mouth, not the kind of direct attack. Sometimes he may not even react when he is scolded.Ji Ran took several detours before he realized that Xu Jisi was insinuating that he liked to drink even though his wine was not good.On his birthday last time, he drank a few more drinks because he was in the mood. Later, it was said that he vomited while singing the horse pole and slept for a whole day and night before waking up.Ji Ran's expression changed again and again, and he was about to say that it was an accident before.As soon as he raised his head, he saw Xu Jisi's eyes falling on a certain place inexplicably, and his eyebrows seemed to be moving.Ji Ran looked around and saw a familiar, slender figure being led through their table, and finally stopped in front of them.The waiter told me exactly the same thing.The man nodded, then raised his eyes with a smile and said in a soft voice: Okay, thank you.The girl took the menu and was about to bow her head. The next moment, he suddenly became aware of the sight coming from here and stopped.Those translucent water eyes passed through the waiter's figure.Then his expression stiffened slightly.Ji Ran raised his eyebrows.What a coincidence.Wasn't it just Chu Ying who had eaten just now?

Chapter 4 Rememberinghaven't seen you for a long time.04What Chu Ying saw at first glance was not Ji Ran.Although the restaurant is called a restaurant, it is not just a place to eat. There was light above the head, but it was still dark. Chu Ying was sitting close to the stage, which slightly reflected some blue light.Someone was hiding in the flickering light, and seemed to raise his eyes slightly. His black eyes were so clear that they almost blended into the dimness, but she could see clearly.Chu Ying's fingers holding the menu were numb for a moment, and maybe her whole body was a little stiff, until someone dragged out his voice and said with some deliberateness: Oh, that's quite a coincidence.Ji Ran's table was only one meter away from her.The lie was caught off guard and exposed nakedly.Chu Ying moved her wrist, her eyes fell on Ji Ran who spoke out, her lips stiffened slightly: Ji Ran.Ji Ran raised his eyebrows and waved to her: "Miss Chu, since we are so destined, why don't you give me face and join us at a table?"It's like nothing happened.Chu Ying opened her lips, as if she wanted to say something, and then said: Hey, anyway, we just finished ordering, and we have bumped into each other, so there is no need to be so unfamiliar.Chu Ying couldn't figure out the other party's temperament, but

Ji Ran's current attitude didn't seem like he wanted to settle accounts with his wife, so he was just looking out for her face.She has refused once, and this will be a face-to-face encounter. If she refuses again, it will be embarrassing on the spot, because she has no vision.Chu Ying could only get up.The waiter on the side looked back and forth.Ji Ran waved his hand: We know each other, so we are all included in my table.As he said this, he pulled out the chair next to him in a gentlemanly manner and looked over there with a smile: How rare it is. Miss Chu is usually very busy, so she let me touch her today.There is something in the words. Chu Ying didn't want to think carefully about the connotation of his words, so she just twitched the corner of her mouth and said, "What's the matter?"The short distance of a few steps was like rushing to hell.Chu Ying closed her eyes and sat next to Ji Ran. She straightened her back and sat stiffly. Her hands were placed on her legs in a regular manner, as if she was being restrained by invisible shackles.Don't be so reserved, just make friends as you said.His tone was light, and after he finished speaking, he turned his head and smiled at her, as if he had no idea what impact his words would have on others.Chu Ying's already forced smile became stiffer.He still remembers this.She also pretended that he didn't mention it before because she wanted to give each other a step forward.This man is worse than she imaginedThis thought flashed through her mind, and the corners of Chu Ying's lips tightened.

She involuntarily raised her eyelashes and quickly glanced at the man opposite who had not yet spoken.At this moment, he was lazily sitting on the back of the chair, his elbows slightly bent and resting on the armrests, his other hand slightly bent, gently supporting half of his head, his eyes half lowered, and his long eyelashes cast a shadow under his eyes.It's not like I want to take care of it.Is heI totally forgot who she isThe moment she realized this, the girl's eyelashes trembled slightly and she clenched her sleeves uncontrollably.Not hearing her response, Ji Ran raised his eyebrows slightly and continued to speak with unclear meaning: Why didn't Miss Chu speak?After a pause, he stretched out his voice again, as if joking: Or, Miss Chu thinks that I am not worthy of being with you.Ji Ran.The finger bones and the wooden board lightly touched, making a crisp sound, followed by a cold voice.Ji Ran paused, turned his head, and saw that the man opposite finally moved. He leaned forward slightly, put his knuckled fingers on the dining table, and cast a cold gaze, which made people feel a hint of oppression.There was no emotion in his voice: enough is enough.After a moment of silence, as if he had confirmed that it was Xu Jisi who was speaking, Ji Ran slowly cast a ghostly look.Even Chu Ying was stunned for a moment, and as soon as she raised her eyes, her figure suddenly froze again.It was as if he just realized how close the two of them were sitting facing each other.Before entering, she never imagined that she would be only an arm's length away from him.Xu Jisi lowered his eyes slightly, and the moment he looked at her, the lamp embedded in the wall suddenly lit up, and his dark pupils were also illuminated.The strings in her heart suddenly trembled for no reason. Chu Ying curled her fingers, as if years passed through his eyes, and the fragments flashed by like time.Humid midnight, shabby corners, dirty skirts.Picture after picture, like torn and scattered pieces of paper, densely falling from the eyes.The final stop was a silent night.The cries of crickets in the trees outside the window were distant and near. The corner of the wooden table that would creak at the slightest movement was lit with a small desk lamp she bought casually on the roadside. She supported her chin with one hand and half-lyed on the table while filling in her test papers. .They were all questions that she had done once, and there were still some memories in her brain. Maybe it was because she didn' t need to use her brain very much, or it was too late. As she wrote, the tip of her pen unconsciously slowed down.Drowsiness swept over her, her brain seemed to be covered with a layer of fog, and her reactions became sluggish. The sound of crickets was a natural weapon to help her sleep. Chu Ying felt that her eyelids were getting heavier and heavier.Just before closing his eyes.The sound of the book being turned suddenly penetrated my cochlea.Chu Ying suddenly opened her eyes.The wooden table shook, and the young man in a white shirt who was leaning against the wall paused for a moment, slowly moved his eyes away from the book, and looked at her with half-closed eyes.The dim lamp could barely illuminate a corner of the desk.The shadow of the book covered half of her face.Chu Ying blinked and raised her head slightly to look at him.The young man's long eyelashes fell slightly, casting a shadow under his eyes. He pursed his lips slightly, with a calm expression, and the dim light reflected in the depths of his half-lidded black eyes towards her, which gradually seemed to coincide with the deserted pupils in front of him at this moment.It also reflected her slightly dazzling eyes.Buzz.The vibrating sound of her cell phone scattered all the unreal fragments and pulled her away from her memories.Chu Ying looked away almost instantly and took out her phone.Wen Zaichen's name flashed on the screen.The next moment, as if grasping a life-saving straw, Chu Ying showed an apologetic look: Sorry, I may need to answer the phone first.As if this reason was not enough to flee the scene, she hurriedly added: to go to the bathroom on the way.Both reasons were reasonable enough. Ji Ran raised his eyebrows and made a spontaneous move.Seeing the girl's pretending to be calm after standing up, her pace obviously became faster as she approached the corner, Ji Ran turned his head thoughtfully.After a few seconds of silence, Ji Ran raised his eyes and saw Xu Jisi retracting his gaze, picking up the glass and taking a sip of water.After realizing something, Ji Ran raised his eyebrows and stared at him for a few seconds: No, what did you mean just now?Xu Jisi paused and raised his eyelids to look at him:Ji Ran narrowed his eyes and suddenly said with certainty: There is something wrong with you.

Chu Ying was so flustered when she left that she even forgot to ask about the location. She wound around two corners and luckily saw the sign for the restroom.The phone was still vibrating. Chu Ying pressed against the wall and waited until her heartbeat slowed down before answering the call.Why did you answer the phone?Chu Ying paused: I didn't hear it just now.The other end didn't have any doubts and asked again: I heard you went to the Spring Breeze.Well, I just arrived not long ago.Wen Zaichen's tone was serious: It's a pity that I'm on a business trip recently, otherwise I would have to come and serve you personally.Chu Ying smiled unconsciously: Mr. Wen is a very busy man, how could I have such great dignity?Don't put a high hat on me, Wen Zaichen seemed to be smiling, you know, if you come, I have to make time no matter what.After chatting with Wen Zaichen for a while, the messy thoughts in Chu Ying's heart dispersed a lot, and she had calmed down when she hung up the phone.Really not ready to continue facing Xu Jisi and Ji Ran, Chu Ying hid in the bathroom, staring at the number in the upper right corner of her phone as it changed from 0 to 0, and her days seemed like years.It took a long time until someone from outside came to urge me: Are the people inside okay?Realizing that she had been hiding for ten minutes, Chu Ying hurriedly pressed the water valve and pushed the door out of the single room.Her brain was running through all kinds of coping strategies after returning. Chu Ying stood in front of the sink. The bright mirror reflected her thin figure. At this moment, her plain and beautiful face was frowning, and her lips were tinged for some reason. white.Chu Ying stared at her obviously unattractive face and deliberately curved her lips.

The reluctance is evident at a glance.Chu Ying couldn't control it anymore. The next second, the corners of her lips bounced back like an elastic rope and pursed into a straight line.The girl took a deep breath, stomped her feet as if to vent her anger, reached out to the induction faucet, took the water, lowered her head, and splashed three ladles on her face.The cold water stimulated her senses. Chu Ying slowly opened her eyes. Water droplets hung on her long eyelashes and dripped down her cheeks as she blinked.The broken hair was wet and intertwined with the earrings that were swinging back and forth, a little precarious, which was annoying to see.She raised her hand, hooked it through her hair, and was about to take off her earrings.Suddenly.In the peripheral vision, a tall figure appeared behind her at some point, leaning against the wall, his eyes falling straight into her eyes.Chu Ying's eyelashes trembled.The man was probably overheated. After taking off his coat, he was left with only a black inner layer. He rolled up his cuffs, revealing his white forearms, with smooth lines and raised wrist bones, hanging casually at his side.Xu Jisi stood there quietly, with sharp brows and cold, dark pupils staring at her with no emotion.Chu Ying froze for a moment and turned around stiffly. The legs that were supposed to escape the scene were tightly restrained by reason.He just helped her out.There is no way to pretend not to see it.Chu Ying failed to think about why he appeared here.The girl gave him a polite smile, nodded slightly at him as a greeting, and then took steps forward impatiently.The moment when we meet.Suddenly, the man moved.A voice suddenly sounded beside her, and the familiar voice called her lightly with the same ending as in the past:Chu Ying.Very light, so light that it would have dispersed silently in the wind.But Chu Ying suddenly stopped in her tracks.A burst of cool woody sandalwood faintly penetrates the tip of the nose.Like water drops suddenly dripping into the pond, causing ripples.There was silence all around, and the frequency of her heart beat uncontrollably faster and faster under this call. She seemed to be able to hear her heart pounding in her ears like a drum.haven't seen you for a long time.

Chapter 5 Rememberingmake cry05With her back to Xu Jisi, Chu Ying couldn't see his expression, but she could feel his eyes staying on her.Every word was like the rising and falling tide on the coast, hitting the rocks and hitting her heart.She never thought that Xu Jisi would speak first.The clear voice has clear enunciation, the final sound is short, and there is no delay in the sound.Just like his neat and tidy character.Thinking of this pointlessly, the tide in her heart suddenly faded away, and Chu Ying laughed silently.As if she suddenly thought about it, Chu Ying breathed a sigh of relief, turned around, and met Xu Jisi's eyes.Mr. Xu, Chu Ying looked puzzled with a formulaic smile. We seemed to have just met yesterday.The atmosphere became stagnant and the air became thin.Chu Ying saw his dark eyes move slightly the moment she finished speaking.The corners of the man's lips pulled slightly, and a short and inconspicuous breath escaped from his throat.You still won't lie.You won't lie.The curve of Chu Ying's lips stiffened.For a moment of daze, it seemed as if there was a distant, cold voice traveling through time and space, pulling her back to remember that rainy night.The night when rumors were spread, papers were hidden, the teacher targeted me, I was punished by running twenty laps on the playground, and finally the equipment room was locked.The lights in the alley corners of the town flicker on and off, and there are not even a few streetlights near the abandoned old house. Only the moon hanging high in the sky emits a deserted moonlight, reflecting the dilapidated outline of the tile-roofed house.The rain was pattering, and she hugged her legs and squatted beside the low and dilapidated tile house.Under the dim wall, you can faintly see the moss that has grown due to years of humidity. The girl's thin body leaned against the mottled wall, her slender fingers clenched her sleeves, and the cold wind that blew from time to time penetrated into her empty sleeves along with the rain. .She buried her head in her arms and let the rain wet her long hair.I don't know how long it took, but suddenly there was the sound of dry branches and leaves being trampled to pieces. Chu Ying moved her fingers and felt that even the strength to raise her head had been stolen away.Soon there was another meow.It's a cat.The girl's effort to raise her head disappeared again.Chu Ying buried herself in her arms and laughed silently.How could she think that someone was coming to find her?This is the first time I have worn the newly bought white dress. It looked clean and fresh during the day, but now the hem of the dress is full of mud. The sweat clings to the fabric uncomfortably tight, and you can tell how embarrassed you are right now without even looking.It was time to go home, but it was too late. Grandma has always been a light sleeper. When she went back, just opening the door would make a creaking sound, which would only wake her up and make her worry for nothing.Where to go?He was accidentally discovered by the security guard and released. It was already late at night after he came out of the equipment room. There were also people at home with his close friends. Wu Ning Town is not a big place. If anyone knows about something, it will spread immediately. It's inevitable that grandma will find out.She just wandered around.There were clearly a few lonely stars hanging in the sky, clearly indicating that the weather would be good the next day, but unexpectedly, it started to drizzle in the middle of the night.Chu Ying usually doesn't exercise much, so the sudden running circle undoubtedly put a huge load on her legs. It was raining again. She originally wanted to rest under the eaves for a while, but as soon as she squatted down, her legs became weak and sore. If her back was not against the wall, she would have almost fallen to the ground.The night wind howled, blowing the ends of her wet hair, making it even more messy.Chu Ying shrank and tightened her cuffs, and thought about the paper that had been hidden at some point.She couldn't complete the papers the class teacher asked her to make up. If there is a blank tomorrow, you will be punished again.In fact, it's nothing to punish her. She's just afraid that her parents will be invited.Grandma is getting older and her legs are getting worse, not to mention it's not a good thing. She doesn't want to hurt her heart.Chu Ying buried her head and didn't know what time it was. Why did she feel that this rainy night was so long?It's so long that I can't see tomorrow.Suddenly, the cold wind seemed to become smaller at some point.The fine raindrops don't seem to be floating anymore.Chu Ying loosened her fingers that were tightening her sleeves. She was quiet for a while, as if she was making a plan. After a while, she raised her head slightly, revealing her eyes.The vision is still dim.He froze when he saw that there was indeed a person standing in front of him.Chu Ying subconsciously shrank her fingers and blinked her eyes, thinking it was an illusion.Then he slowly raised his head.Under the very pale moonlight, someone stood against the light, and the light and shadow outlined his clear and tall outline.He held the umbrella and leaned his hand forward, landing on her head.The young man held the umbrella handle with his slender and well-joined fingers, and lowered his head slightly. His expression under the dark broken hair was dark and difficult to distinguish. His narrow and cold eyes moved slightly, and he looked at her with half-lidded eyes.Just like this, standing in front of her like a dream.I don't know how long it was silent.The girl realized later, her eyes widened suddenly, and she didn't know where she got the strength to stand up.Her eyes suddenly went dark for a moment, and her weak legs were still a little weak. She shook her body and leaned forward unconsciously.Chu Ying subconsciously stretched out her hand, trying to find some support point to stabilize her body.The warm palm of a hand rested on her shoulder.The young man used a little force to steady Chu Ying, who was about to jump forward.As her eyes gradually returned to normal, Chu Ying shook her head and regained consciousness.There was a steady stream of warmth in the palm of her shoulder, and her heart was beating unconsciously. Chu Ying blinked and looked at the young man with silent eyebrows in front of her, and then she felt a sense of reality.Xu Jisi murmured his name.The young man stared at her gray face, his eyes swept over her scattered hair stuck to her cheeks, her slightly swollen eye sockets, and down to the dirty hem of her white dress stained with pure gray.His sharp jaw tightened slightly, and his expression became colder. Under the high bridge of his nose, his thin lips slightly opened, and he paused: "Who did this?"He didn't even ask what was going on.It's like you can tell at a glance what she's been through.Chu Ying's eyelashes trembled slightly, and she wanted to say it for a moment, but thinking of the rumors in school, she looked down at the dirt-stained white skirt and pursed her lips again.After a long while, she looked at him carefully and whispered: No one.After a pause, she gently touched off the fine gravel and sand that had stuck to her while squatting with her fingers, trying to cover up in a poor way: she had fallen.Xu Jisi said nothing, only looked at her with his dark eyes.After staring at her until she reached out and rubbed the back of her neck uncomfortably, he spoke very quietly and called her name:Chu Ying.The boy's cool voice always spoke softly when he called her name.Others like to draw their names when calling her, but Xu Jisi is the only one who is calm and short.The girl lowered her head quietly, her fingers deceiving herself as she repeatedly kneaded the waist of her skirt. I wonder if she had been blown by the cold wind for too long, but her head felt a little hot. She muttered to herself as if she didn't want to hear what he said next:It's dirty and I can't let grandma see it.

I have toYou won't lie.His words still reached her ears clearly.It is a straightforward and affirmative statement.The voice seemed to have been taken away by someone for a moment. Chu Ying opened her mouth and couldn't spit out even a single word. She could only freeze.Xu Jisi stared at her reddish eyes and repeated:You won't lie, Chu Ying.

It's obviously just a few words.But Chu Ying felt that her heart was grasped by invisible hands, and she was so painful that she couldn't breathe.How could he always be so cold and unscrupulous in digging out the emotions she wanted to hide inch by inch? Woolen cloth.It was five years ago.Even now.Her eyes seemed a little hot. Chu Ying clutched her phone tightly and her breathing became rapid, but she still stared at those dark pupils without blinking, as if she wanted to see something from them.The girl in front of her didn't seem to have changed much from what she remembered, except that her eyebrows had grown longer and she became more beautiful.The eyelashes under the crescent-shaped eyebrows are curled up, embedded with a pair of clear and bright black eyes.But these eyes were covered with a thin mist at this moment. She looked white, so the redness in her eyes became more and more obvious.Xu Jisi's eyebrows suddenly wrinkled slightly.He opened his lips slightly and raised his wrist, as if he wanted to say something.I don't understand what you are talking about. Chu

Ying's trembling voice was forcibly restrained, and she raised her lips:Mr. Xu's pick-up techniques are very old-fashioned.After saying that, she didn't care about being polite and didn't want to pretend at all. Chu Ying turned around and walked away.It was probably too large, and something fell silently at this moment.Xu Jisi didn't seem to have recovered from her words. Xu Jisi stood motionless, with an unclear expression.After a long while, his eyes slowly dropped to where she just stood.A little blue comes into view.No one noticed that the footsteps suddenly stopped at the door of the women's restroom.The girl who had just come out of the private room to wash her hands was sorting out the information she had just heard, and looked at the handsome man standing in front of the sink with a strange look.She's not bad looking either. Why did that girl refuse so simply just now?He's not a gamer, right?The girl's eyes changed again and again, almost imagining a big drama in her mind, and finally her eyes gradually turned to contempt.The man is handsome, but he is indeed unreliableXu Jisi glanced sideways as if he was aware of his gaze, and glanced at the girl whose expression was changing expressionlessly.The girl was so frightened that she hurriedly looked away, moved to the mirror in a small step, touched her hand casually, and left in a hurry.His mind was filled with Chu Ying's red eyes when she looked at him, and Xu Jisi frowned even more tightly.After a while, he returned to his calm appearance and walked out.

It was close to six o'clock, and a pretty girl was already singing on the stage. The lights above her head were changing from blue to purple, and it was ambiguously dark. The whole restaurant was mixed with clinking glasses and noises, and the unique nighttime atmosphere became hot.The phone kept vibrating. Xu Jisi lowered his eyes and saw that the question marks sent by Ji Ran were still popping up.Not far away, you can see him sitting half-slumped at the table with his head bent on the screen.After taking a few steps forward, I saw him holding down the bottom of the screen to send him a voice message: Mr. Xu, what are you doing again?Shout out the soulXu Jisi's cold voice sounded above his head.Ji Ran raised his chin when he heard the sound, and saw his sharp jawline, and above it were the clear eyes that glanced at him lazily, with an expression as if nothing had happened.He couldn't help but think of the girl who just spoke with a nasal sound, as if there was a savage beast behind her, and fled in a panic. The unhappiness in his heart had not dissipated, but when he encountered that girl's expression, he couldn't even express his anger, or even said it was okay. I haven't even finished talking yet.Ji Ran looked at Xu Jisi with a strange expression and asked in a tentative tone: Did you just run into Chu Ying?Xu Jisi paused, tapped his finger on the table and turned around: What?When he didn't get a negative answer, Ji Ran's eyes widened: "What's the matter?" What did you say that made me cry?After the words fell, he realized something was wrong again and denied himself: No, what can you say to others? The two of them couldn't get along at all, and Xu Jisi wasn't someone who would take the initiative to talk to others. Then why is Chu Ying crying? Ji Ran glanced at Xu Jisi again. Although he did act a little weird just now, Xu Jisi has always been unpredictable in his actions and has a very weird temper. What's more, he asked just now. Xu Jisi just asked him to say one, two, three, four with a half-smile. He held it in for a long time and said that his face was obviously colder after eating yesterday. Xu Jisi asked him if he was taking a thermometer. You can see that his face is colder than before. He lost his voice. It felt outrageous but reasonable. He felt that Xu Jisi's cold face was a very subjective judgment on his part, and it really couldn't prove anything. So he went on to talk about how his cell phone was taken away from him on the road. Xu Jisi glanced at him and asked who asked him to see the record first. He couldn't refute the record at all. He was the one who let him see the record. When he held it up, Xu Jisi couldn't see it clearly. He really couldn't confirm it. When he took it away and looked at it carefully, there was no problem. In the end, Ji Ran could only ask in an aggrieved tone why he interrupted him. What he got was a sneer from Xu Jisi, telling him not to embarrass himself and embarrass a girl because he had swallowed his education. He wanted to say that he usually didn't see you being considerate of others, but when he saw Xu Jisi's obviously impatient look, he swallowed his words.This temper, this look, it really feels right now.At that moment, Ji Ran began to suspect that he was really thinking too much.He has known Xu Jisi for such a long time, but he has never seen a woman who is not related to him by blood, not to mention Chu Ying, whom he has never heard of or met. What is there for him to talk about, and what can he do to others? I couldn't help but cry.impossible. It is impossible for the sun to rise in the west.Ji Ran withdrew his gaze, shook his head to himself, frowned, and was still analyzing: That was the problem with the phone call she just answered. What situation made her leave in such a hurry?People can leave if they want, you don't care about that muchXu Jisi lifted up the coat he had just taken off with one hand and spoke coldly.No, she hasn't eaten anything yet.He was not happy from the beginning. Xu Jisi put on his coat, glanced at him, and said in a cold voice, "You are so aggressive. I don't know who can eat it."Being choked by him and speechless for a moment, Ji Ran opened his mouth for a long time and tried to make amends for himself: Then didn't I talk nicely at the beginning? She lied to me and let me bump into her. I can't be angry anymore.Xu Jisi sneered: What does this person have to do with you? We only met once and then we have to listen to you when we go out to eat.Who spoiled you?He showed no mercy, and Ji Ran was completely speechless.I am used to being sought after on weekdays, I have never encountered any obstacles, and I come and go as soon as I ask the people around me, so I have never been rejected.After all, he was a little frustrated. He wanted to get some face back after losing face. He said he didn't care about his identity and just made friends, but in action he used his identity to the extreme. Didn't he really know?Xu Jisi knew Ji Ran's temperament very well.Glancing at him, Xu Jisi thought of something again. Xu Jisi's hand in his pocket flexed, his fingers touched something, and he paused:Don't worry about it. This girl is not interested in you, so don't rush to make her unhappy.Ji Ran's face froze, and he wanted to save some face for himself: I told you to make friends.Xu Jisi acted as if he hadn't heard, straightened his sleeves, and looked up at him: Don't forget, you have a fiancée.Ji Ran almost immediately retorted:Don't talk to me about this. In what age are we still doing arranged marriages? Girls are not willing to join me in this marriage. Wait, why are you standing chatting with me all the time?His eyes fell on the coat he put on again, and Ji Ran realized that Xu Jisi didn't mean to stay any longer. When he saw him, he was about to turn around and said hurriedly:Hey, wherever you go, the food has just been served.Xu Jisi glanced at him, ran her fingers over the cool earrings in her pocket, and her eyes flickered:Return something.

Chapter 6 Rememberingoffice romance06Autumn started early this year, just after six o'clock, and the sunset was already drowsy.Stepping out of the spring breeze, the music and noise gradually faded away, and my ears became quiet. I could only hear the occasional rustling of the wind and the laughter and scolding of the students arm-in-arm.When Xu Jisi noticed Chu Ying's back, she had already left the pedestrian street, was hailing a taxi, and sat in with her thin back bent.In the blink of an eye, a burst of exhaust gas was already left on the roadside.It was obviously not a hot weather, but there was a trace of boredom in my heart.The tight lips revealed the displeasure at the moment. Xu Jisi looked gloomy, frowned slightly, and slowly took out the blue object he picked up from the bathroom half a quarter of an hour ago.He held the ear hook lightly with his fingertips, and the small earrings dangled in front of his eyes. Xu Ji thought for a moment, then raised his eyes to look at the taxi driver who had already left.Suddenly a familiar call sounded from behind: Xu JisiXu Jisi held the earrings in his hands, tilted his head, and saw that Ji Ran had already taken a few steps to his side. He must have just been driven out, his chest was heaving and he was still breathing.Ji Ran put a hand on his shoulder: What is so important?Xu Jisi calmly put the earrings back into his pocket and raised his eyebrows: "You don't want to eat anymore."You're gone, what good do I have to eat.Originally, today was just a matter of luck, and I stopped by to see if the band was there. I picked up Xu Jisi just to have some company, but he had already left, and there was nothing interesting for him alone.However, the atmosphere here is indeed good, and the audience is composed of energetic college students, who are much more energetic than the old, stoic faces he saw in the company. He has not experienced this youthful atmosphere for a while since returning to China.Just as he was about to leave, he still felt a little pity. Ji Ran persisted and asked: "You haven't said anything yet. Why didn't I know who gave you something and when?" If you don't pay it back sooner or later, you just picked the time when you come with meJi Ran's voice was so noisy in his ears that Xu Jisi's temples jumped when he heard it. He looked down at the screen of his phone and interrupted: I won't return it yet.Ji Ran was stunned for a moment, and when he came to his senses, he was about to say that he would go back with him for a while, when Xu Jisi glanced at him, as if he had predicted what he was going to say, and refused decisively: "I won't go."He lowered his eyes and clicked on the screen, sending a location to someone.By the time Ji Ran reacted, Xu Jisi had already put away his phone.Ji Ran couldn't believe it. He didn't expect that he could really ruin the fun to this extent: You're going to leave me now.Meeting his gaze, Xu Jisi raised his chin slightly and pointed in the direction they came from before: Didn't you drive?

Ji Ran's eyes widened even more.I need Uncle Chen to drop you off.Ji Ran blurted out: At this point, it is better for me to go home than to let me die.It was an expected reply. Xu Jisi slapped away his hand on his shoulder: Well, feel free to do it.Ji Ran:The next time I talk to Xu Jisi, his surname is not Ji.

Dusk fell when we got home.The corridor was empty, and Chu Ying stood at the door of her home, which she was very familiar with. She repeatedly pressed the phone screen with her fingers, stared at the time on the phone for a moment, and then pressed it off.The consequence of the complete conflict with Zhu Ruoxuan is that now even going home has become a torture.After staying at the door for five minutes, raising and lowering her fingers several times, Chu Ying really didn't know how she would face Zhu Ruoxuan if she was at home.The sensor light dimmed quietly, Chu Ying took a deep breath in the darkness, finally made up her mind, and put her finger on the fingerprint lock accurately.The door opened in response.The sensor light came on as she took steps forward, illuminating a corner of the empty and quiet living room.Chu Ying subconsciously looked towards Zhu Ruoxuan's room.The door was closed, and no light came out from the crack.Chu Ying breathed a sigh of relief for no reason. She turned around and closed the door. When she walked around the dining table in the living room, she suddenly caught a glimpse of a piece of paper pressed by a vase.Chu Ying came closer, lifted the vase, and picked up the note.I'll go back to my hometown for two days, so don't disturb me. After reading it in a low voice, Chu Ying was stunned for a moment, feeling that Zhu Ruoxuan was also deliberately avoiding her.Regardless of whether this is true or not, it is true that she was given two days to relax.Chu Ying was lost in thought for a moment, pursed her lips, put away the note, took her mobile phone and sent a message to Moments, asking if anyone needed to share the apartment.Not wanting to continue to cause trouble to others, Chu Ying stayed up late and checked a lot of rental information.When she was woken up by the alarm clock in the morning, her brain was still a little sluggish. Chu Ying walked out of the room and subconsciously walked to Zhu Ruoxuan's door and knocked on the door, wanting to ask her if she wanted breakfast.No one answered for a while. The living room was dimly lit and so quiet that even the ticking sound of the clock in the living room could be heard clearly. After a while, Chu Ying regained consciousness, her vision gradually became clearer, and she remembered that Zhu Ruoxuan was not at home.Finally, I casually cooked a bowl of clear soup noodles for breakfast.The place where she rented a house was half an hour away from the company, so Chu Ying checked the rental information again.Facts have proved that it is indeed a very unwise choice to have conflicts with roommates.Chu Ying glanced at the red numbers between four and five thousand, and pressed her temples with a headache.Would it be better for her to endure it a little longer?The shared house with Zhu Ruoxuan has two bedrooms and one living room. It is said that it is the house of her senior relative, and it was rented to her at a friendly price. In addition, Zhu

Ruoxuan's room had multiple balconies. When it was decided to share the room, Zhu Ruoxuan offered to pay the majority of the rent herself, while Chu Ying only had to pay two thousand per month.It is almost difficult for her to rent a house at such a price in Lizhou. The one bedroom and living room she saw now cost more than 2,000 yuan, unless she looks for it in a remote place, but there is no subway around the place that is too remote, plus the cost of travel expenses. higher.Chu Ying's tense body leaned back slightly, leaning against the window, and sighed unconsciously."Little girl, what's going on?" the sighing driver asked familiarly.Well, I suddenly realized that every inch of land in Lizhou is precious.The driver nodded in agreement and looked at her in the rearview mirror several times. Seeing that she looked young, he asked casually: "Are you here to study in Lizhou?"Chu Ying nodded: I just graduated.Have you found a job?Found it, pretty stable.That's pretty good.The man smiled and thought of something again. His expression showed a trace of worry involuntarily. My daughter is in Wushi and has just graduated. I don't know how she is working there. Every time I ask her, she always says it's good. ofSeeing that he was already talking to himself, Chu Ying leaned forward slightly, hooked her fingers through the hair beside her ears, and her plain and beautiful face came into view.She raised her clear eyes and showed a serious expression.The girl's quiet look of listening completely opened up his conversational box, and a few white hairs could be vaguely seen in his hair. The middle-aged man murmured that he was too busy making money to spend more time with his daughter, and he didn't understand now. Regarding my daughter's current situation, I am worried about whether she will be bullied in other cities.Chu Ying responded appropriately and comforted: Don't worry, she is not a child anymore. You have to believe that she can live a good life.I also know that she has grown up, but I still can't help but miss her. When the red light turned green, he stepped on the accelerator and said with emotion: Poor parents in the world feel sorry for you when you are alone in Lizhou. Your parents must also miss her.Chu Ying's black eyes trembled slightly, and she suddenly curled her fingers.The car was silent for a moment.No one responded for a while, and the man looked in the rearview mirror again, only to see that the girl had lowered her eyelashes at some point, and her scattered black hair blocked her expression, making it difficult to see clearly.It seemed like a long time before I heard the girl's soft response from behind: Maybe.This answer was a bit strange. Before the man had time to think about it, the system automatically announced that he had arrived at his destination. He looked out the window, found an open space, and parked slowly.It wasn't until the car came to a steady stop that the girl moved, as if nothing had happened. She tapped her finger on the phone screen, smiled at him, and stretched out her hand to open the door: "Thank you, thank you for your hard work."No need to thank you, men subconsciously say this, so be careful on the road.The car door was closed, and through the car window, the girl waved to him again, signaling goodbye.The man turned around when he saw her and walked towards the huge cultural and creative park.The girl's delicate back is straight, and a section of her slender neck is exposed in the wind under her thick black hair, making her look even more white. The light blue dress swayed slightly in the wind, like a blue hibiscus swaying in the wind, as if it had stepped out of the painting, vivid and vivid.That moment of silence seemed like an illusion.

All short episodes were gone as soon as Chu Ying entered working mode.She had never particularly liked anything until she came into contact with dubbing and met Ling Tingyang. If someone asked her about her interests now, she could probably say that voice acting is what she loves.When a hobby becomes a career, it can become a grind. But when her career was accepted and transitioned into a good environment and became what she loved, Chu Ying was quite happy with it.Dubbing different characters is like experiencing the different lives of each character. Although it is indeed boring to a certain extent, Chu Ying does not think so.Ling Tingyang's satisfied call came from the earphones, and Chu Ying glanced at the clock on the wall.Four p.m.It feels like I've only been here for half an hour.Chu Ying took off her headphones in a familiar manner, stood up and walked to the control room. When she opened the door, she saw Ling Tingyang trimming the audio.Hearing the noise, Ling Tingyang didn't even look up. While cutting, he asked: How did you think of using such emotions in the scene just now?Chu Ying sat aside and thought about it: I just feel that sometimes despair does not have to have too strong emotions, and the more desperate you are, the calmer you will be. The performance of the actress here is not particularly heartbreaking. Too much is superfluous.Ling Tingyang nodded: It was handled very well.The same was true for the notes he took during this section. He thought he needed to explain the drama to Chu Ying, but he didn't expect that Chu Ying realized it on his own and passed it in one sentence.Listen to the effectLing Tingyang was still staring at the screen, clicking the mouse on the audio, seemingly asking casually. Chu Ying said hello. Ling Tingyang still needed some time to cut the audio, so she waited quietly aside and took out her phone to look at it.I posted a message to Moments last night, but I haven't seen anyone reply this morning. I haven't looked at it for a few hours. Now when I clicked on WeChat, I saw that two or three people had sent her messages one after another.However, after sending a message with full of expectations and asking a few questions, the results she got were either too far away or not in Lizhou. Chu Ying couldn't help but feel a little disappointed. She scrolled down the records and saw that there was another aaa that she didn't know when it was added. The real estate agent asked her if she was looking for a house.Chu Ying couldn't remember when she had joined an agency. She clicked on her profile picture and looked at her circle of friends. When she saw the person's selfie, she realized that it seemed to be one of her high school classmates. She didn't know when she started working as an agency.Where would she get the money to buy a house? Chu Ying sighed and typed to decline.Ling Tingyang's voice suddenly sounded beside him: You are looking for a house.Chu Ying raised her eyes and asked subconsciously: What are you doing?Before she even finished saying the two words, she saw Ling Tingyang reaching out to open the phone on the side and waving it in front of her.You didn't post it on Moments.Chu Ying blinked and then remembered that she forgot to block Ling Tingyang.It wasn't that I couldn't tell Ling Tingyang, but it was still strange for the boss to know about these private matters.Chu Ying suddenly felt a little embarrassed, and couldn't deny it. She could only hum. Then she quickly said: Brother Yang, don't worry, I won't affect you.I remember that my friend's house happened to be vacant. The location was pretty good. It was just a few minutes' walk from the subway station and about half an hour away.Chu Ying almost didn't react. She stared blankly as Ling Tingyang clicked on a contact on her hand and said to her: I'll ask about the situation, maybe

I can help you.You mean, Chu Ying finally came to her senses under these clear words, her black eyes opened wide, and she paused mid-sentence, hurriedly waving her hands, "This is too much trouble for you, I can look for it myself"The words have not yet fallen.Ling Tingyang stared at the screen and suddenly raised his eyebrows, interrupting her: Replied.He said he was leaving this week and could go see it tomorrow.

Chu Ying really couldn't find any reason to refuse Ling Tingyang's kind help. This problem had been bothering her for many days, and people had asked it for her. If she still refused, she would be ignorant.The most important thing is that Ling Tingyang said that they were acquaintances anyway, and his friend wanted to charge only 3,000 yuan for the rent, so it was a smooth favor.Or two bedrooms and one living room.She and Zhu Ruoxuan shared a room, and her dubbing equipment was placed together with the room, which actually took up a lot of space. If it was two bedrooms and one living room, she could use one as a recording studio.What's the difference between this and pie in the sky?If Ling Tingyang hadn't said it, she wouldn't have believed that such a good thing happened.It's just that Chu Ying has a delicate mind. After thinking about it after returning home, she always felt a little uneasy.After washing up in the evening, she still called Ling Tingyang and asked if the price was real.She was a little worried whether Ling Tingyang would make up the difference in price.Ling Tingyang has always been very kind to the company's employees and always helps out when needed. Last year, a colleague's mother was hospitalized for surgery and couldn't afford the money. When Ling Tingyang found out, he paid for it without saying a word.The other end paused for a moment, as if he didn't expect that she would ask this question when he called me at night. He said in a funny way: I colluded with my friend and asked him to quote a low rent for you to watch, and I will give it to him privately. Make up the difference. Chu Ying, do you think I'm a little too good-natured?Chu Ying was silent, and her cheeks suddenly began to heat up.Although she did have this suspicion, once the words were repeated by the person involved, why did she feel so ashamed?like.It seems like she is so narcissistic that she can make others pay so much attention to her.The target is still the boss.Let her dieChu Ying suddenly regretted making this call.Her tone was very serious at the beginning, because she was afraid that Ling Tingyang would fool him with jokes because of his temper.I, Chu Ying, opened my mouth, but only one syllable came out, and I didn't know how to reply.Fortunately, there was no intention to continue teasing her.I am your boss, no matter what, I will not do anything to give you money. Just asking for you is just something I can do conveniently, so you don't need to take it too seriously.Ling Tingyang's words gave her a positive answer. Chu Ying felt relieved a lot. She was about to apologize when she heard the other end add:If one day I do something like this, it will definitely bring me more benefits.The implication is that acting in front of her would do him no good.Chu Ying thought about it seriously and found that even if he really did this, he would only get a good person card from her and be rejected.There is no second benefit other than gains and an awkward atmosphere for employees.Even if he advanced money to his colleagues before, he just had the money to help him and didn't say he didn't have to pay it back. But he didn't rush him, and his colleagues were always grateful and worked hard, paying back a little every month.To sum it up, she really thought too much.Chu Ying touched her burned ears and whispered: I was presumptuous.Don't be pressured, Ling Tingyang knew her temper all too well, so he smiled and said it would be the best reward for you to make sure there are no mistakes in your dubbing.

The next day was Friday, and Ling Tingyang was worried that he would be late due to traffic jams during the evening rush hour, so he asked Chu Ying to finish the dubbing in advance.With her efficiency not far behind, Ling Tingyang sent Chu Ying out of the shed after sending messages to her friends.After handing over the progress with the assistant director, Ling Tingyang arrived at the lobby late. Chu Ying was already waiting for him at her desk. When she saw him coming out, she put away her phone and stood up to walk towards him.As the two walked towards the elevator, they said: "He is in a hurry to leave first. The key has been sent to the security room. Let's go get the key first."Chu Ying was stunned for a moment: Is he not worried at all?Ling Tingyang chuckled: He is my roommate in college. We have a good relationship. He is a rich second generation and very casual. By the way, he is the one who occasionally comes to the company to hang out. Strictly speaking, he is also one of the bosses. You He asked me who he was before.I told him that you were looking for her, and he had a good impression of you. After saying that, he looked at her again and joked, otherwise, how could he rent it to you at a discount?The tips of Chu Ying's ears turned crimson almost instantly.It was at this moment that the two of them were bumped into by Ji Ran and Xu Jisi.Xu Jisi was still wearing the gray suit from yesterday, her eyes were indifferent, her lips pursed into a line, her long and cold eyes swept over the two of them, and finally settled on the girl.At that time, it seemed to Ji Ran that the two of them were talking and laughing without paying attention to them in front of them, and then he didn't know what Ling Tingyang said. The girl who spoke officially yesterday and had always been restrained suddenly turned red at the tip of her ears and became shy. He lowered his head, revealing a slender neck that could make people stare straight at him.What a fucking eye-opener.No wonder I'm so unfamiliar with him.The co-author is having an office romance with the boss here.

Chapter 7 RememberingThe warmth of contact07Ji Ran looked at the two of them with a complicated expression, not knowing whether to speak or not.Ling Tingyang just happened to turn his head, raised his eyes to meet the two people who suddenly arrived, and was stunned.Ling Tingyang stopped, and Chu Ying also stopped. She was still thinking about the embarrassing phone call last night. She wanted to dig her head into a hole in the ground. She squeezed the bag tightly with her hands and almost took off the decoration on the bag.Until Ji Ran was the first to speak out: It seems that we came at an unlucky time.He raised his eyebrows: He is goingSuddenly hearing a familiar voice, Chu Ying thought it was an illusion. When she raised her head, she suddenly encountered a pair of dark pupils that seemed to be raised lazily.Xu Jisi stood beside Ji Ran, his eyes still looking dull and emotionless.It seemed like they didn't meet the day before yesterday.The clips of the encounter two days ago flashed uncontrollably, from being forced to share the table to the confrontation in the bathroom.And that sentenceMr. Xu's pick-up techniques are very old-fashioned.This sentence came to mind without any warning. After Chu Ying realized what she had said just to show off, she stiffened up and trembled all over as if a gust of wind had blown by.She's really crazyPerhaps it was the formal recognition the day before yesterday. Chu Ying could clearly feel that the person's gaze was not just a passing glance before. He did not hide his gaze at the moment. As long as someone glanced at him, they would know that he was looking at her.At this moment, the word "scorching" may not be suitable to describe Xu Jisi, but it can be used for her.Everywhere Xu Jisi glanced at was burning, and his unclear expression made her feel on pins and needles.Chu Ying turned her head stiffly, moved her steps imperceptibly, and hid behind Ling Tingyang.Unexpectedly, Xu Jisi's dark eyes darkened slightly after he noticed her movements, and the corners of his lips twitched slightly.Sorry, I didn't know you would come to the prison shed today.Ling Tingyang quickly came to his senses and explained: "I have some personal things to do today and need to leave early. It will not affect the progress of the project. Don't worry."Private things.Ji Ran raised his eyebrows and really didn't avoid it.private matterJi Ran lazily chatted, his eyes wandering around the two of them, meaningfully: What are you doing?He intentionally prolonged his tone. Ling Tingyang reacted, frowned slightly, and glanced to the side. Seeing that Chu Ying was distracted abnormally, he paused, took a step forward, and intentionally stopped in front of her, standing in front of her. She blocked most of Ji Ran's hinting glances.We don't mean to neglect our duties. We do have some things to do urgently, and we hope that the documentary film producer will understand.In one sentence, it not only explained that they were not there for fun, but also explained that there was no close relationship between them.Ji Ran's eyebrows moved. Whether it was his tone or expression, Ling Tingyang was too calm. He already believed it.After all, it was a cooperative relationship. The other party had already lowered his profile and ensured that it would not affect the progress of the project. When he pressed further, it seemed unreasonable. Ji Ran shrugged: Okay, then we won＇t waste it. It's your time.Ling Tingyang breathed a sigh of relief almost imperceptibly, and showed an apologetic look: the reception was not good enough. If you want to know the progress, you can contact Jiang Qi. He is the dubbing assistant director of the project and should be in Studio 2 now.Ji Ran nodded calmly: It's okay, we'll just stop by and take a look, and we're leaving now.Ling Tingyang nodded, then turned around, raised his hand slightly, and silently said to Chu Ying to leave.Finally able to leave, Chu Ying hurriedly stepped to follow.The next moment, a cold voice suddenly sounded.I have something else to do.Chu Ying's steps stagnated, and she began to panic for no reason.Isn't it aimed at her this time?Did Xu Jisi want to take revenge on her and file a complaint with Ling Tingyang?Ji Ran was stunned for a moment, then turned to look at him: What's the matter with you?I didn＇t even tell him.Xu Jisi glanced at him coldly, turned slightly, his tall and superior figure facing away from the light, and the falling slender shadow came into the girl's field of vision.This angle was obviously looking at her.Chu Ying's heart beat like a drum, and she didn't know where to put her fingers. In just a few seconds, countless thoughts flashed through her mind. What should Xu Jisi do if she really doesn't care about the past relationship and avenges her.Xu Jisi raised his black eyes slightly and looked at Chu Ying's background, clearly noticing her stiffer back.I'm here to return the favor. He spoke slowly, his voice was light, neither loud nor quiet. I didn't know if he was responding to Ji Ran or talking to someone.He paused, raised his eyebrows and looked towards Chu Ying without concealment, and moved his lips slightly:Miss Chu's earrings.Ling Ran's voice passed through the gentle air, and the atmosphere was dull and silent for a moment, and then suddenly exploded like thunder on the ground.

Why do you have Chu Ying's earrings?On the way out of Lingting Building, Ji Ran didn't even come back to his senses.He had never felt like such an outsider. He was also present when he met Chu Ying twice. How could Xu Jisi inexplicably get into such an ambiguous situation as returning the earrings?What on earth did he do to get good earrings into his hands?It couldn't have been dropped, right?Ji Ran almost began to doubt his life, and his tone was shocked and accusing: You guys even met each other behind my back in private?Xu Jisi did not refute. In Ji Ran's eyes, it was as if he had admitted. He turned his head, feeling a strong sense of betrayal: "Xu Jisi, tell me honestly, what happened?"Halfway through the words, in the flash of lightning, the words Xu Ji couldn't help but say when he left in the spring breeze flashed back to his mind.wrongHis brain suddenly connected many pictures and words together. Chu Ying's appearance of escaping hastily appeared in front of his eyes. Ji Ran suddenly clapped his hands: Could it be that they really bumped into each other the day before yesterday?Xu Jisi's thoughts were completely messed up by Xu Jisi's glance but without explanation. The questions in his mind were about to turn into snowballs. Ji Ran's eyes were so wide that they seemed to fall out. He held it in for a long time:you, you

youThe autumn wind is always cool.The uneven green belts on both sides of the road receded, and the wind blew gently, blowing the hair on the side of the girl's face.Staring at the scenery outside for a long time, her eyes were a little achy due to the wind. As if all her strength had been relieved, Chu Ying suddenly leaned to one side tiredly, still nestled between the car door and the backrest.Ling Tingyang hesitated for a long time before asking you.His tone seemed casual, but his eyes turned sideways several times uncontrollably.In fact, he shouldn't ask more.But Chu Ying's condition was indeed not quite right.When she took the sapphire blue earrings from Xu Jisi's hand at the company, she remained calm and even thanked her very politely.From his perspective, the girl's waist was straight, her thin neck and shoulders were straight, and although her figure was thin, her posture was inexplicably stubborn.He couldn't see what the two people's expressions were like in those few seconds.But the voice doesn't lie.He knew Chu Ying's voice too well.Others may not notice these details, but he can. Chu Ying's voice trembled slightly when she spoke, clearly revealing that her mood was not as calm as she appeared.Faintly aware of a hint, Ling Tingyang remembered that when the film crew came for the first time, Chu Ying seemed to be in something wrong.At that time, Xu Jisi and Ji Ran were also there.If you have to think about it too much, Chu Ying may have some kind of bond with one of them.The green light suddenly turned yellow as the car approached the intersection. Ling Tingyang was lost in thought for a moment and lightly stepped on the brakes. The sunny doll hanging on the rearview mirror shook. Ling Tingyang subconsciously glanced into the mirror and saw Chu Ying's obviously tense body.I happened to bump into her in the spring breeze the day before yesterday. She looked a little unnatural. She paused after her words, her long eyelashes drooped, and she stared at the blue spot in her palm. I must have accidentally dropped the earrings.She was in a bad mood at the time and forgot that she had planned to re-hang the earrings. She didn't even notice it all the way. It was only when she got home and washed up that she realized in the mirror that she had lost one of her earrings.Maybe it was lost somewhere on the way out of Chunfengli, or in a hastily hailed taxi, she thought at that time.I never expected that it would be in Xu Jisi's hands.The moment this name flashed across his mind, the way the man looked at her half a moment ago with his neck bent and his eyebrows lowered came to mind.His cold eyes were half down, his slender finger bones were slightly bent, and the small earrings were in his palm.He handed it forward.Chu Ying didn't know what her expression was like at that time. Her mind probably went blank for a moment. When she reacted, the warmth between her fingertips and her palms seemed to burn a hole in her heart.His palms were warm and dry.Chu Ying's fingertips felt slightly cold and she froze for a moment. The next moment she realized something, her face tightened as if she wanted to prove something.She wanted to look as calm as possible, and took the earrings from his hand very quickly without looking at him. The words "thank you" seemed to be squeezed out, and then she turned around without pausing for a second.It seemed that in this way, she could ignore the gaze he cast on her, as if he could see through her.

Nothing has changed.He was always so high and mighty.After the reunion, every look in their eyes was dull, but they showed an expression of knowing everything.It seemed as if all her disguises could be defeated easily.Chu Ying's throat suddenly became sore, and her palms tightened unconsciously.The earrings in her palms seemed to be covered with sweat. The pain stimulated her nerves until her palms were numb. She did not relax at all, as if she wanted to remember something.Perhaps it is to remember that ordinary autumn day when the sun sets in the west, or perhaps to remember those days and nights in front of the hospital bed.Remember the phone call that I couldn't reach that day, and also remember the response I didn't get until the end.

Chapter 8 RememberingI knew it five years ago08On the day of moving, Ling Tingyang specially gave her a holiday.Zhu Ruoxuan still hasn't come back.Chu Ying got up early and looked up at the sky. It was foggy and drizzling.The things to be moved have already been packed up. She has a lot of things and a lot of things. It is a bit over-qualified to find a moving company, but she would have to move it several times herself.Chu Ying stood at the entrance of the stairs, with several packed suitcases next to her. She moved her fingers back and forth among the contacts, and her eyes fell on Wen Zaichen's name several times.There is no doubt that if a coolie is needed at this moment, Wen Zaichen is the best choice.To a certain extent, Wen Zaichen was her brother. She deliberately hid it from Wen Zaichen when she was looking for a house, just because she was afraid that he would interfere too much. If he found out, she would definitely let her go home to live.And when she made this call, there was a high probability that Wen Zaichen would talk about it.Her finger paused at the top of the screen and hesitated for a while. Chu

Ying wondered if she could move all the luggage in one day if she relied entirely on herself.Otherwise, just spend some money to hire a moving company.The moment this thought flashed through his mind, his phone suddenly vibrated.She lowered her head and saw an incoming call from Wen Zaichen that happened to light up on the screen.Chu Ying blinked and answered the phone. Before calling out his name, Wen Zaichen's depressed voice sounded on the other end: Chu Ying, where are you?I'm at the company. She subconsciously interfaced.The voice on the other end was silent for a moment, and seemed to laugh angrily at her: In, company, companyThen why don't you turn around and take a look?Chu Ying blinked and turned her head slightly.Not far away, a man in a suit stood in front of the car, holding an umbrella in one hand and holding a phone to his ear in the other, giving her a smiley expression.Chu Ying saw the man open his mouth, and then through the rain curtain, the other person's voice came clearly into her ears from the other end of the phone.Chu Ying, you are very capable.

You don't discuss a big thing like moving with me. If I hadn't stopped by today, how long would you want to keep this from me?As expected, Wen Zaichen's mumblings were endless. Chu Ying put her finger on the fingerprint lock, and the door opened. She looked back at Wen Zaichen, who was still frowning to show dissatisfaction, but honestly carrying her recording equipment in his hand, and her voice softened. soft:I originally planned to tell you after the move was completed, but I was worried that you would be busy and would disturb your work.Chu Ying said as she opened the door. Worried about knocking her baby, Wen Zaichen subconsciously took a few steps back and carefully raised the device in his hand. He waited until she walked through the door before following her. He looked at her with a half-smile but said, "You see, believe it or not."Chu Ying responded seriously: Really, I wanted to call you just now.This set of words just deceived him.In fact, he had a suspicion in his heart, just because he was afraid that he would interfere too much. If Chu Ying really mentioned it to him, he would either let Chu Ying go home, or he would directly give her a place next to the company.Chu Ying has always been measured. She usually looks gentle and easy to talk to, but in fact she has made up her mind and is more stubborn than anyone else.There is a red line in her heart. Above the red line, it is easy to talk about anything. Below the red line, no one can get into it.After four or five years of getting along with him, he had a clear idea of Chu Ying's temperament.Wen Zaichen knew what he was doing, so he didn't continue the discussion with her and put the device gently on the ground: "Then I have wronged you."Chu Ying nodded seriously: But for the sake of helping me move, I forgive you.Wen Zaichen chuckled: He got an advantage and acted like a good boy.With Wen Zaichen's help, the efficiency has become visibly higher. The living room had been tidied up as early as the afternoon. It was so bright and bright that even the off-white polished tiles reflected the blue sky outside. It was clean and refreshing. When dinner was approaching in the evening, Chu Ying only had the bathroom left to buy daily necessities.Finally, she wiped the bathroom mirror, washed her hands, and stuck her head out from the door to ask Wen Zaichen what she wanted to do with dinner.Wen Zaichen was leaning on the wall outside the bathroom, lowering his head and pressing his cell phone to send a voice message to the man, saying to leave it until he went back to deal with it. It was probably something at work.After replying, she looked up at her. Chu Ying met Wen Zaichen's gaze and asked thoughtfully: Do you want to go and do some work first?Wen Zaichen turned off his phone and stuffed it back into his pocket, raising his eyebrows: Why did I work as a coolie for you all day and didn't even include food?No way, Chu Ying thought for a while, if you are not busy, I will treat you to a nice meal. If not, I will make up for it later.After finishing today's work, Wen Zaichen straightened up, put the coat hanging on his arms back on, tilted his head towards her, and left.

In a mansion with a river view somewhere.Next to the floor-to-ceiling windows is a bright living room. At a glance, you can see the tall buildings rising from the ground in the center of the city. The sun sets in the sky and the afterglow overflows from the clouds and falls on the luxurious flat floor.The sunlight was dazzling. Ji

Ran raised his hand to cover it. After a few seconds, he felt tired again. He took the remote control nearby and pressed a button. The floor-to-ceiling curtains were half closed, just enough to block the half of the light that was shining on him.After completing this set of actions, Ji Ran threw the remote control aside and continued:Anyway, the old man wants to give you a joint product, so that you can't find fault with it on the surface, and it also allows me to learn more from you.I really can't understand these bad old guys. Regarding this project, the group is lifeless. They just give progress reports every day. What's there to keep an eye on?Ji Ran lay lazily on the sofa, eating melon seeds, and scrolling through his phone with one hand. After a few seconds, he didn't hear a reply. He spit out the melon seed shell, stretched his neck to the side, and tapped the table with his fingers: What do you think? squeakThe man sitting on the single sofa on one side has one long leg slightly bent and the other slightly stretched forward. He looks dignified. The legs of the ironed suit trouser were pulled up a bit due to this posture, failing to cover the bulging cold white ankles. He leaned to one side, holding a pen in his bony hand, and circled a number on the document before glancing at it:Uncle Ji mentioned it to me yesterday.Ji Ran put his hands on his temples, stood up, and immediately asked: What did he tell you?It's pretty much what you said, let me take you through it.He really has the nerve to imitate you and learn like you. After returning home, he will read these boring documents all day long, attend those boring meetings, and listen to them arguing about this and that all day long.Xu was neither thinking nor annoyed. He lowered his head again, scanned the document with his dark eyes, and turned back the page.Ji Ran clicked his tongue and asked again: "Then how did you respond?"He must refuse it. What does this matter have to do with you, he thought.As if he suddenly felt depressed, Xu Jisi spread the documents on the table, taking Ji Ran's words as background, raised his wrists and curled his fingers, the muscles on the back of his hands were slightly convex, loosened his tie, and then responded calmly: I said good.I said you won't agree. That old man just wants to be beautiful. Wait, what did you say?There was silence in the air for five seconds. Ji Ran looked at him stiffly. Xu Jisi's eyes fell back on the document, as if he didn't know what impact it would have on him, without even looking up.When did you become so enthusiastic? Ji Ran's expression fell apart for a moment, and he collapsed on the sofa. Why did you agree to this kind of thing?Xu Jisi said quietly: "Your dad, let me give you some face."Ji Ran gritted his teeth: You haven' t even given me my face.I really don' t understand what kind of medicine you took recently.Ji Ran put a hand on the back of his head, and raised his legs to the table without any pretense and crossed them. There is also the matter of Chu Ying. I don't usually see you so fond of doing good deeds, but now you have become a 'Lei

Feng', and an earring is enough. Specially sent to people.At that time, he really thought that Xu Jisi was just stopping by for him.He still finds it unbelievable. When he heard the sentence about returning the earrings, his mood was no less than when he heard that his sixty-year-old man had married a twenty-year-old wife.When asked later on the road, Xu Jisi just said that he saw it by chance.This reason was far more reasonable than the vague guess in his heart. Ji Ran's heart dropped and he skipped this matter.But now, how could Xu Jisi be able to cope with such a ridiculous thing.No wonder his father was so natural when he called him. The co-authorship had already been agreed upon.The old man doesn't think that his life span will be shortened. He has watched Xu Jisi grow up. Can he not know what kind of character Xu Jisi is? Can he agree to such a thing without doubting it?The more Ji Ran thought about it, the more his head became numb. He took a breath and wanted to ask Xu Jisi what his plan was. However, he raised his head and met his cold profile, looking through the documents with an indifferent expression. He opened his mouth and then The words were swallowed back.There was no way he could ask Xu Jisi what he didn't want to say.He already knew it.I knew it five years ago.Ji Ran stared at him for a long time, sighed, and slumped back to the sofa. He took a back pillow and put it on his chest. He took the mobile phone on the table and continued to scroll through it while asking: What should we have for dinner?He thumbed up a few times and scanned some content in his circle of friends in boredom. Suddenly, his eyes fell on a photo full of luggage. Ji Ran's eyes fell on the top of the photo, staring at that After taking notes for a second, he suddenly sat up.Xu Jisi glanced at him out of the corner of his eye, not knowing what was going on with him, and didn't respond.Ji Ran obviously forgot what he asked before, and his mind was entirely on that photo at the moment.Click it, zoom in, zoom in again.Then from a pile of boxes of various sizes, he accurately saw the half hand on the far right in the mirror.Only about a third of it is on the wrist in the shot, where a men's watch comes into view.Two blurry letters were printed on the bottom of the watch. Ji Ran's brain was racing and he quickly matched the numbers in his mind.It is a low-key luxury brand. He had seen it at Liang Xuqing's house. He had no impression of the brand at the time and even asked about it.But it's not certain that this is a male hand.He squinted his eyes and slid to the left.The second picture seems to be in a restaurant. Opposite the owner of the mobile phone, you can vaguely see the knife and fork half in the frame.Turning to the right, the third picture shows the sunset through the clear floor-to-ceiling glass. Buildings stand tall in the distance, and vehicles are constantly flowing down below. If you look carefully, you can vaguely see her figure reflected in the glass.But she's not the only one.The figure of the person opposite was really unclear, but that was probably the case, and Chu

Ying didn't notice it either.Ji Ran saved the picture, opened the photo album, adjusted the contrast of the photo, and could barely make out the outline of the man.He was quite tall, and his hands were folded casually on the dining table.short hair.Moving his eyes downward, the familiar watch just now came into view, reflecting the light and making it very conspicuous.Good guy.What a man.Judging from the style, it's not Ling Tingyang either.Why did you change it again?Ji Ran's eyes twitched: Why are there so many wild bees and butterflies around Chu Ying?

Not knowing what keyword he heard, Xu Jisi darkened his eyes.After a long while, as if he was finally willing to divert his attention from the paper in front of him, Xu Jisi raised his eyelashes slightly, his eyes fell on Ji Ran's cell phone, he tapped his half-bent fingers on the pen holder, and then rubbed it slowly. .Then he lowered his eyes, held back the pen, and wrote something on the document paper, as if he just mentioned it casually, with a calm and cold voice:let me see

Chapter 9 RememberI fouled her nose first09Ji Ran really wanted to see a doctor for a moment, otherwise he would have been hearing hallucinations recently.When he hesitantly glanced at the only person beside him, he didn't meet his gaze, and it seemed that he was silent. Xu Jisi didn't even raise his head, but felt a little tense. He put down the pen and loosened the button on his wrist.As if just noticing his gaze, Xu Jisi slowly raised his eyes: What?Nothing, Ji Ran stared at his boney and white wrist, muttering to himself as if to express his thoughts, I think I should make an appointment with a psychiatrist.Xu Jisi raised his eyebrows, thinking something was wrong.Ji Ran nodded: You are right, maybe you should go to a psychiatric department.

Xu Jisi ignored his nonsense, glanced at his mobile phone, put his finger on the pen, and asked casually for a moment: How is the progress of the project here?Dubbing hereUm.I didn't pay much attention to it. They would report it in the group, and it was usually too old. Ji Ran's attention was diverted for a moment, and he suddenly remembered something. If you want to take over, I'll just drag you into the group to understand.Xu Jisi picked up the pen and circled it between the slender finger bones, saying in a calm voice: OK.It was so smooth that it made people think that he was just waiting for this sentence.Ji Ran pulled people into the group, and then he felt a little strange and had to look away to the side. Xu Jisi's expression was still natural, and his beautiful fingers were scratching on the screen, and he could faintly see that he was flipping through records.After a long while, he slowly and concisely summarized: The process is very fast, I will keep an eye on it for a few days when I have time.Although Xu Jisi would agree to the behavior of his old man, which surprised him, he couldn't control it too much, and even wished that someone would take over.Ji Ran had long wanted to be the hands-off shopkeeper, so he hurriedly said: This is what you said.Then he lay back on the sofa and said lazily: Then I can feel free to ask someone out to play.Don't forget that your dad is still watching.Isn't it enough to have you? He just wants to get some glory from He Jing. He really thinks he wants me to learn something.What was said on the table was true and false. Ji Ran looked at the dude and knew everything in his heart. And Xu Jisi couldn't be unclear about this that he knew.He has nothing to show off.What's more, Xu Jisi agreed even though he knew everything.Although he didn't know the reason, this decision just happened to suit him. Ji Ran didn't like to explore these motives, which would make him feel that his friendship was cheap, so he usually didn't mention it at all.Ji Ran started eating melon seeds again, unaware that there was anything inappropriate about talking about these things.Anyway, in front of Xu Jisi, he was probably more transparent than the floor-to-ceiling window next to him.Not two seconds after the words fell, Xu Jisi paused, as if thinking of something, he rubbed the cap of his pen with his fingers, and his dark eyes half-closed: OK.Oh, Ji Ran raised his eyes and teased, "Young Master Xu is so happy today and always responds to requests."Xu Jisi was too lazy to pay attention to him and glanced at the records casually. He didn't see Chu Ying in the group saying anything.Scanning his eyes across the upper right corner, he slowly clicked on the group member information.I saw the familiar avatar at a glance.It's still that sideways photo at the beach.Xu Jisi thought about whether his fingers would fall, and suddenly said: "Let me take a look at your phone."What for?Look at the first document.Oh, OK. Ji Ran withdrew from the circle of friends and handed it to him.Xu Jisi took the phone, swiped the screen, and clicked something.Ji Ran stared at his movements for a few seconds before he realized: No, if you want the documents, I'll just send them to you, right?Xu Jisi swiped his finger to the right, found a file and clicked on it, then looked away and raised his eyes.Yep.He handed the phone back to Ji Ran: Send it.Why do I always feel like something is weird?Ji Ran lowered his head and looked at the screen.It's just a file, nothing more.Where did this weird feeling come from.Ji Ran had a flash of confusion and didn't notice that Xu Jisi picked up his phone and naturally entered a string of letters into the add friend in the upper right corner.The account that popped up was Chu Ying's.But when staring at the words added to the address book, Xu was thoughtful and showed a rare hesitation.It took a while until Ji Ran remembered his original question again and asked him what he wanted for dinner. Xu Jisi moved his fingers slightly, crossed the screen, touched the bulge on the side, and dimmed.Either way.He deserves the cold shoulder.

On the other side, the housing problem that has

been bothering her for many days has probably been finally solved. Chu Ying is indeed in a good mood today.When it was time to check out after finishing the meal, Chu Ying got a reply from the waiter that the order had been paid half an hour ago.Suddenly remembering that Wen Zaichen went to the bathroom during the meal, Chu Ying's confused expression gradually faded, and then she slowly turned her head.However, Wen Zaichen entered the elevator first as he had expected this scene.She had no choice but to thank the person quickly and ran to the elevator in three steps at a time.Just as he was about to step into the elevator, the door began to slowly close automatically. Chu Ying stopped subconsciously and raised her eyes in annoyance. She met Wen Zaichen's teasing expression through the crack in the door, and she was very flattered.Wen ZaichenIn her aggravated tone, Wen Zaichen raised his hand in time and pressed the button to open the door.The door that was about to close was opened again. Wen Zaichen raised his wrist and turned it twice, making a gesture of inviting her in.Still teasing herChu Ying walked into the elevator expressionlessly, without looking at Wen Zaichen's expression. She lowered her head and clicked on WeChat to find his profile picture, and said in a strained voice: "How much is it."Wen Zaichen looked down at her and saw that she was pressing her lips tightly and had already clicked on the transfer.So angryChu Ying ignored him and asked again: How much.It's only a few hundred yuan, so it's not that big of a deal. I told you that you wanted to come here. Wasn't it because you were going to bleed?In fact, he was just joking at the time. Seeing Chu Ying's blank expression and then widening her eyes, he thought it was cute, but he didn't expect that she would grit her teeth and actually agree.In her words, a trip here is no different from the cost of finding a moving company.He replied at the time that what he ate into his stomach was different from what he gave directly to others.So Chu Ying thought about it for a while before deciding to come here.One thing comes back to another. The elevator is transparent and you can clearly see the darkening night. Chu Ying paused, her voice was still muffled. Since you said it's my treat, it's my treat.There was silence for a few seconds, and the elevator was still descending slowly, jumping from 7 to 6.Staring into her serious eyes, Wen Zaichen sighed softly, then admitted defeat and reported a number.Chu Ying's expression softened a little and she quickly transferred the money to him.When he was about to turn off his phone, he suddenly saw a string of numbers sent by Ling Tingyang.Chu Ying's attention was quickly diverted and she clicked on the profile picture. Ling Tingyang just happened to send two consecutive voices.Thin white fingers touched the screen.Regarding the rent issue you asked earlier, he said he was too lazy to hand over this, so he just asked you to transfer money into it every month. This is the bank card number.But I also gave him your WeChat account and he should add you. Just pay attention. He doesn't like to chat much, so you don't need to send him a message if there's nothing wrong, and you won't necessarily get a reply if you do.The voice sounded in the closed elevator. Wen Zaichen stared at her side face and slowly moved to her mobile phone: Your bossChu Ying told him about this while eating earlier.Chu Ying typed her reply and responded: Yes.Wen Zaichen paused and asked again: Is your boss treating your employees so well?yes.Oh, Wen Zaichen turned around and pretended to look at the scenery outside, and said after two seconds, I know your company is quite famous in the industry. How old is your boss? He is very powerful.It seems that he should be in his early thirtiesChu Ying didn't think much. She raised her eyes and recalled it. Just halfway through her words, she saw a red number pop up in the address book and a black avatar appeared among the new friends.What she was about to say stopped abruptly. The girl stared at the profile picture of this account for a long time, and instantly thought of the voice message that Ling Tingyang had just sent.The pure black avatar, with nothing visible, is in line with the simple style of the rich second generation in my impression.So fast.Chu Ying muttered softly, lowered her head and passed her friend smoothly.The elevator finally reached the first floor slowly, and the door opened in response. The girl lowered her head and said some polite words as she was about to walk out.Before he could send it out, his arm was suddenly pulled by someone, and he staggered two steps to the side, passing by the person in front of him.Watch the road.The man holding her arm reminded her.Chu Ying was stunned for a while, then looked sideways, and saw that the man who almost bumped into her just now was a tall and strong man, who looked like he was not easy to mess with.Chu Ying turned back with lingering fear and saw Wen Zaichen frowning: It's too late to come back later.makes sense.What's more, Ling Tingyang just said that the other party didn't like to chat.Chu Ying nodded and put the phone back into her pocket.As the night fell, the two of them were walking along the pedestrian street together. Wen Zaichen was walking casually, as if he were just wandering around, so he asked her if she wanted to take a stroll.Chu Ying's eyes slowly fell on the mobile phone in his hand that frequently turned on the breathing light. She raised her chin slightly to indicate: Mr. Wen, work must be urgent.In the afternoon, she could tell that he was probably busy with something, but he still insisted on going to dinner with her. Chu Ying thought that it might not be that important, so she followed his wishes.However, while eating, she noticed that Wen Zaichen repeatedly took out his cell phone several times to reply to messages.Now that news was popping up all the time, she was not a fool and could realize that Wen Zaichen obviously had something important to do next.Wen Zaichen paused and looked at her helplessly: I'm so busy that I rarely have time to see you. It's not easy to see you today.I am no longer the child who always needed someone to accompany me when sleeping. Chu Ying suddenly interrupted him with a serious expression. If you have something more important to do, if you want to find me, I will always be here.The girl's clear black eyes looked straight into his. Wen Zaichen opened his mouth, tightened and loosened his fingers, and after a while he responded: "Okay."Chu Ying originally wanted him to go work directly and she could just take a taxi home, but Wen Zaichen insisted on sending her back on the grounds that the company was on the way to her new home.She knew the address of Wen Zaichen's company, recalled the route, and confirmed that it was indeed the right way, and then got into Wen Zaichen's car.The night gets quieter when I get home.With a gentle pull, the door automatically closed slowly, and the click of the gusset seemed to block out the complicated world. A feeling of tiredness suddenly washed over the body.When Chu Ying returned to the room, she threw herself into the bed and slowly closed her eyes.Being alone will make it easier for her to regain her energy.For a moment, she felt uncomfortable living alone. Chu Ying closed her eyes for half a minute, then suddenly remembered something and opened her eyes. She clicked on her phone and found Zhu Ruoxuan's WeChat account.She paused with her fingers in the air, and then Chu Ying typed: I have moved away.After staring at the words for a long time, he typed again: "Go back."About to send out.An incoming phone call interrupted her movements.After looking carefully at the notes on the screen, she realized that the caller was Zhu Ruoxuan, the person she wanted to send a message to.Chu Ying was stunned for a moment, recalling that after the quarrel, Zhu Ruoxuan didn't even send her any more messages. She always left notes when she went out.Why call her at this time?Within a few seconds of distraction and hesitation, the call was quickly hung up again.Chu Ying raised her finger hesitantly.Although the relationship between the two has indeed become tense recently, she has moved out now and they have been living together for a year, so there is no need for the relationship to get to this point.Besides, with Zhu Ruoxuan's temperament, she probably wouldn't call her if nothing happened.Feeling something was wrong, Chu Ying dialed back again.The phone was not connected immediately. Chu Ying tightened her fingers to catch up with her daily posts in Qi'egu Wu'er 490 Bar 192. She couldn't stop eating meat. The fatigue was suppressed, and there was an ominous foreboding. The cold came over me, and my beautiful eyebrows frowned unconsciously, and I stared at the number on the screen without blinking.Probably ten seconds, maybe twenty seconds.The ringing suddenly stopped, indicating that the call was connected. Chu Ying breathed a sigh of relief and was about to speak when a male voice came from the other end: HelloChu Ying made a move and frowned unconsciously: Are you?The male voice was faster than her: Is your name Chu Ying?yes.I am a policeman, Zhu Ruoxuan is your friend, right?Chu Ying was stunned for a moment: What happened to her?She drank, had a conflict with someone on the road, and injured someone. The other party did not accept the settlement. The police briefly summarized what happened. If you are free, come over now.Chu Ying subconsciously asked: Is she injured?There were no flesh wounds.Chu Ying calmed down and was silent for a moment, thinking that her relationship with her was not that good.But she couldn't write a record in her current state. The police added that we should give priority to mediation. Everything must be negotiated after she sobers up. It's not early today, so it's best to take her back first.Are you free? The other end asked again.There was silence on both ends of the phone for a few seconds.Chu Ying unconsciously looked out the window at the dark night.A long while.good.She touched the keychain on the table with her fingers, stood up, and whispered: I'll be right over.

It wasn't until she arrived at the door of the police station that Chu Ying stared at the big word "Public Security" above that she realized what she was doing.Zhu Ruoxuan clearly had so many friends, so why did he call her?And she actually came.Chu Ying pursed her lips, her expression changed from a momentary daze to calmness.Just think of it as the last time. After this time, the two owe each other nothing.Chu Ying exhaled and walked to the glass door.Just as he was about to open the door, an annoyed male voice penetrated the crack in the door and entered his ears.Chu Ying raised her eyes and saw a man sitting in the corner wearing a Hong Kong-style shirt. He looked young, his hands were draped on the armchair, his legs were crossed, his face was slightly red, but he was extremely ugly:I don't accept it. I'm bleeding. Can't you see? Do you know who I am? Do you dare to let her go today?This was really not a friendly word, and the content in Ting Ting's words was probably something he had been asking for for a long time. The policeman's expression was serious, implying a warning:This is the police station. I have told you that we are not not dealing with it, but in her current state we cannot make a record to determine what happened. Without a thorough investigation, we cannot directly detain her. You can go to the hospital for examination first. Preserve all evidence.Her eyes passed over the flowered shirt and the policeman, but she didn't see Zhu Ruoxuan's figure, so Chu Ying paused.Then let her stay here until she sobers up. If this woman doesn't apologize to me, she won't be able to leave.Chu Ying frowned and was about to interrupt the conversation between the two.There was a sneer from the corner that I didn't pay attention to at first, and the voice was hoarse and a little floaty: If I apologize again, I will still hit you.Chu Ying turned around when she heard the sound and finally found Zhu Ruoxuan.She was wearing a long black dress, her long hair was a little messy, her earlobes and neck were still a little red, probably because she hadn't fully sobered up, and she could vaguely see a few scars on her shoulders, I don't know when they were left.The flower shirt's eyes widened when he heard the sound, and he exploded instantly. He pointed at the woman in the corner, turned his head and complained to the police: Did you hear that? She has no repentance at all. Doesn't this count as evidence?She is still drunk. From a legal perspective, her words at this moment cannot be used as evidence. The police tone is objective. Please trust the public security organs. We will investigate and deal with it in accordance with the law and give you justice.Hua Shirt almost laughed angrily, and seemed to be furious the next second.Chu Ying tightened her fingers and walked to the police first before he had an attack and said:Hello, I am Chu Ying.The sound was neither too loud nor too quiet, but it was enough for everyone present to hear it clearly in the silent police station.Chu Ying pursed her lips. From the corner of her eye, she could see Zhu Ruoxuan in the corner stiffening when she heard her name. She instantly raised her eyes as if she had sobered up. After looking at her for a brief second, she quickly looked away. .Hua Shirt's temper, which was about to break out, finally found someone to vent to. Before the policeman could open his mouth, he stood up and walked to her in a few steps.Looking back and forth between her and Zhu Ruoxuan, the man suddenly sneered: You are that crazy woman's friend.Chu Ying frowned and was about to speak.no.The voice in the corner was still mute, and everyone's eyes turned to her. Chu Ying moved her fingers, raised her eyes, and saw Zhu Ruoxuan standing up at some point, probably because she drank too much, and she was shaking when she stood up. Akira, holding on to the wall.After a moment of silence, the police officer frowned and looked at her suspiciously.Chu Ying paused, as if she didn't hear anything. She glanced past the flowered shirt and looked back at the police calmly: You said she was drunk and you can't believe what she said.She opened the call history on her phone and handed it over: This is the number you just called me from.The policeman walked up and took a look, then relaxed his eyebrows. When he looked up, he saw the man in the corner with his fingers pressed against his temples, his eyebrows tightly knitted, his eyes slightly closed, and he was obviously drunk.He didn't know what the conflict was between the two little girls, but if one of them came to the police station to pick her up in the middle of the night, he had a gut feeling that their relationship wouldn't be too bad.The policeman sighed softly, walked a few steps to the corner, helped the woman who smelled of alcohol sit down, and whispered, "Sit down and rest for a while."I don't have to worry about her.The police just thought she was drunk and said: OK, OK, no matter, drink some water first to sober up.Chu Ying's eyes stayed in the corner for a while, and then she slowly took back her phone. Her eyes fell back on Hua Shirt's face. She took a deep breath and spoke calmly: Please respect her. She is my friend, not what you call crazy. woman'.Hua Shirt stood aside for a long time and listened to talk about whether friends were friends or not. He was already impatient. He didn't care about the relationship between the two. He just snorted from his nose and pointed to his forehead:Have you seen this? This is the masterpiece of your 'friend'. After drinking at night, he went crazy and hit someone with a bottle. Just now he said he would hit me again if he did it again. Doesn't this count as intentionally hurting someone?There was some dried blood on his forehead. Chu Ying pursed her lips tightly and was about to say that if she wanted compensation, she could ask for it.Before he could open his mouth, he suddenly pushed forward.The distance between the two suddenly tightened, and Chu Ying subconsciously stepped back slightly to distance herself from him.There was nothing he could say to a drunk person, and the police kept repeating those few words over and over again. Xu Kaiyuan had never been so aggrieved before, and now he was easy to handle with just one glance, but he couldn't let him vent his anger.Regardless of the policeman standing nearby, Xu Kaiyuan lowered his voice, leaned forward, and approached the girl. His tone was cold, as if he had read her thoughts:I won't be private anymore.Unless she kneels down and apologizes to me.Xu Kaiyuan spoke one word at a time, and after finishing his words, his eyes glanced at the pretty girl in front of him.As if he noticed something just after he got closer, his eyes fell on her regular facial features, fair and smooth skin, all the way down, and then focused on her slender neck and beautiful collarbone.The man squinted his eyes slightly, something flashed across his eyes, his expression changed again, he seemed to be smiling but not smiling, his tone changed from the cold tone just now, and became frivolous: OrHis eyes were glued to Chu Ying like a snake. He spoke softly and slowly, passing by her ears: Apologize for her.Squinting eyes wandered over her body, the word "apology" was ambiguously pronounced, the breath almost touched her cheek, and the subtle smell of smoke from the man also penetrated her nose at this moment, any memory that she wanted to delete with all her strength. The fragments of the past seem to be awakening at this moment.A feeling of discomfort hit her face, Chu Ying's face suddenly turned pale, her blood seemed to start flowing backwards, her long and curly eyelashes trembled uncontrollably, and there was a roar in her ears.She wanted to retreat, but her legs felt like they were filled with lead and couldn't move at all. Chu Ying's thoughts were complicated, messy memories were running around in her mind, and her eyes were getting dark uncontrollably.The girl staggered and could hardly stand.The next moment, a pair of slender and distinct hands touched her shoulders.Warm and powerful.Chu Ying waited for several seconds before her vision gradually returned to clarity.Gradually she came back to her senses and realized that someone had helped her. The person behind her seemed to have not moved. She reacted for a while before turning back lazily, wanting to say thank you.Rising chest, broad shoulder line, sharp Adam's apple, thin jawChu Ying paused suddenly.Before she saw the man's face, the cold woody sandalwood scent wrapped around her nose.A familiar breath filled his body. In a daze, his breathing suddenly stagnated, and his heart beat uncontrollably amid the sluggishness.That face instantly came to mind.Chu Ying's fingers were numb and she froze for a moment.at the same time.She heard a tentative, yet somewhat disbelieving voice coming from her side.elder brother

Chapter 10 Rememberlove debt10elder brotherThe cry instantly brought her back to reality.Chu Ying stared for a moment, then slowly raised her eyes and met the man's dark eyes.The light and shadow above his head depicted his still cold and desolate face. Under the fine black hair, the man's expression was still indifferent, but the superior brow bone and sharp jaw were unusually tense.If they weren't very close, others wouldn't be able to see this detail.Sure enough, it was Xu Jisi.Although she had a premonition, Chu Ying was still distracted for a moment when she faced his face.Why do I seem to keep running into him lately?The frequency is almost unreal.Some thoughts flashed through her mind, and Chu Ying tightened her fingers, suddenly feeling a little ridiculous.For her to believe this, it is better to believe in coincidence.While his thoughts were in turmoil, the man's gaze slowly dropped from the front, and then penetrated into her eyes.Without saying anything, Chu Ying miraculously understood his glance, probably asking how she was doing.Chu Ying looked away, paused, and squeezed out a dry thank you from her throat. She turned her head and looked at the flowered shirt with a stiff expression as if she hadn't recovered yet.The policeman on one side finally realized the situation belatedly, stepped forward in a few steps, and looked at the deserted but oppressive man behind the girl.Just when he was about to ask about his identity, he didn't expect that the flower shirt who was so domineering just now spoke first, with a hint of fear in his tone: Brother, why are you here?Xu Jisi's eyelashes were half lowered. He raised his eyes slowly when he heard the voice. The corners of his cold lips were slightly raised. There was sarcasm in his cold voice: Why don't you ask your good father who is abroad?Quite capable, the news spread through several hands and went round and round until it reached his ears.The flowery shirt immediately turned pale: My dad also knows.He subconsciously looked around, and then suddenly realized that the eyeliner next to him was gone.No wonder he always felt like something was wrong.You are afraid too.He himself felt a little upset after being ordered to run. Xu Jisi lightly passed by the girl who was still stiff in front of him, suppressing some emotions unnoticeably.He has always had a bad temper, and he didn't want to give any face to him at this time. He glanced at the policeman who was hesitating whether to speak, and then turned back to the flowered shirt. He lazily pulled his lips and said, "I'll explain myself."He knew Xu Kaiyuan's character very well. He had been used to being a bully since he was a child, and he was even more arrogant than Ji Ran. Ji Ran also knew that he had to restrain his temper in some situations and pretend to be a fake gentleman occasionally. Xu Kaiyuan had to be supported wherever he went. Anyone who made him unhappy would not end well, and everyone was afraid of him.Due to his great reputation, no one in the circle dared to provoke him, except for a few sworn enemies.As for those who don't know him, he has a domineering aura that anyone with a bit of discernment will know is not to be trifled with. No one is free to stir up trouble, let alone a woman.A sense of pressure came towards him, Xu Jisi's expression was cold, and the gaze that stayed on him was like needles. Xu Kaiyuan swallowed, he really didn't feel that he was at fault, his tone was very aggrieved, and he was not as arrogant as before. arrogance:Brother, I really didn't cause any trouble this time. Look at meHe came forward, wanting Xu Jisi to look at his forehead.Before he had taken two steps, the pretty girl in front of his brother's eyes trembled, and he stepped back in fear, almost touching the chest of the person behind him.An indescribable annoyance came to his head. Xu Kaiyuan was stimulated by her actions for a moment: What do you mean, I can still eat it.Xu Kaiyuan.The cold voice contained a warning. Xu Yuan's face froze. When he raised his head, he saw that the mockery on his brother's face had faded, and the sharpness in his eyes gradually faded.Something suddenly came over his mind. Xu Kaiyuan trembled all over and his mouth stiffened: I, I was just joking.Xu Jisi glanced at him with a dull look, then slowly lowered his voice and said in a moderate voice: "You wait nearby, I'll handle it from here."The voice above her head was cold and indifferent. Chu Ying was stunned for a while before she realized that Xu Jisi was probably talking to herself.The girl curled her fingers, turned her head, and looked into his half-cast eyes.It was unclear when he had said the same thing before, and Chu Ying responded unconsciously:good.Xu Kaiyuan hadn't come back to his senses yet, watching blankly as his brother's eyes fell on the girl named Chu Ying, until she walked to the corner and sat with the woman in a black skirt.The two looked at each other for a brief moment. The girl tilted her head first and lost sight of him.His brother slowly moved his eyes away and returned to him.They seemed to know each other.When more ominous thoughts came into his mind, Xu Kaiyuan's face became even stiffer: BrotherXu Jisi's expression was obviously a little impatient, but he still suddenly raised his lips at him and looked at him: "Talk to me."

At Xu Jisi's request, the police took the two of them into a nearby room.It was already midnight, and the corner of the police station was so quiet that only the roar of motorcycles speeding past on the road outside could be heard.Chu Ying thought for a long time and didn't know what to say to Zhu Ruoxuan.No matter how you ask, it's like exposing a scar, and Zhu Ruoxuan probably won't want to tell her.It seems that we can only wait for the police to come out and tell the result.Chu Ying stared at the lamp above her head in ecstasy, not blinking for a while.Until Zhu Ruoxuan suddenly said in a confused voice: I am just drunk.Don't expect the police to call you.Chu Ying blinked her somewhat astringent eyes, slowly tilted her head, and saw that Zhu Ruoxuan still had her head lowered, and her fingers were pinching her eyebrows in discomfort. She didn't look at her, and then said to herself: I haven't thought about you either. will come.In fact, she should have contacted her parents, but when the police asked her, she calmly said they were dead.It doesn't matter whether it is true or false, because living is no different from being dead.The policeman was speechless for a few seconds, and when he took her cell phone, she didn't react.Until the other party took her cell phone and suddenly asked who Chu Ying was.Her brain was still a little groggy, but she subconsciously recalled that she was a friend.It wasn't until there was a ringing sound in her ears that Zhu Ruoxuan suddenly came back to her senses and saw that the police had dialed the phone.Thinking of the quarrel with Chu Ying, she panicked for a moment and hurriedly grabbed the phone from the policeman and hung up.The policeman frowned, and she remained silent under his gaze. She stared at the note for a long time, then laughed to herself and said she wouldn't accept it.How could he be considered a friend? At the end of the day, he was just an ex-roommate.Unexpectedly, as soon as he finished speaking, the call came back.The policeman took the cell phone while she was stunned and answered the call.She didn't know what she was thinking at the time, but she didn't stop him.But when she really saw Chu Ying coming, she regretted it again.For a moment, Zhu Ruoxuan seemed to have withdrawn from her memories.No matter what she did, she couldn't change anything. She finally slumped her shoulders as if relaxed and stared at the reflective tiles on the ground. She didn't seem to want Chu Ying to say anything, and continued to speak hoarsely:I was drinking in a bar, and he whistled at me, but I ignored him. He told others that I looked like someone had died in the family because I was wearing all black, and he thought it was unlucky to sleep with him. I'd better be as aloof as I am now in bed.Chu Ying didn't realize that she suddenly took the initiative to talk to him, and he didn't expect that she would say this to her directly.These words were too unpleasant to hear. Chu Ying came back to her senses and flashed the arrogant face of Hua Shirt. She opened her mouth several times, but nothing came out.After a pause for a few seconds, Zhu Ruoxuan lowered her eyelashes and said: Today is the death anniversary of my grandma.Chu Ying's expression was dazed for a moment, her black eyes were blank, and her fingers on her side moved slightly.she alsoThen we will settle the matter according to the wishes of both parties, and at the same time, the other party will bear the medical expenses and other compensation losses for you, and then both parties need to write a letter of guarantee.The door on one side was pushed open, and three people stepped out one after another. The police's voice interrupted Chu Ying's thoughts.As the policeman spoke, he took out the receipt. Before he handed it over, the man at the front said in a calm voice: He doesn't want compensation.Although Xu Kaiyuan didn't like the few hundred yuan, the original result of the settlement was frustrating enough. Now even the symbolic punishment of compensation has to be wiped out. Doesn't it mean that his beating was in vain? If his friends knew about it, how could he still fool around?Xu Kaiyuan couldn't hold it back and said angrily: "Then I will suffer this blow for nothing."I don't know whether your injury is serious or not.Xu Kaiyuan froze.This is true.If he was really seriously injured, he wouldn't have made a fuss here at all. The area on his head looked like it was bleeding, but in fact it was just a scratch, not even a minor injury. There would be no case to be made, otherwise he wouldn't have Will be so angry.In silence, Xu Kaiyuan gritted his teeth tightly. He always felt that the eyes of the two people in the corner were mocking. He tightened his fists and frowned, his face full of dissatisfaction:I'm just lucky. If she had hit me harder, she would have given me a concussion.Xu Jisi suddenly stopped.Xu Yuan was overjoyed and thought he had convinced Xu Jisi.Unexpectedly, the next moment, the man in front of him slowly turned his head. There was no smile in his eyes, and his voice was as cold as falling into an ice cellar: You deserve to be beaten to death.Xu Kaiyuan's hands and mouth have been bad for a day or two, and he still doesn't feel that he is at fault.From the beginning, he stuttered and said that he was just joking and said a few not-so-nice words, but when pressed, he said that it was bad luck for him to wear black clothes, and then he said something cheerful, and he hesitated to say no. After saying those words, Xu Jisi knew that what he said would only sound worse.What kind of father is what kind of son. The father is living and drinking abroad, while the son is doing evil at home.As expected, the Xu family has the same origin, and no one is a good person.So does he.Xu Jisi's eyelashes were half drooped. He ignored Xu Kaiyuan's expression that became even more ugly as he froze. After a while, he raised his eyelids again and his eyes fell on the two girls in the corner.At this moment, the movement on their side has attracted the attention of both of them. The woman in the black skirt tightened her hands when her eyes touched Xu Kaiyuan, while Chu Ying quietly put her hand on the back of her hand.She seemed to be stiff, and the hand on the other side moved, but she did not avoid it.Xu Jisi looked away, turned slightly sideways, and said in a calm voice: Apologize.Xu Kaiyuan looked at him in disbelief: BrotherThe man glanced at him with languid eyes, opened his lips and repeated: Apologize.It was an extremely calm tone, but it made people feel invisible and frightened, as if a storm was about to come.The fainter Xu Jisi's voice became, the more frightened he became.The fear of being held by Xu Jisi's expressionless neck and pushed into the water over and over again when he was a child was reawakened. At that time, he also gently and calmly asked him again and again if he wanted to apologize.Swallowing uncontrollably, Xu Kaiyuan finally felt a trace of regret at this moment.If he had known it earlier, this would not have been true. He was just trying to save face in front of his friends.He was the one who blew the whistle, but he didn't know that the woman would give him a cold and mocking look, as if she was looking at some rubbish. When had he ever been wronged like this, how could he endure it?After a few words of excitement, the man went crazy and suddenly hit him with a wine bottle, catching him off guard.He didn't even come back to his senses.Knowing that the news spread so quickly and would attract Xu Jisi, he pretended to be magnanimous and tolerant.Xu

Kaiyuan's mind was spinning again and again.The spy today is probably a different person. After all, he had warned and threatened him in the past, and no one really dared to complain.He is used to being domineering, and his vigilance has dropped. Originally, he relied on his father to be able to control him abroad, but unexpectedly, he overturned today.Xu Kaiyuan gritted his teeth in his heart, but did not dare to show any dissatisfaction on the surface. He could only look at him secretly and smiled awkwardly: Brother, let's talk about this in private.Xu Jisi's eyebrows were slightly raised, and the corners of his slightly hooked lips were straightened. He tilted his head, a trace of impatience finally leaked out of his eyes, and his thin lips touched lightly.Just a second before he was about to speak out, Xu Kaiyuan's alarm bell blared, fear flashed in his eyes, and he gritted his teeth and squeezed out: I'm sorry.Xu Jisi glanced at him and asked quietly: Who should I apologize to?Xu Kaiyuan froze, his eyes falling on the two girls in the corner who had not yet recovered.Taking a deep breath, he closed his eyes as if he was humiliated: Miss Zhu, I'm sorry.There was silence for a moment, and the two people in the corner looked at each other slowly and seemingly in unison.Xu Jisi's gaze passed over Chu Ying very lightly, and he saw the girl's dark eyes looking at the person beside him and then raising them slightly to fall beside him. She pursed her lips tightly and her face was unusually tense. She seemed to be pale just now. It hasn't faded.Xu Jisi's expression paused, and his mind flashed back to Xu Kaiyuan's behavior approaching Chu Ying when he first entered the door. His eyebrows jumped suddenly, and he became upset.The gloomy eyes suddenly glanced at Xu Kaiyuan again. Xu Kaiyuan's forehead jumped and his heart started to rise again. He pursed his lips and didn't dare to say anything. He didn't even dare to look at him.Xu Jisi frowned, suppressed his thoughts, and spoke in a slow tone: "Just one person"Xu Kaiyuan was stunned for a moment, and soon realized something. He gritted his teeth and bowed to Chu Ying: I'm sorry, Miss Chu. I made a mistake just now.

Chu Ying was stunned as if she didn't expect it.Xu Kaiyuan spoke very softly at that time, and the police probably didn't hear what he said.Xu Jisi heard somethingIn a blink of an eye, the girl's eyes glanced at Xu Jisi very quickly, and she saw that the man still had the same calm expression, with his eyebrows lightly pressed, as if he just mentioned this sentence in the most objective way.Her long eyelashes trembled lightly, and the shoulder that had been supported half an hour ago seemed to be starting to feel hot after a while. Chu Ying clenched her fingers, her thoughts were confused, and she opened her eyes in panic.After a few apologies, there was no reply. Xu Kaiyuan had never experienced such humiliation, but Xu Jisi was beside him, so he didn't dare to get angry even half-heartedly.Finally, it was the police who broke the tense atmosphere, turned around and asked the two girls next to them: Do you accept this apology and reconciliation?Chu Ying's eyebrows moved slightly and her gaze turned to Zhu Ruoxuan.Zhu Ruoxuan lowered her eyes and said nothing.From the beginning, I didn't expect Xu Kaiyuan to truly acknowledge his mistake and apologize from the bottom of his heart. The harm caused to the other party cannot be compensated by an apology. It was expected that he would not receive a response.After a few seconds of silence, Xu Jisi looked at the woman in the black dress and said calmly: Miss Zhu, if you suffer any mental damage, we will compensate you.Zhu Ruoxuan paused and finally raised her eyes.Then he met a pair of dark eyes, cold and distant, with no emotion.Somehow, the other party clearly took a step back, gave room for choice in the plan, and safeguarded her interests, but she somehow felt a bit of a coercive aura.but.If it weren't for the man in front of her, let alone compensation, she wouldn't even receive an apology.She knew very well that the person she had offended today was of high status, and she had even made the worst plan to consider herself unlucky. The result now was better no matter how she looked at it.Zhu Ruoxuan's face looked drunk, and her brain was indeed a little confused at first. After staying in the police station for several hours, she has now become more awake and can still clarify the basic logic.She was silent for a moment and nodded slowly.Xu Jisi finally relaxed, asked for a piece of white paper from the police, wrote a series of numbers on it and handed it over: Within a month, if you want to go to the hospital, you can contact this number at any time and someone will accompany you.Zhu Ruoxuan took the paper and her eyes fell on the black numbers on the back of the paper. She glanced at Xu Kaiyuan, whose eyes were obviously suppressing his dissatisfaction, and paused: Then heI will never have anything to do with Miss Zhu again.Xu Jisi was calm and neat, and his tone made people feel safe. Zhu Ruoxuan gradually relaxed and accepted the result.After a while, she suddenly remembered something again. She tilted her head and her eyes fell on Chu Ying, who had not spoken a word until now. The girl narrowed her eyes slightly, as if she was distracted and had no reaction.Zhu Ruoxuan paused, then moved her eyes to look at the tall man.After communicating with the police for a few words, he stretched out his hand to loosen his tie. He glanced this way, then looked back after a pause.Zhu Ruoxuan withdrew her eyes, glanced at Chu Ying, and whispered: I'm going back first.Chu Ying came back to her senses, frowned slightly, and subconsciously said: No, how can you go back like this?I'm not drunk.Say this to me again when you can stand firm.

Zhu Ruoxuan's eyes fell on Chu Ying's white wrist, which was holding her arm.When she stood up just now, she was indeed shaking a little.But that was only physical. She felt that she was still conscious at the moment.Zhu Ruoxuan explained: I'm really not drunkI'll take you back.The man's cold voice sounded from above her head, interrupting her words.He obviously noticed that the girl beside him stiffened, and the hand on her arm seemed to tighten.Zhu Ruoxuan paused and raised her eyes.She saw the man's eyes slightly lowered, obviously looking at Chu Ying.If she guessed correctly, that glance just now was also looking at Chu Ying.Perhaps, she was able to receive this treatment today because of Chu Ying.Zhu Ruoxuan glanced sideways, clearly aware of the subtle atmosphere between the two.During the shared tenancy, I didn't hear that Chu Ying had a boyfriend.Could it be a previous love debt?After a thought passed by, Zhu Ruoxuan suddenly froze.

What is she thinking about? Is she really drunk?The word "love debt" has nothing to do with Chu Ying.She would rather believe that the man in front of her is chasing Chu Ying now.Maybe it's an ambiguous period.Zhu Ruoxuan shook her head slightly, trying to get rid of those irrelevant thoughts.Chu Ying beside her finally said: Don't bother Mr. Xu, we can do it ourselvesIt's not easy to take a taxi at this point.Xu Jisi tilted his head and gestured to the clock hanging on the wall. Chu Ying unconsciously raised her eyes and saw that the hour hand had passed twelve.It's early morning.Chu Ying paused slightly, her brain working rapidly, trying to find a reason.But the other party seemed to have noticed her thoughts and said calmly: Your friend's situation is not suitable for taking a taxi.This place is far away from the city center, it is indeed a bit remote, it is too late, two girls, one of them is drunkChu Ying hesitated for a moment.From a safety perspective, Xu Jisi is obviously a more suitable choice.But for her, being in a confined space with Xu JisiNot finished thinking yet.Suddenly there was a heavy feeling on my shoulders.Chu Ying suddenly came back to her senses, turned around and saw Zhu Ruoxuan, who was supporting her, frowning tightly, and put her head on her shoulder as if she was feeling uncomfortable.DizzinessZhu Ruoxuan's voice became hoarse.Chu Ying hurriedly went to support her, but Zhu Ruoxuan seemed to have no strength. She raised her arms but was unable to swing them down. His face seemed to be getting redder, and he didn't know if it was because he was drunk, but his legs seemed unsteady.Chu Ying bit her inner lip lightly and had no choice but to turn her head to look at Xu Jisi.Please Mr. Xu.

Chapter 11 Rememberingboarding.11The three people next to him said something, as if they were separated from him by a barrier, Xu Kaiyuan's background board stood aside, their faces turned green and red, they had never been ignored like this before.The girl's response was obviously forced by the situation. Xu Jisi's face remained as usual, his chin slightly raised, he gave her a gentle tap, and walked out the door.Chu Ying supported Zhu Ruoxuan and slowly followed the man. At first the man strode quickly, but then he didn't know if he didn't hear the movement behind him and looked back.After a pause, he slowed down again.It wasn't until the three of them left the police station that Xu Kaiyuan finally came to his senses and hurriedly passed through the two girls and followed Xu Jisi.Xu Jisi had already walked to the car. He raised his eyes slightly and saw that Chu Ying and Zhu Ruoxuan were still some distance away. He leaned to the side, bent his knees slightly, lowered his head and straightened his sleeves.When he looked up again, the two of them were getting closer, and he opened the rear door.Xu Kaiyuan, who was in front of him, suddenly braked and stopped in front of the car. His eyes widened in fear. He looked up at Xu Jisi, who had no expression. He froze, feeling as if he had been beaten and given a bullet. Candied dates, my brain is so messed up.He wasn't dreaming, was he?Xu Jisi was famous for being aloof and arrogant, and now he was actually opening the car door for him.Is there a scam? Is Xu Jisi waiting for him to make another mistake so that he can have a reason to deal with him?Xu Kaiyuan's brain has never turned so fast. He gritted his teeth and was about to say thank you, but he could just sit in front.Xu Jisi's somewhat impatient and cold voice sounded above his head.Stay out of the way.Xu Kaiyuan paused, his downed brain running slowly, and he looked up to see a man with a cold and handsome appearance, his eyebrows slightly furrowed, suppressing the chill, and his slightly lowered eyes cold.Xu Kaiyuan's expression froze, and he suddenly came around the corner. Turning around, he saw that Chu Ying and Zhu Ruoxuan were already standing behind him.

After swallowing what he almost said, Xu Kaiyuan turned his head and opened his mouth nonchalantly: I'll go sit in front of you.Before he finished speaking, Xu Kaiyuan saw his brother's eyebrows suddenly raised, a sneer seemed to hang on his lips, and his voice was so cold: I will be your driver.

Xu Kaiyuan spoke with difficulty: Then I'll sit downXu Jisi was too lazy to talk nonsense to him: he contacted Uncle Zhang himself.Uncle Zhang is the steward of Xu Kaiyuan's family and his father's loyal subordinate.His father said that when he was away, Uncle Zhang had the right to control his behavior.He got into the police station today and let his father know about it. Uncle Zhang must also know about it.Although he didn't know why Uncle Zhang didn't come now, he always felt that it was the calm before the storm.Xu Jisi thought that this would make him take the initiative to contact Uncle Zhang, which would be tantamount to asking for his own death.Xu Kaiyuan's face turned pale, and his tone was reluctant: I, I can just go back by myself.Fortunately, Xu Jisi didn't seem to care about this. His eyes swept over him, fell behind him, and said lazily: "It's up to you."Xu Kaiyuan mechanically took two steps to the side and watched helplessly as Chu Ying helped Zhu Ruoxuan into the car. Xu Jisi closed the door and walked around to the driver's seat.It wasn't until the car's taillights quickly disappeared from sight that Xu Kaiyuan slowly came back to his senses.He looked around blankly. The surroundings were eerily quiet, with only the sudden wind blowing across the fallen leaves on the ground.Gazing dully at the seemingly endless dark road where the black Maybach was heading, Xu Kaiyuan realized later that fragments of memory suddenly came back to him, and scenes flashed back, and his expression became horrified unconsciously.What the hell.Xu Jisi opened the car door for someone.Whose figure did he turn to several times?The hand on the delicate shoulder offered to take the person home.In the flashback of the messy scene, a delicate and pretty face was fixed in my mind.The name also came to mind.Chu Ying.The girl's long eyelashes are slightly curled, her upright facial features are pure and small, her thick black and soft long hair falls on her collarbone, and her black and white eyes are so clear that they don't contain a trace of impurities. She can really amaze people at a glance.But Xu Jisi must have seen many women.In more than twenty years, I have never heard of anyone of the opposite sex around him, let alone him taking the initiative to have physical contact with anyone. Today, no one would believe Xu Kaiyuan's behavior even if he said it, and he would still be asked if it was true. Didn't wake up from the dream.Where did this Chu Ying come from?Xu Kaiyuan's horrified expression gradually became complicated, and he couldn't even care about the annoyance of being abandoned on a lonely roadside. There was even a hint of fear.If Chu Yingzhen had anything to do with Xu Jisi, if he had been closer at that time,A chill ran down Xu Kaiyuan's spine. The first thought that flashed through his mind was whether he should find an opportunity to come to the door and apologize again.What if she is a real sister-in-law?

It was extremely quiet on the dim path. The street lamps stood quietly on the street, and the light and shadow cast by the branches and leaves swayed by the wind passed through the car windows.The car was so quiet that it was dull. Zhu Ruoxuan tilted her head, no longer feeling weak as before. She still held the white piece of paper with her mobile phone number in her hand, and her eyes fell on the car window in a daze.The blurred outline of the girl next to her was reflected vaguely on the car window. She could be seen leaning on the back seat, her head resting on the edge of the window. She was silent all the way, as if she was a little tired.In the middle of the night, maybe he had been busy all day and was about to take a rest, but he rushed to the police station because of a phone call from an ex-roommate with whom he had no relationship.Where did Chu Ying come from?If someone hadn't met her by chance, how would she have ended up?She is a bad person, Chu Ying should not have a relationship with her, and moving away is the best choice.Zhu Ruoxuan's heart felt as if something was stuck in her heart. She had something to say but seemed unable to say it. In the end, she could only let out a breath silently and turned her eyes away.Until we gradually passed a road that was being repaired, the wheels rolled over fine gravel, and the car began to shake.Zhu Ruoxuan's eyes fell to her side involuntarily.Chu Ying put a hand on her temple, closed her eyes slightly, her eyelashes trembled slightly, her face was a little pale, and her eyebrows could not be stretched.Closed space, unstable road, and pungent smell of alcoholEverything is a nightmare for Chu Ying when riding in a car.Suddenly, the slight sound of the car window being lowered fell upon my ears, and the cool night breeze poured into the car, and most of the smell of alcohol dissipated.The coolness stimulated her senses and made her sober almost instantly. Chu Ying subconsciously turned her head and happened to see Zhu Ruoxuan turning back as if nothing had happened.Chu Ying paused: You can't blow the air directly after drinking.Zhu Ruoxuan didn't look back: I woke up.Chu Ying pursed her lips lightly, wanting to say something, but saw Zhu Ruoxuan closing her eyes again.never mind. There seems to be nothing to say.Chu Ying lowered her eyes, tilted her head again, held her temples with one hand, and leaned against the window.Unexpectedly, Zhu Ruoxuan suddenly opened her eyes again, and the corner of her eye fell on her. After a while, she said something very softly, and was taken away by the night wind again.Half an hour later, the car arrived at the downstairs of Zhu Ruoxuan's house.Chu Ying was feeling sleepy in front of her and fell asleep for a while. She didn't react when the car stopped. It wasn't until she heard the sound of the car door next to her being opened that she slowly opened her eyes.I happened to see Zhu Ruoxuan get out of the car.After shaking her head forcibly to regain consciousness, Chu Ying moved two steps to the side and held against the car door that was about to be closed.Zhu Ruoxuan's eyes met hers for a moment.Chu Ying pushed the door open with a little force.Zhu Ruoxuan said in a very calm tone: I can go upstairs by myself.Not bad at this time.Chu Ying was still worried and raised her wrist to hold her arm.The next moment, she almost blurted out: But I don't want to owe you anything anymore.Chu Ying's wrist that was just halfway raised was slightly stiff.Zhu Ruoxuan seemed to realize that these words were too unkind. After Zhu Ruoxuan finished speaking, she froze up and her lips seemed to move, but in the end she still didn't explain anything and looked away in silence.After a few seconds of silence, Chu Ying said hello slowly.As if pressing some non-existent switch, the silent air finally revived. Zhu Ruoxuan intentionally did not linger on her face, turned around and left.Before he had taken two steps, he stepped back again and glanced to the side as if he noticed something.The dignified man in the driver's seat was as silent as the driver all the way, and the window was half-opened at some point.Zhu Ruoxuan paused, turned her head slightly, bent down slightly, and whispered: Thank you, Mr. Xu.The man's slender fingers lightly touched the steering wheel, his long legs were slightly bent, and he leaned casually on the back of the chair. He didn't know whether he heard their conversation or not. He was behind the words, so he looked at her without raising his eyelids very hard. Eye.He didn't seem to be someone who would respond to such words. Zhu Ruoxuan didn't expect to get any reply. After speaking, she planned to turn around and leave.Unexpectedly, as soon as she straightened up, she heard the man say no thanks in a cold and perfunctory manner.There was a slight pause, and just when she looked sideways into the car, thinking it was an illusion, the man moved his fingers slightly and tapped lightly on the edge of the steering wheel.Then the corners of his lips curled up slightly, his dark eyes glanced slightly, and he continued unhurriedly: By the way.

Chu Ying stood in the night wind for a long time, until Zhu Ruoxuan's figure completely disappeared, then she blinked slowly.She didn't know what Zhu Ruoxuan said to Xu Jisi, and she didn't really want to know. She just wanted to ask herself what she had gained this night.A worse relationship and a tired bodyStill a person whom I never want to meet againChu Ying suddenly came to her senses at this thought.Then she suddenly realized that next, she would be alone in the same closed space with this person.It had only been a few days since he came to return the earrings, so she had no idea how she should face Xu Jisi.What concerned her even more was Xu Jisi's attitude towards her.It was because he left cleanly in the first place, and it was because he was distant and cold towards her when they reunited.It happened that he came to help under Ji Ran's pressure, revealing his seemingly ambiguous relationship with her in front of everyone, and asking Xu Kaiyuan to apologize to her.She had no idea what Xu Jisi wanted to do.Just like when he suddenly broke into her world and left quietly without saying goodbye, she could never see through him.Chu Ying's hand that fell to her side was clenched unconsciously, and her pursed lips were so tight that the curve of her jaw was unnatural.At this moment, she heard the cold voice of the person in the car.boarding.The smooth forearms of the man in his eyes were propped up by the window, half of his face was hidden in the darkness, and his broken hair fell on his forehead, casting a shadow that blocked part of his sight. Chu Ying could not clearly see the emotions in his eyes.

She really couldn't move her feet, and the man didn't push her.It was so rare that he sat there patiently, as if he could wait for as long as he wanted, without looking away at all.Chu Ying was stared at and felt numb all over.Finally, he lowered his head and walked to the car in small steps.She put her slender fingers on the car door handle and bent it slightly. The fingertips were slightly white from the exertion of a little force. The moment the door was opened, Chu Ying felt that the sight that was so hot to her was caught. Take it back compassionately.With the car window down halfway, Xu Jisi turned the steering wheel with one hand and reversed the car with a familiarity, about to drive out of the community, and then asked: Where do you live?The light from the roadside that was not too bright shone slantly into the passenger seat. In the half-darkness, Chu Ying put her fingers on the phone with a black screen and curled up slightly.She didn't want Xu Jisi to know where her home was.There was no reason to feel that if Xu Jisi knew about it, her supposedly peaceful life would be disturbed even worse.As the car approached the gate at the entrance of the community, Xu Jisi slowed down, as if waiting for her reply.Chu Ying tightened her fingers.Suddenly, a light shone into the dark car, getting brighter and brighter, and then there was a car honking despite the silence of the night. Chu Ying's temples were hit by this, and she looked back. The low-beam headlights behind her dazzled her. My eyes hurt as they adjust to the bright light.Chu Ying hurriedly turned around, and the car behind her that was going somewhere in the middle of the night flashed its lights.Chu Ying turned her head and saw that the expression on Xu Jisi's face was still calm, and her fingers even curled up lazily, tapping regularly on the edge of the steering wheel, as if she didn't hear anything, and her mood was as calm as if she was waiting for the waiter to serve in some high-end restaurant. .Just by looking at his expression, it was impossible to tell who was waiting for whom.The car owner behind was obviously a little impatient, and the horn sounded more quickly and sharply.The car owner was waiting for Xu Jisi, and Xu Jisi was waiting for her.Xu Jisi could afford to wait, but neither the car owner nor she could afford to wait.Chu Ying was still shy, biting the tip of her tongue, she hurriedly said an address, with a hint of haste in her voice.Xu Jisi then slowly stepped on the accelerator, turned the steering wheel slightly, drove out of the community and headed for a road.There was no sound along the way.The car drove smoothly all the way. If she hadn't known that she couldn't afford the car even if she sold it, Chu Ying would have thought she was taking an ordinary taxi.The tight nerves in her heart were intertwined with the fatigue in her body, and the sleepiness she was supposed to have just disappeared. The evening breeze blew coolly across her cheeks, and Chu Ying stared out the window. For a while, she saw the cold moon reflected in the water as she crossed the bridge. The color, for a while, was the bright spotlights outside the towering buildings in the distance. It was not until the scenery and buildings on the roadside became more and more familiar that my wandering thoughts returned.Ling Tingyang's so-called house in a good location is almost close to the city center. I heard that Ling Tingyang's friend bought it when he came to play and saw the beautiful surrounding scenery. It is called Jiananhui. It is not an ordinary community. It is a bit luxurious but not high-profile. It is said that There were many low-key industry elites living there, and she suspected that she was the only one renting there.In fact, when Chu Ying came to see the house for the first time, she felt that she was a little out of place.Ling Tingyang said it had two bedrooms and one living room, and her impression was that it was similar to the one she lived with Zhu Ruoxuan. When she entered the house, she saw that the living room was twice as big as her previous bedroom. Ling Tingyang then said that her friend In order to make it easier for me to play with my friends, I knocked down a wall and created a two-bedroom apartment.She flinched for a moment, and suddenly realized that the so-called rent charged by Ling Tingyang's friends was 80% for fun.At that time, Ling Tingyang probably saw what she was thinking. He said that the project was urgent and there was no time for her to adjust her mood because of the roommate relationship, and he gave up her retreat very coldly.After driving into the community, the speed of the car slowed down, and Chu Ying finally came to her senses.There was a winding intersection in her field of vision. Chu Ying paused. She always felt that something was wrong, but she couldn't remember it.Until I felt the car gradually stop at the intersection ahead.There are several numbers engraved on the wooden road sign beside it.She quickly realized that what Xu Jisi meant was to tell her the specific building number. Chu Ying pursed her lips and spoke for the first time that night.

After all, everyone had been sent in for her. If he was allowed to stay here, she would Putting it down is really a bit shameful.She recalled the route and repeated it to Xu Jisi. After a pause, she added a more obvious sign: there was a small bridge next to it, which seemed to be No. 17.Although Chu Ying has a good memory, after all, she just moved here and is not very familiar with the road yet. She only remembers the general direction, not to mention it is late at night.I thought Xu Jisi needed to find a way, but after she finished speaking, he responded with a faint "hmm" from his throat and sent her downstairs within a few minutes.The moment when she parked the car was the moment when the tense nerves in her heart were the most relaxed. While unbuckling her seat belt, Chu Ying thanked her very quickly and said politely, "Be careful on the road." She put her white fingers on the door handle. .Just before pulling away.The click of the door latch filled the still air.Chu Ying froze, thinking that this was just an illusion, and curled her fingers unwillingly.Can't pull it apart.The street lamp next to the building was cold, making the interior of the car feel particularly cold. Even the sudden wind seemed to cool down a bit.The nerves that had finally relaxed suddenly tightened up again. Chu Ying took a deep breath, turned her head suddenly, and blurted out a question that seemed to have been endured for a long time.However.She couldn't even call out Xu Jisi's name, so she was caught off guard and faced the man's dark eyes that were as cold as the moonlight.Chu Ying,Xu Jisi stared at her with his eyes slightly pressed, the corners of his lips slightly pulled, his cold voice a little hoarse, he drawled, as if he was smiling.You really think I'm the driver

Chapter 12 Rememberingconfinement12The air was dead.The man's gaze was too direct. Chu Ying stiffened her body and unconsciously tightened her fingers on the seat belt hanging by her side.Subconsciously avoiding the hint in his words, Chu Ying reluctantly raised the corners of her lips after a while: Mr. Xu, you misunderstood. I just think it's late now.She paused, deliberately leaving a blank space, trying to make someone a little self-aware, and did not say anything further.But the man didn't seem to understand, and said lazily: Well, it's really late.

I can't tell from your attitude that you feel it's too lateWhat I mean is that Chu Ying's fair little face was tense, she suppressed her temper, and spoke calmly, "Going to bed late is not good for your health."There was a brief silence in the car.Chu Ying's heartbeat increased for no reason, she tightened her fingers, and deliberately looked away, and then she heard a breathy sound coming from her side that sounded like a smile.The man put his fingers on the steering wheel and tapped it lightly. He lazily raised his eyelids, kept the curvature of his lips, and responded with unclear meaning:Miss Chu is quite concerned about my health.

Chu Ying could no longer maintain her polite

smile.When did Xu Jisi become so free that he would choke at her even saying something that was immediately obvious to her as a courtesy?It's obviously intentional.But it was a fact that he helped her today and sent her back late at night. If she really said this, it would make her look ungrateful.Chu Ying took a breath and tried to control her expression. She looked at the display screen on the center console and said politely:You see, it's already two o'clock. Mr. Xu, your precious daughter, today's trip has taken up a lot of your time. I don't know how to thank you.The words have not yet fallen.A hand that looked cold white under the moonlight and had clear joints suddenly came into view.Chu Ying paused, stared at the phone in her hand showing the address book page, and blinked slowly.Then he slowly turned his head and looked into Xu Jisi's slightly drooped, lazy black eyes.WhatChu Ying asked subconsciously.The hand waved slightly, and Chu Ying's attention returned to the illuminated mobile phone in front of her. She heard Xu Jisi's lazy voice ringing in her ears: Thank you for the way.

Touching the confusion that shone in Chu Ying's eyes, he slowly added with rare patience: I don't believe in verbal promises.

Why is this the key point Xu Jisi is looking for?Is that what she meant?Why doesn't he just ask her to write another contract and fingerprint it?She never expected this development, and all the words in her mind were overturned. Chu Ying's thoughts were stuck, and her eyes were confused for a moment.Young Master Xu's hand was really just waiting. His smooth forearm was half-flexed against the armrest box, and the other hand was loosely stretched forward to rest on the steering wheel. His bony fingers fell on each other one after another. At the edge, his eyes wandered over her delicate profile.Half a minute passed, and the girl's dark pupils finally moved. She probably came back to her senses, but the curve of the corners of her lips was obviously unstoppable. She took an inconspicuous deep breath, and her chest rose and fell slightly.It seemed that she had put up a great struggle in her heart. After a long while, Chu Ying finally exhaled silently. As if she had no choice but to do so, her voice was a little tired: What do you want?Xu Jisi doesn't want anything, what can he get from her?It was easy for him to contact her, and there was no need to go through such a special process.It's better to just talk about it directly.That's what she thought.The girl's voice in his ear was less polite than before. It was the closest thing to his true emotion in today's conversation with him. Xu Jisi lowered his eyes, his dark eyes half hidden in the darkness, and his eyes fell on her particularly serious expression. On the facial features.She seemed to really think that he had some other purpose.It's hard to tell what emotion came out of her. Xu Jisi's originally dark eyes seemed to be darker. Chu Ying accidentally bumped into this look. She was stunned for a while, but before she could react, she saw that he seemed to have returned to his original state in the blink of an eye. , as if it was just an illusion.Chu Ying blinked and calmed down, and the man was finally willing to respond.Not so good, his cold voice was tinged with a hint of romance, he moved his wrist slightly, raised his chin slightly, his eyes fell on the mobile phone, and he lowered his eyes to indicate, otherwise, who would I ask for a 'thank you gift'?Chu Ying suddenly raised her eyes and stared into those black eyes.Xu Jisi met her gaze calmly.The two looked at each other as if facing each other, neither of them looking away first.Time passed by, and I don't know how many gusts of wind blew outside the car window. The moonlight was half covered by the drifting clouds. The night became deeper and quieter. The man's deep eyes seemed to melt into the dark night, and his face was clear. He was careless, but the true emotions in his eyes were hard to see through.The time on the screen on the center console slowly changed.There is no chance of winning against Xu Jisi in endurance competition.Chu Ying was finally defeated and took the phone with a dull face.Halfway through inputting the number, she paused for a second before turning her eyes slightly to look at him and hesitantly testing: After giving it, she would cancel it.Xu Jisi glanced at her and smiled, "Miss Chu's contact information is quite expensive."

Chu Ying's eyebrows and her heart skipped a beat, and her tone was a little annoyed: Do you want love?Xu Jisi's lips curled up slightly and he nodded calmly: Well, I can't open the door either.

Why didn't I realize he was such a rogue before?Chu Ying took a deep breath and pressed her fingers on the screen so hard that her fingertips turned white.She enduresAfter typing in the number with her slender fingers very quickly, the girl handed the phone back to the person who was leaning loosely on the back of the chair with an expressionless face.Xu Jisi didn't notice her reluctance, glanced at the screen, and dialed it out.Chu Ying's cell phone then lit up.Inexplicable frustration and annoyance arose. Chu Ying hung up the phone and moved her lips at him with a smile: My grandma taught me to keep my promises since I was a child. Mr. Xu can rest assured.Something doesn't sound right about this. The words "keep your promise" are pronounced clearly intentionally or unintentionally. It always seems like there is a next sentence, which is probably to accuse someone of not keeping their promise.Xu Jisi glanced down at her, paused, and softened his voice: LanCan Mr. Xu open the door?Chu Ying suddenly spoke up.Xu Ji thought quietly for a moment.Then, the click of the door lock being unlocked was heard.Chu Ying didn't hesitate at all, and opened the car door with her back foot, as if waiting for another second would cause trouble. She stepped on the granite brick with her slightly higher heel. After a slightly muffled landing, she said goodbye with a polite voice. The car door was closed immediately.Chu Ying walked around the front of the car, and out of the corner of her eye, the man's dark eyes were slightly dark but showed no emotion, they just fell straight on her.Unconsciously, she quickened her pace, and Chu Ying slowly stopped until she isolated that scorching gaze outside the cold porcelain wall.Her finger gently pressed the elevator up button, and the numbers displayed on the dozen or so floors began to flash slowly. Chu Ying's black eyes were half-cast, a little lost in thought.Until the elevator door suddenly reflected a little red in the field of vision.Chu Ying paused and saw the breathing light on the phone next to her was on.He lowered his head and picked up the phone and clicked on the screen. What came into view was the call page showing the unfamiliar number that had been hung up on.Messages from this number are floating in the information bar.Remember to remarkThe man sent four words.Chu Ying stared at the numbers for a long time.The fingers holding the edge of the phone moved.Some thoughts buried in the memory were brought out again.She seemed to have had this thought at some point in the past.She thought it would be nice if she had a way to contact him.If only I could contact him.In fact, he didn't have to do anything, it was enough to let her know that he was there.After all, at that time, during those silent nights with nowhere to talk, he was her only sustenance.But it was so difficult. It wasn't until the end that she realized that she only knew him by his name.The name that occasionally appeared on the paper in my trance became so unfamiliar at some point.Later, when the frost withers and the summer turns green, she realizes that their relationship was anything but equitable from the beginning.It turned out that as long as he closed the door on her, she had no ability to resist at all.The numbers on the display kept beating, as if they never stopped waiting for someone's time.Until her phone went off screen after she hadn't used it for a long time.The floor also jumps to 1 at this moment.The elevator made a short, sharp chime.Chu Ying slowly raised her head and saw the elevator door slowly opening to her.The trance reminded her of the last winter day five years ago, when the monitor continued to beep and the sun rose slowly.

The dream was very confusing and bizarre.I don't know if too many things happened today, and many people appeared in the dream.When I was very young, my grandma went out to catch up with Po Wen every day. She was eating meat in Qi'egu Wu'er 490 Bar 192 and couldn't stop buying food for her, so she accidentally locked herself out. At that time, she was not as tall as the jujube tree that had just been planted in front of her house. She was holding a baby that had faded from washing and wanted to go to the mayor. But she heard someone chatting in front of the mayor's house, talking about her. The fact that I have no blood relationship with my grandma.After a while, her classmates in high school found out that she was an orphan, and many people gave her strange looks. She was eating alone at noon, and a handsome boy suddenly sat across from her and asked stiffly if he could join her. eat.She was not very good at rejecting people, so she nodded at that time, so for several days in the morning there would be an extra bottle of milk on her desk, and occasionally some snacks.Her intuition was that it was the boy. Just when she was about to ask him, the nightmare started.She would be bumped into for no apparent reason while walking on the street, she could never find all the homework she had to hand in, and her test papers were always missing.I frequently get locked in the bathroom when I go to class. Every time I come out, the class is halfway through. Several times a week, I am punished by the teacher for being late and running laps on the playground.Too many unfounded malices and unfounded rumors hit her like a sudden rainstorm at that time.Later, she found out that the daughter of the grade director liked the boy. The boy was usually very reserved and unknown. He had few friends and did not take the initiative to contact anyone. She was the first one and probably the only one. The girl later said that mainly It was because she was so beautiful that she felt in danger.It's quite ridiculous. She is like the unlucky guy who was accidentally hit by a falling vase while walking on the road. She didn't even have the ability to reason.Messy scenes flashed through each scene, and Chu Ying looked at her past experiences calmly like an outsider.Until another blink of an eye, she appeared in the police station.The ferocious face in the flowered shirt suddenly magnified in front of her, causing her to take several steps back in shock. Before she could realize when she could control her body in the dream, her feet slipped.But no one appeared behind her, and she was caught off guard and fell backwards.The reality of her heartbeat suddenly slowing down made her subconsciously close her eyes.However.bangThe pain he imagined did not come.The back is soft.She opened her eyes in confusion, and suddenly realized that she had fallen into a car.The next moment, a pair of familiar dark eyes like a deep pool looked straight into her frightened eyes.She couldn't figure out why she suddenly appeared here again. After looking around in a panic, she realized that the other party was leaning towards her at this moment.Even, it was less than two fingers away from her.She subconsciously wanted to hide away, but her whole body was imprisoned between the chairs and could not move.She closed her eyes in despair.But at this moment, he heard the man's slightly hoarse voice.Remember to make a note.

Chu Ying opened her eyes suddenly and gasped heavily.Before she realized what kind of dream she had, she opened her phone in a daze and looked at her text message records.Someone's number is really lying inside, and the dialogue still only shows the four words he would send.She didn't reply.No notes either.Is she crazy or is Xu Jisi crazy?I would actually dream of such a scene.After a while, she finally came to her senses, and

Chu Ying's breathing gradually became calmer.She didn't know whether she was afraid or worried that it might become a reality. She stared at the numbers for a moment, gritted her teeth gently, and wrote down his name vigorously.

After all, she had just moved to a new home and was not yet familiar with the commuting route, so Chu Ying set off half an hour early.Arriving at the company earlier than usual, Chu Ying walked into the elevator and pressed the floor button. Just as the door was about to close, a fiery figure appeared in front of the door and hurriedly reached inside: Hey, wait, wait, wait.Chu Ying pressed the door button with quick eyes and hands, and the figure came in quickly. She patted her chest and thanked her: "Thank you."A familiar voice rushed into her ears. Chu Ying turned her head slightly and finally saw the person clearly.It's Luo Hui.Sister Huihui. Chu Ying spoke up.Luo Hui turned her head, looked into Chu Ying's clear eyes, and raised her eyebrows: Yingying is so early today, has she had breakfast?have eaten.Chu Ying nodded, and the next second, Luo Hui suddenly hooked the broken hair on the side of her face, as if she had discovered something, stared at her eyes for a while, and asked: Didn't you sleep well last night?Chu Ying was stunned for a moment: What?Luo Hui reached out and tapped her lower eyelids: they were a little blue.Chu Ying blinked her eyelashes lightly, and the outrageous dream just now flashed through her mind. Xu Jisi's face seemed to appear in front of her eyes again. The girl's expression froze slightly: she was having a nightmare.Luo Hui saw that there was no change in her expression, but there seemed to be a trace of indescribable depression and gritted teeth in her voice.It's rare to see Chu Ying like this, but he sensed that she didn't want to talk too much, and Luo Hui didn't ask any questions. She just said that she hadn't slept well and took a nap for a while. He glanced at her and remembered something within two seconds, jokingly saying: Yesterday I saw that your circle of friends moved to a new home. Congratulations. When will you invite us to visit your home?The elevator door opened in response, and the two of them went out one after another. Chu Ying blinked and smiled: Sister Huihui can do it anytime if she is free.Then I have to find a good day.The two entered the door chatting and laughing, and chatted for a few more words before they dispersed.Chu Ying took out a bag of honeysuckle tea from the drawer, brewed it in her cup, added a few spoons of sugar to it, and walked slowly to the shed holding her thermos cup.Before Ling Tingyang arrived, Chu Ying had already familiarized herself with the drama she would be filming today in advance.The original plan for the dubbing of "Wild Tangzhi" was to be completed within two weeks.At first, Ling Tingyang was worried that she would not be able to adapt to the role of a TV series for the first time, and that it might take a lot of time to adjust to her habits, but in fact, Chu Ying was only pointed out some details in the first two days of contact, and then nothing happened. A self-taught teacher, he has fully adapted to the professional requirements of TV drama dubbing.In just one week, the dubbing progress of "Wild Tangzhi" has reached two-thirds.Today's plot is stuck at the turning point in the middle and late stages. The heroine has experienced a major change and the character's temperament has changed greatly. Chu Ying has several ideas in her mind, but she is not sure which state is more suitable.After Ling Tingyang came, Chu Ying took the initiative to try several different ways of interpretation, but she always felt that something was missing.Rarely stuck in progress, Chu Ying had a few bites of rice at noon, and even took the initiative to send a message to He Hong to ask him for more details.It was here that Chu Ying discovered that there was one more person in the group.The man's ID only had an X, and a familiar cold style came to his face.It was so vivid that she could only think of that one person.Chu Ying hung her fingers in the air and paused for several seconds before clicking the blue X.The face of the person in the dream appeared in the avatar not unexpectedly.I don't know who took the photo of him. It was probably a snapshot. The outline of his face almost blended into the dim background. Only the black eyes that suddenly raised their eyes towards the camera seemed to penetrate the screen.It felt like I was being stared at.Chu Ying was shocked and suddenly put her phone on the table with her backhand.He took a sip of the milk tea at the table as if he was shocked.Just when he was about to look up again.In the peripheral vision, a slender shadow under the slanting afternoon sunlight on the wall suddenly approached.Luo Hui's surprised voice sounded not far away.Mr. Xu, why are you here?Chu Ying's hand holding the milk tea shook.He could feel that the man's eyes were fixed on him.Then the corners of his lips slightly raised with unknown meaning, and his voice came out lazily.Let's confirm whether our heroine can receive the information from the communication device normally.

Chapter 13 Rememberingtake advantage13Our heroine.Chu Ying didn't know why the keyword she caught in her mind at the moment was this. The slender finger bones turned white inadvertently, the transparent milk tea cup was pinched and dented inward, and the water level of the milk tea after only taking a few sips rose. It almost overflowed from the slit opened by the straw, making a small sound.Chu Ying finally came to her senses and was about to let go.In the brief silence, Luo Hui was obviously confused.But when she mentioned the heroine, a vague face appeared in her mind. Luo Hui paused, glanced subconsciously at the window not far away, and hesitantly said: Are you looking forThe words have not yet fallen.The dull clatter of something falling to the ground interrupted her thoughts.Luo Hui subconsciously looked towards the source of the sound, and at this moment she heard a slightly panicked sound of the chair legs rubbing against the tile floor.In the sight, the person who caused these movements in the corner seemed to freeze inconspicuously, and then quickly squatted down in confusion. The coffee-colored liquid spreading on the ground came into view. Luo Hui reacted instantly, and Luo Hui hurriedly walked over there. Past: Yingying, be careful with your skirtAfter a pause, Chu Ying finally remembered that she was wearing a long skirt today, and she wanted to get up in a panic. However, the moment she squatted down, the hem of her skirt was stained with brown, and even expanded.Luo Hui arrived in time and handed over a few pieces of paper: wipe it quickly.While picking up the milk tea cup at her feet and throwing it into the trash can, Luo Hui took out some paper and helped Chu Ying wipe the corners of her skirt.She frowned tightly and sighed as she wiped it: Ouch, how could such a good thing fall down?Chu Ying's movements froze imperceptibly.How should I put it? It was only after hindsight that she realized what Xu Jisi meant in the second half of his sentence, and she was so panicked that she knocked over the milk tea.The hem of her skirt rubbed against her legs from time to time as she moved, and the indescribable sticky feeling irritated her skin. Chu Ying pinched a corner of her skirt in a somewhat embarrassed manner. Luo Hui glanced at the messy scene: I'll clean up here, you go first. Go to the bathroom and tidy up.Chu Ying nodded hurriedly, showed a grateful smile, and hurriedly left around the corner without noticing the gaze.After finishing this matter, she remembered that Xu Jisi was still there. Luo Hui immediately stepped forward and apologized: I'm sorry for making you laugh.This point lies in the fact that there are only two or three people in the company. In the office area, there are Luo Hui and Chu Ying. Luo Hui is the most senior and naturally needs to be responsible for welcoming Party A.After apologizing, still remembering the interrupted conversation, Luo Hui asked tentatively: What did you mean just now, did you want to find someone?just kidding.Xu Jisi's tone was leisurely and nonchalant, and in his eyes, the man who was halfway around the corner seemed to pause imperceptibly at his feet.Then he almost accelerated his escape.There was no more shadow until around the corner.The corners of his lips gradually flattened, and he slowly withdrew his gaze.Luo Hui was stunned for a moment, then reacted. When she looked up again, she saw that the looseness he had just now had faded away, and his tone returned to its usual cold tone: I'm here to take over from Mr. Ji and follow up on the project.Luo Hui subconsciously glanced behind him, quickly sorted out her thoughts, and nodded:But Mr. Ling is not here right now. Everyone has just finished eating at this time and should be on their way back.Luo Hui said as she picked up her phone and sent a message to Ling Tingyang. Then she immediately raised her head and continued: I just sent a message to Mr. Ling. He should be back soon. In this case, I will take you to Mr. Ling first. Office etc.Need not.Xu Jisi raised his hand, Luo Hui was stunned for a moment, and quickly calmed down: "If you don't mind, I can take you to visit our company."No need, this time he went back faster than before. After a moment of pause, Xu Jisi glanced at Luo Hui, who was a little frozen for a moment and didn't know what else to say. He gave the steps in a rare and considerate way. I just took a look.Ah good.Luo Hui nodded dullly: If you need to call me, I'll take care of this first.The man nodded slightly, his eyes carelessly passing over most of the office area, and finally slowly landed on the corner where the girl left just now.After a while, he walked towards that place.

The skirt stained with milk tea was on the back side. Chu Ying turned her head, reluctantly hooked the skirt corner, and wiped the wet area with a paper towel soaked in water over and over again.She forgot to bring paper when she came in. The few papers Chu Ying had in her hand were all given to her by Luo Hui just now. They quickly became a mess after getting wet.However, once she went out, she would inevitably run into Xu Jisi again. Chu Ying stared at the wet paper in her hand, feeling like she didn't know where to throw her anger.Every time, every time I see Xu Jisi, I will be troubled.It wasn't enough to scare her in the dream, now he also came to the company.just kiddingWhat kind of bad taste is this?But yesterday he joined the project group, does that mean he has now directly become her client?Chu Ying moved slowly, and in her lowered vision, she saw that the white canvas shoes she was wearing were stained with brown spots at some point.Suddenly, another water droplet dropped, falling on that spot, causing the sudden brown color to spread.Chu Ying blinked, came to her senses, held a clean corner of the tissue and bent down to rub it twice.Just when he was about to straighten up.A pair of black leather shoes suddenly appeared in the peripheral vision.Then, a slightly curved, slender hand appeared in sight.Chu Ying's eyes paused for a moment, and she passed by the pieces of paper clutched in this hand, and then her attention was suddenly attracted by this man's wrist.There was a trace nearly three centimeters long, glowing with white.The edges were dark pink and looked like they had been there for a long time.She didn't get up for a while.The man didn't move, but glanced at her slightly disheveled skirt, and said lazily: "I'm quite welcome."

Chu Ying paused.There is no need to give such a big gift.There seemed to be a bit of teasing in the cold tone.Chu Ying's forehead jumped and she straightened up suddenly.When she raised her head, the person in her field of vision was indeed smiling, and her usually indifferent face curved in such a straightforward manner. Chu Ying was stunned for a moment, and for a moment she wondered if the person in front of her had been taken away from her.The sun is rising in the west, and Xu Jisi can tell jokesWhen did it start? Why does it feel like every time she meets him, he is teasing her?To be honest, this was even more creepy than Xu Jisi pretending not to recognize her.It gave her a sense of uncertainty about her life that was beyond her control.Xu Jisi waved the tissue in front of her eyes and looked back to indicate the hem of her skirt.Chu Ying forced a stiff smile: No, thank you Mr. Xu.After saying that, I had to rub shoulders with him.The man happened to take a step in her direction and stopped in front of her.Chu Ying paused and tried to pass through on his left side.Whether it was a coincidence or something else, the long legs wrapped under the suit pants also took a leisurely step to the left.Chu Ying slowly raised her eyes:While staring at him, he took a step to the right.The man stopped pretending and openly blocked the way she was going in front of her.A pair of black eyes looked down at her lazily, with a slightly raised eyebrow, an expression that said, "What can you do to me?"But Luo Hui's voice suddenly sounded outside, asking her if she was okay and saying that Ling Tingyang was back.Then there was another muttering, saying why Mr. Xu was not seen.Chu Ying's eyelids twitched.Mr. Xu.Isn't it here?Chu Ying slowly turned her gaze away, staring at the rightful owner in front of her who had nothing to do with her. She acted as if she hadn't heard him. Her expression didn't change at all, as if she was just passing by.She gritted her teeth gently and urged in a low voice: "You go out first."Xu Jisi raised his eyebrows slightly, and suddenly bent down and approached her, his dark eyes level with hers. He drawled his voice, pronouncing individual words clearly intentionally or unintentionally, and the meaning of his tone was unclear: In what capacity is Miss Chu asking me?The man's warm breath almost sprayed on her cheeks, and his faint woody fragrance lingered faintly on her nose. The bathroom, which was not cramped, seemed to start to heat up for no reason. Chu Ying froze, and her brain suddenly went blank for a moment.too close.So close that she could clearly see every one of his long eyelashes.In a daze, she even felt that this scene overlapped with her dream last night.Until the footsteps outside suddenly got closer and closer.Every sound of the heels touching the tiles made her heart beat faster. Chu Ying finally came back to her senses, her eyes focused for a moment, and she looked into the man's dark eyes that seemed to be deep in thought.Xu Jisi had no intention of avoiding him at all.Not only that, but he seemed to notice that her expression was getting stiffer and stiffer. The man moved his eyebrows and even moved closer to her.Chu Ying suddenly took two steps back and pressed against the cold washstand.At the same time, the footsteps outside the door suddenly stopped at this moment.Chu Ying's heartbeat also stopped.The company is generous. There are three bathrooms on each floor. They are all single rooms and the design is more home-like. Ling Tingyang said that he arranged all the small details to make everyone feel like they are at home.Xu Jisi closed the door just now when he came in. He seemed to hear some movement, probably thinking that someone was going to the toilet inside. Luo Hui stood in front of the door and knocked hesitantly.Yingying, are you in there?In an almost confrontational posture, Chu Ying's slender waist pressed against the washstand, and the coldness crawled up her spine, stimulating her nerves.The man's narrow, dark eyes stared at her casually but deeply. Chu Ying's whole body was tense, her nails clenched tightly on her knuckles, for fear that Xu Jisi would make some noise and let people outside hear something.Not hearing anyone respond inside, Luo Hui paused, muttering whether it was an illusion, and put her finger on the door to push it open.Chu Ying's voice suddenly sounded at this moment.I'm here. My stomach feels a little uncomfortable. I'm sorry. Please tell Sister Huihui to tell Brother Yang. I'll be back in a minute.Her voice was indescribably urgent and depressed. Luo Hui slowly put down her hand and asked worriedly: Hey, are you okay? Yingying.Within two seconds, Luo Hui seemed to have realized something, and then asked with concern: Is it her menstrual period?Chu Ying froze, and clearly noticed that Xu Jisi's gaze also paused. The previous panic had not faded away, and the indescribable embarrassment ran up her fair neck again, making her blush.The girl gritted her teeth gently, not daring to move her eyes away. Xu Jisi was undoubtedly a time bomb. His every move seemed to pull a thread in her heart, and every breath made her fearful.After an inexplicable silence for a long time, Luo Hui became even more worried: Yingying, are you okay?Xu Jisi straightened up, slowly raised his eyebrows, and touched his thin lips lightly, as if he was about to make a sound.Chu Ying quickly raised her hand, her slender fingers made a half-circle in front of her eyes, and then she unexpectedly covered his lips.The warm and slightly cool fingers touched the soft lips, but Xu Jisi didn't seem to react, and he blinked slowly.Before Luo Hui got suspicious, Chu Ying glanced at him and finally answered: "Yeah."I'm fine, she said vaguely, Sister Huihui, please go and do your work first, don't worry about me.There was a moment of hesitation outside. She probably had something to do, so Luo Hui said hello and said he would send her a message if he had something to do. Then he gradually walked away.Chu Ying finally let go of her worries.Until bursts of warm and regular breathing gently brushed her fingertips, and she suddenly realized something. She looked back stiffly, and saw that the man in front of her was half-lowering his eyes, seeming to fall on her hands. After a while, he slowly raised his eyes again. Eye.A very low laugh lightly shook her slightly cold hands.The hot temperature spread between her palms, and even her tailbone began to feel numb.Chu Ying came to her senses instantly and retracted her hand as if she was electrocuted.The person opposite her pursed her lips inexplicably, and his eyes followed her hand hanging by her side.Sensing his gaze, Chu Ying unconsciously tightened her fingers and hid her hands behind her back, as if the burning sensation was rekindled.So Xu raised his eyes thoughtfully and leisurely, and raised his lower lip lightly under her inexplicable guilty look: Are Miss Chu and I familiar?He paused, whether intentionally or unintentionally, his fingers slightly flexed, his knuckles lightly brushed against his lips, and his eyes glanced at her hand hidden behind her for the second time as if it was suggestive.Why did Miss Chu still take advantage of me?

Chapter 14 RememberingWhat if I say, it's important?14Why did Miss Chu still take advantage of me?

What's cheapWho takes advantage of whomChu Ying's eyelids twitched again, and she was so shocked that her hot fingertips felt cold when they touched the sink.When her mind went blank, she didn't even know where to focus her attention.Is it because he can say such words without shame, or because Xu Jisi can actually tell cold jokes?What kind of dirty thing had got on him?Chu Ying's figure, which was already close to the edge of the stage, took a step back and raised her toes slightly.Seeing the expression on Chu Ying's face changing again and again, Xu Jisi looked at her with interest: Miss Chu has thought about how to explain.explainHow did he have the nerve to say it?Chu Ying finally found her voice, sneered, raised her lips and asked: What 'explanation' does Mr. Xu want to hear?If he hadn't just wanted to make a noise, would she have done it?If he hadn't deliberately blocked the road, she wouldn't have been so startled and worried.The more she thought about this, the more Chu Ying's previously depressed emotions surged in her heart.The crisis was over, and now all those worries came out like a tide. Her tone was a little irritating unconsciously: Could it be that Mr. Xu first appeared here inexplicably, and then blocked my way inexplicably?I appeared at the wrong time. The man's voice was calm, and his dark eyes fell casually. He slightly passed the girl who was stunned because she didn't expect him to make a sudden sound. He turned around and said, "I'll leave now."Chu Ying's clear black eyes blinked slowly. Seeing that Xu Ji was lagging behind in his thoughts, she walked straight out the door. This time it was neat and tidy.but.There is only one bathroom up to the end here. Luo Hui just left. If he goes out now, he will have to meet people directly.After reacting for two seconds, Chu Ying had already grabbed the man's forearm uncontrollably before she came to her senses completely.And almost the moment her hand came up, the man stopped as if he had expected something.Xu Jisi tilted his head leisurely.His eyes fell on her slender, white hands tightly grasped in his arms.Then he slowly raised his eyes, and the smile appeared in his eyes again.This is a repeat of the same old trick

Realizing that she had fallen into Xu Jisi's trap, Chu Ying suddenly let go of her hand.Xu JisiShe was so angry that she called out the name for the first time since the reunion. As if she was really annoyed, Chu Ying gritted her teeth: Don't go too far.Unexpectedly, the man turned around leisurely and gently pulled up the corners of his lips.The tone suddenly seemed like: It turns out that this name is not a ban.

Chu Ying came to her senses later and almost laughed angrily: Are you sick?The surroundings were suddenly quiet for a few seconds.Chu Ying paused and realized what she had said. She curled her fingers slightly and raised her eyes.But unexpectedly, he bumped into those dark pupils whose smile had faded.I just heard the man suddenly ask confusedly: What are you afraid of?Chu Ying was stunned for a moment.The man's narrow, clear eyes were half lowered, and his sharp mandible was retracted inwards. He was looking at her with slightly closed black eyes, and the emotions in his eyes were dark and unclear.When he is not smiling, his thin eyelids will droop, the corners of his lips will be slightly curved, and his dull face will always make people feel alienated and unapproachable.I still remember that my first acquaintance with Xu Jisi was not a pleasant one. His attitude was not friendly and he was even stingy about raising his lips to her. In addition, he had an innate aura of aloofness, as if he was an isolated island. He rejected everything around him. She once thought that they would never meet again.Until she unexpectedly discovered that he lived next door to her.That cold face just had the words "Don't approach strangers" on top of it. Sometimes Chu Ying would wonder if he couldn't laugh or if he didn't know what happiness was.So later she always wanted to make him smile.It seemed that as long as he smiled, the snow on the mountain tops that could not be reached would melt, and she would be closer to him.It's a pity that no matter how much she does, it's all in vain.He would show his confusion at the funny jokes she had found from nowhere. He didn't want to know the logic of the joke, so he would just skip the topic and ask her coldly if she had finished her homework.Listening to her talk about someone in the class who missed the ball when playing football, but kicked out his shoe, hit the head of the passing principal, and flung the principal's wig away. She couldn't help but start mid-sentence. Laughing, the young man only looked at her for a long time and then asked her blankly if she was an idiot.He was not interested in the bits and pieces she shared, nor did he want to understand.But her life is made up of boring bits and pieces.She just wanted to share everything in her life with him.It might be the stubborn little flower in the corner on a rainy day, or the bold puppy sleeping with its belly turned over on the roadside on a sunny day.It may be boring and meaningless.But that was the only way the girl in love could think of to express her love.clumsy.But sincere.She thought being sincere was enough.She didn't know at the time that there was more than just a thin layer of snow between them.But this side of the mountain and the other side of the shore.It's a natural moat.It is insurmountable.They are as different as clouds and mud.She found out on

Christmas Eve after a sleepless night.What are you afraid of in the endThere was no reply for about a long time, and the man stared at her with his dark eyes and asked again reluctantly.Chu Ying's vision gradually became focused.Seeing Xu Jisi's unblinking eyes, it was rare to see any hint of emotion in his deep eyes.He looked depressed, as if he was a little bored.

He asked obviously not just what happened just now.Not for a moment did she realize as she did now that she knew Xu Jisi so well.She always thought she never really knew him.Chu Ying blinked slowly, watching the man purse his thin lips tightly and frown slightly.He seemed genuinely puzzled by this.Somehow, she suddenly wanted to laugh.he does not know.Of course he doesn't know.How could the aloof young man know that his sudden behavior would cause a tornado in Texas like a butterfly effect?How could she know that as long as he appeared, he could easily blow away the heavy dust on the dusty photos in her heart, and open up chapters that she least wanted to remember.It was like a pool of spring water that could wrinkle her just by accidentally brushing against each other.He comes and goes freely and can leave silently at any time.Little did she know that every time the butterfly's wings slowly flapped, the gust of wind would flutter in her heart.Five years of days and nights cannot cover that short autumn and winter.From the moment he appeared in front of her again, the huge gears of fate began to turn, and she didn't know how it would disrupt her peaceful and stable life.Of course he didn't know any of this.Chu Ying slowly met his gaze.It was probably the first time in the several reunions that she felt so calm.She asked softly: Is it important?Xu Jisi's expression was slightly condensed, and he saw that the girl in front of him seemed to have suddenly lost all her emotions. The corners of her lips were clearly raised, but her eyes were so calm that it made people panic.The scene suddenly became quiet again.The girl raised her head slightly, staring at him with her dark eyes, and saw a trace of confusion flashing through the man's eyes.Then there was a long silence.He pursed his lips tightly, frowned slightly, and his smooth and sharp Adam's apple slid up and down.After ten seconds or twenty seconds, until her eyes became dull, Chu Ying slowly blinked her eyes, raised her lips slightly, and seemed to smile.She said nothing.The silence just now clearly laid the answer before the two of them.Chu Ying looked away and breathed out slowly. When she raised her eyes again, her eyes were full of unfamiliarity and etiquette. She smiled politely and said in a calm voice: I still have to work, so I won't accompany Mr. Xu on the 'visit' .She stepped toward the door, took two steps, and paused when she was about to pass him: I hope Mr. Xu will come out in a few minutes, thank you for your cooperation.The man didn't reply.Chu Ying didn't pay attention, but when they rubbed shoulders, the tip of her nose suddenly felt sore for no reason, and her eyes felt hot for a moment.Realizing something, those uncontrollable emotions were quickly suppressed by her. As if nothing happened, she walked to the door.She put her finger on the metal doorknob, and the cold temperature ran down her fingertips to her nerves, calming her mind a little.Just before the door opens.The man's slightly cold voice sounded from behind, as if he was a little hoarse.What if I say, it's important?

When Chu Ying came out absentmindedly, she happened to bump into Luo Huizheng at the corner reporting the situation to Ling Tingyang anxiously.You can vaguely hear words like "I was there just now" in the words.That silent face flashed through her mind instantly. Chu Ying's heartbeat skipped a beat for no reason, and she subconsciously glanced back.I don't know if he will cooperate.When he turned around again, he happened to meet Luo Hui's eyes looking up unintentionally.Hey, Yingying is here.Luo Hui took advantage of the opportunity to greet them, and Chu Ying put aside the messy thoughts in her mind and quickly approached the two of them, just about to apologize to them.But Luo Hui stared at her for a few seconds as if she had noticed something. She suddenly frowned, leaned into her ear and whispered: "Can you still hold on? Do you want to take a rest? I'll get you an ibuprofen."Chu Ying didn't react for a moment. Just as she turned her face, she heard Luo Hui's concerned tone:I asked you why your voice is muffled in front of you. Look at you, your eyes are red. Your health is the most important thing. We are here to help you.Only then did she realize that Luo Hui had misunderstood. Chu Ying opened her mouth and subconsciously wanted to explain. However, she thought of the lie she had just told and the corners of her lips moved. Finally, she followed Luo Hui's words and found a reasonable reason:It's okay, Sister Huihui. I have some medicine. Just now, an insect flew into my eye. I rubbed it and my eyes became red.Luo Hui looked at her suspiciously: Is it true?Really, Chu Ying nodded hurriedly, I felt really uncomfortable so I just asked for leave.Well, Luo Hui said and looked away. After a pause, she remembered something again. She turned her head and asked her, by the way, did you see Mr. Xu was here just now? I don't know now.He replied.Ling Tingyang, who had been silent for a long time, finally raised his head and spoke.The two looked at each other and then looked at him together. Chu Ying's heart tightened and she subconsciously asked: Where is he?He said that he was visiting the recording studio and Shizune didn't hear it just now.Luo Hui said ah, and asked: In which shed is it?1 shed.Luo Hui thought about it and looked puzzled: I have obviously been to Shed 1.Maybe he happened to be somewhere else when you went there. Chu Ying took advantage of the situation and interfaced.The studio is large, even with three floors, and there are many sheds. It is reasonable to miss something. Luo Hui did not doubt it and nodded: Yes, it will be fine if he found it anyway. I was worried that I did not entertain him well and he just left. Then I have sinned.

If Xu Jisizhen left, then the problem could only be hers.Thinking of the dispute just now, Chu Ying felt inexplicably guilty and curled her fingers. Ling Tingyang's eyes passed over her, and finally fell on Luo Hui. He waved to her: I'll come here, you can go on your own first.Knowing that Xu Jisi was still there, she felt relieved. Luo Hui said hello, turned to tell Chu Ying and told Chu Ying that she had a warm baby in the cabinet before leaving.She subconsciously said thank you, but when she came to her senses and looked up, she only saw Luo Hui's back leaving in a hurry. Chu Ying blinked, clenched her phone tightly with her fingers, and suddenly felt a trace of guilt in her heart.Luo Hui was so kind to her that she didn't want to hide anything from her.But once the matter between the two of them was revealed to her, there was too much to explain.She didn't want to have anything to do with Xu Jisi anymore.Chu Ying sighed silently, turned her head and met Ling Tingyang's scrutinizing eyes.The girl blinked and called tentatively: Brother YangShe's terrible at hiding her emotions.Luo Hui has a carefree personality and doesn't think deeply about some things. She can fool her, but Ling Tingyang can't.From just now, he noticed something was wrong with her.The clenched fingers, the hesitation to speak several times, and the frowning frown on her face that looked like she was relieved, all told him that she was hiding something.The man's cold face flashed across her face almost instantly, and she remembered the conversation a few days ago, explaining that she was obviously hiding something.You, Ling Tingyang, paused slightly.Chu Ying's clear black pupils were slightly raised, showing an unclear but listening expression.The girl's unpainted little face is delicate and delicate. If you look closely, you can see the soft down on her face. She is white everywhere, so when she looks into those clean and clear eyes, the light red ring under her eye sockets is particularly attractive. Notice.After staring into her eyes for a few seconds, Ling Tingyang turned to what he wanted to say and finally swallowed it. He sighed and waved his hand.You go to the recording studio to prepare first.Chu Ying blinked. Although she had doubts in her heart, she knew that there was no need to ask what others didn't want to say. So she nodded, said hello, took the script and thermos cup from her seat and walked to the recording studio.At noon, I discussed the plot with Stanley Ho, and Chu Ying's thoughts became clearer. She sat in the recording studio, trying to figure out the characters' emotions, while using a pen to write down key points on the script.The more she analyzed, the more she entered the state. Chu Ying muttered to herself and tried a few sentences, and it turned out that the effect was better than that in the morning. The urgency to show Ling Tingyang the results suddenly emerged at this moment. She looked at the time and saw that it had passed. Ten minutes later, there was still no movement in the control room.After sending a message but not getting a response, Chu Ying decided to get up and go out to take a look.As luck would have it, as soon as she stood up, the door on the other side opened.Chu Ying's eyes lit up and she was about to walk through the control room to share with Ling Tingyang.But behind Ling Tingyang, a very familiar figure came into his eyes.Chu Ying froze suddenly.The man still put his hands casually in his pockets, his cold face expressionless, his eyebrows slightly lowered, as if he was listening indifferently to what Ling Tingyang was saying, and after a while he tapped his chin again, probably in response to something.After Ling Tingyang finished speaking, he glanced over here and saw that she was standing frozen in place, her fingers slightly bent and spread out, gesturing for her to sit back down.Then, the person behind him also noticed something and slowly raised his eyelashes.Make eye contact with her.Half a quarter of an hour ago, the man's response from behind seemed to ring in his ears again.What if I say, it's important?How did she reply?She said, if you use "if" to fool people, does Mr. Xu think that I am still so easy to deceive?This was indeed the truest thought in her heart.But when she said these words at the time, she did forget that as a film producer, he was naturally qualified to watch the studio in person.The impatience she had just now was instantly extinguished by the dark look cast by this person. Chu Ying sat down stiffly and heard Ling Tingyang say that Mr. Xu would take over from the documentary producer to follow up the progress.Chu

Ying's brain slowly received this information.After capturing certain keywords, the expression on his face froze.Whatever it is called, it will happen nextHe also plans to come every day

Chapter 15 RememberingYou're with him, right?15Chu Ying stiffened up and her eyes were blank for a moment.For a moment, I didn't even hear what Ling Tingyang said, until I looked up in a daze and saw Ling Tingyang's complicated expression on the other side of the transparent glass.Chu Ying.He frowned tightly and called her name in a deep voice.Suddenly withdrawing her consciousness, Chu Ying's eyes slowly focused. The man next to her had already stopped looking and sat down nearby.Her broad back under the suit was leaning on the leather sofa, her long legs were slightly bent and crossed over each other casually, one hand was loosely clasped, the other was bent, her elbow was propped on the handrest, and her well-jointed fingers were touching her chin, as if aware of her gaze. , he raised his eyelashes again.The gaze was very light, but Chu Ying felt a burning sensation, which made her avert her eyes in a panic.Ling Tingyang's voice entered the ear canal at this time, with some dissatisfaction: Look at the lines.Chu Ying moved her somewhat numb fingers, and her mind finally came back. She tried her best to control herself and ignore the scorching gaze. She took a deep breath, trying to regain the feeling she had just discovered.However, as soon as he opened his mouth, his voice became hoarse for some reason.Chu Ying froze, and subconsciously looked up at Ling Tingyang's expression. She saw his brows moving slightly and his frown getting tighter. Then she looked to the side, as if she was explaining something to Xu Jisi, and leaned lazily against her. The man on the sofa then cast another unclear look and nodded leisurely.Sorry, I moistened my throat.Chu Ying looked back embarrassedly, as if she finally got a chance to breathe, and took the thermos cup on the table hurriedly. She lowered her head deliberately, wrapped her slender fingers around the water cup, and twisted her knuckles to the right with slight force.like a statue.Chu Ying quickly glanced up, then lowered her eyes immediately. From the corner of her eye, she could see the two of them waiting for her. The two eyes staring straight through the glass made her scalp numb.Probably because I poured too hot water before, the air pressure dropped when it cooled down, and it was really not that easy to open for a while.It was originally to calm down while drinking water, but who knew that this could also go wrong.Is there anything more embarrassing than being watched by the boss and Party A at the same time and trying to unscrew the cup but failing to do so?The temperature in her neck spread to her earlobes. Chu Ying gritted her teeth gently, buried her head lower, put a little more strength in her hands, and finally unscrewed the cup before she felt that the person outside was about to speak.Breathing a sigh of relief, Chu Ying immediately took a cup and poured some water into her dry throat almost without any image. Her long and white neck was raised high. Chu Ying could only rely on these few seconds to calm down her emotions.It only took half a minute, but being watched made her feel that the time had been stretched several times, making it extremely long.It seemed that she was drinking in a hurry, so Ling Tingyang softened her tone: "Slow down, don't panic."After a pause, he shifted his vision slightly, glanced at the man sitting on the side who could not see his emotions, and said slowly: I believe Mr. Xu is a very objective person, just play your part as usual.There seems to be something in the words.Xu Jisi raised his eyelids, looked away from the girl whose movements were slightly stiff, and glanced at her lightly.After receiving his gaze, Ling Tingyang's expression did not change, but she seemed to be asking for his opinion: Right?The man raised his eyebrows slightly, and after a long while, he said in a long, cold voice: "Of course."Ling Tingyang smiled politely at him, then turned around and asked Chu Ying, who had put down her water glass, if she was ready.Chu Ying nodded, her previously bloodless lips were much moister, and under the cold white light above her head, they looked like jelly and glowed with a light pink color.After the girl moistened her throat, her voice became much more normal.Chu Ying tried the sound test and made an OK gesture to the other end.The screen in front of her began to play the original film. Chu Ying tightened her grip on the script and spoke to the heroine's lips.Fortunately, everything went smoothly afterwards.The man's presence was so strong that Chu Ying couldn't really pretend that he didn't exist. At first, his attention was a little distracted, but under Ling Tingyang's guidance, he gradually got into the mood.Just when the plot was about to explode with emotion, Chu Ying brewed her emotions and completely immersed herself in the role, focusing only on the plot and lines.Later, I didn't know when Xu Jisi left.In short, by the time she noticed a hint of thirst, took a sip of water, and looked up again, Ling Tingyang was the only one left in the control room.Chu Ying blinked slowly and turned her gaze.He saw Ling Tingyang lowering her head and sketching something on the script while she was resting.As a supporting director, he needs to know the emotional state of each character at every stage. Ling Yang's scripts are always full of details, and he will mark and highlight everyone's lines.Chu Ying opened her mouth and was about to ask something.At this moment, as if he had a telepathic connection, Ling Tingyang did not raise his head, but spoke: He left ten minutes ago.Chu Ying froze, and her eyelashes blinked quickly unconsciously, as if she suddenly realized something. She almost choked in her throat with a mouthful of water, and her cheeks turned red for a moment due to the blockage of her trachea.I do notLing Tingyang's sigh cut off her desire to hide her emotions. He slowly raised his head and stated in a tone: This is not the first time.Chu Ying subconsciously clenched the script with her fingers, almost rubbing the corners of the paper through.Ling Tingyang stared at her, looking at her tense expression, stiff body, and hands with nowhere to rest, as if he wanted to see through every micro movement she made.You had dinner with Luo Hui that day.Just because he didn't say it before doesn't mean he doesn't know.As soon as they arrived, Luo Hui sent him a photo and complained to him about leaving the employees to eat.At that time, when he thought about it, he initially realized that something was wrong.Based on his understanding of Chu Ying's character, she was not the kind of person who would be a disappointment on important occasions.Chu Ying was usually emotionally stable, but her reaction that day could almost be said to be out of control.Later, Xu Jisi came specially to give her earrings, but she was distracted in the car.Now it is affecting her working mood even more.After spending so much time with Chu Ying, he knew that Chu Ying was a girl who took her work extremely seriously. She would do her best even if she was recording a group of miscellaneous works.Not to mention her professionalism, even when the producer suddenly arrived that day, she performed extremely well, and her words and demeanor did not show any timidity.This is the first time in three years that something like this has happened today.If before entering the shed, he was still thinking about giving Chu Ying some privacy to adjust his emotions, then at this moment, after seeing her state just now, Ling Tingyang felt that he had to say something.Chu Ying is a rare good talent with extraordinary talent. He has always doted on talents. Moreover, Chu Ying was discovered and brought up by himself. He has reasons to talk to her both in public and private matters.His straightforwardness obviously made Chu Ying feel at a loss for a moment.Ling Tingyang saw that her ears were visibly reddened, and paused, as if a little surprised: "You really think I don't know?"She remembered that Luo Hui took the photo at that time, but the topic was suddenly interrupted at that time, and she did not think about it later.In fact, she knew.This is a lie that can be easily exposed.I just didn't expect that in this situation, Ling Tingyang would say it so bluntly.Chu Ying bit her inner lip gently, as if she wanted to hide it: it was just uncomfortable at that time, but it got better later.Ling Yang was almost amused by her quibble.So, today too

Chu Ying didn't dare to look at him again.Whether she realized that she had passively told so many lies today, or realized that lying in front of him would be futile, Chu Ying's eyelashes trembled slightly and she lowered her neck.When Luo Hui said she didn't find Xu Jisi, were you with him?Even though he was confident in his heart, Ling Tingyang still asked this question out loud as if he was confirming it.

Chu Ying still didn't make a sound.But the silence at this time was no different than admission.Somehow, after confirming the situation, he breathed a sigh of relief.The first thought was that it would be better to be related to Ji Ran.If it were Ji Ran, with his understanding and intuition, Chu Ying would definitely be in trouble, let alone whether the project could progress smoothly.But if it's Xu JisiXu Jisi's uncertainties are naturally greater than Ji Ran's, and his character and city are more difficult to figure out than Ji Ran's.But one thing he knew.Whether it was his intuition, or his sophisticated vision developed from years of dealing with all kinds of people, he could tell that Xu Jisi had a bottom line.Maybe he has his own interests and purposes, but he will not harm Chu Ying.Ling Tingyang exhaled slowly.After a long while, he suddenly said: OK, I believe it.Chu Ying raised her head, blinked, and her brain slowly analyzed the meaning of his words.It took a while before I remembered anything.Ling Tingyang was replying to her first and only reply.Although both of them knew it tacitly.Although for Ling Tingyang, he had every reason to ask her clearly on the grounds of the project.But he didn't press.Chu Ying breathed a sigh of relief, but also felt a little guilty.I just let go of my anxiety.But there is one thing.The next second, Ling Tingyang's voice was deep, and he spoke clearly every word: I don't care how you plan to deal with it.Chu Ying's breath froze.Ling Tingyang lightly swept her long trembling eyelashes, and then said: I only look at the performance. You have to show your professionalism and let your work speak for itself.Chu Ying unconsciously raised her eyelashes and saw that his expression was calm, but there was a rare sense of oppression.You're new and it's definitely a challenge.But 'Lingting' only produces high-quality products, and my requirements for you will only be stricter.Ling Tingyang's tone was calm, as if it should be so.Being used to Ling Tingyang's friendly image, I almost forgot that he is also a businessman at heart.Chu Ying came back to her senses and met Ling Tingyang's slightly bent gaze. Her mood was not consciously affected by his words, and she nodded blankly.Ling Tingyang's expression relaxed a little and his voice became softer. He didn't waste any more time and got to the point:OK, continue.

After being woken up by Ling Ting, she didn't know what she wanted to prove. Chu Ying closed her eyes, took a deep breath, completely cleared her mind of all the messy thoughts, and finished a few episodes in one breath.Her job is almost gone, so how can she have the chance to make her sad?Ling Tingyang finally couldn't stand it anymore when he saw that her soft voice was tinged with gravel and she was still just moistening it with a few drops of water.The solemn look on their faces had long since faded. The atmosphere was always relaxed when they were dubbing, but today it was a bit too heavy.Chu Ying didn't seem tired, asking him over and over again which would be more appropriate. In fact, the state was no different from usual. They still discussed the emotional issues in the lines together, and also worked out the details of the tone together, but there were fewer of them. Joyous laughter.Chu Ying took a sip of water, cleared her throat, lowered her head and scratched the surface of what she just said. She still felt unsatisfied, so she raised her head again and wanted to ask: Did I feel too emotional about what I just said?Let's stop here today.Ling Tingyang sighed softly and interrupted her.Chu Ying was stunned, blinked her eyelashes, and tried to persuade him: "Let's finish this part first. I'm pretty smooth now."Don't overdo it. Ling Tingyang looked at her. Failure to maintain a good voice will affect the progress.As soon as she finished speaking, Chu Ying felt that her throat was indeed dry and itchy, and she couldn't help coughing.A little embarrassed, she stretched out her hand to rub the back of her neck. Chu Ying pursed her lips and then whispered: Okay.It happened to be the evening rush hour when I left the company.The autumn breeze was cool, Chu Ying walked out of the Cultural and Creative Park and subconsciously walked to the opposite side of the road.After walking some distance, I suddenly realized that I was going the wrong way.Crossing the road is the direction to Zhu Ruoxuan's home. Her new home only needs to be walked along the road to the nearby subway station.After all, they had lived together for more than half a year, and now they suddenly moved away. Chu Ying was really not used to it.After sending Zhu Ruoxuan back yesterday, it was hard to say whether the relationship between the two had eased. But this morning, she received a message from Zhu Ruoxuan, saying that she had left her earphones at her house.I just moved to a new house not long ago, and some daily necessities have not been fully used. Chu Ying happened to be busy recently, and I really can't remember if there are any small items that I didn't bring back.In the past, she had various opinions against Zhu Ruoxuan, but now she has moved away. For her, everything in the past has been reconciled, and she has no need to deliberately avoid suspicion.Chu Ying thought for a while and replied that she would get it when she had time.There was no reply from there.The girl stood at the intersection at dusk, the lights of passing cars flashing in her eyes.Within a few seconds, the red light on the other side of the zebra crossing jumped and the traffic stopped. People in twos and threes chatted and rubbed shoulders with her, but Chu Ying suddenly felt lost.In fact, she knew that Zhu Ruoxuan was not that bad.It is true that she hangs out every night and rarely comes back. She is occasionally sloppy and has a bad personality.But Chu Ying also remembered that she would bring breakfast for herself when she came back in the morning; if she came back in the middle of the night or early in the morning, she would take off her shoes and try not to make too much noise.Zhu Ruoxuan's embarrassed appearance yesterday came to mind again. Such a hoarse voice and depressed look were something she had never seen before.And what she mentioned was grandma's death anniversary.How similar they are.But she didn't know which side of Zhu Ruoxuan was the most real.Until the traffic light started flashing again and turned green.All kinds of cars passed by, sweeping away the dim light of the sky and opening the curtain of sunset.At seven o'clock, the street lights on the roadside came on on time.Vehicles were whizzing by, and when someone passed by her, the BGM of a short video was played on her phone. The roar of the surroundings was approaching and then getting further away. From time to time, long or short car honks were heard in the distance and blended into the ambient sound.There was a streetlight on one side, and a long shadow stretched out from Chu Ying's feet, straight to the bottom of the tree beside the road.She stood there, looking at the sky that seemed to be darkening suddenly in a daze.Suddenly, a trumpet sounded close to my ears.He made a short sound, as if he just wanted to attract her attention. Chu Ying suddenly came back to her senses, looked at the source of the sound, and saw a black car slowly stopping under a tree nearby.After double flashing, the spot where the opponent stopped was blocked by dense branches and leaves. Chu Ying could only vaguely see the outline of the man in the driver's seat.His eyes slowly moved down, and finally landed on the silver-framed license plate with white characters on a blue background.It looks familiar.Chu Ying took two tentative steps that way: Excuse meBefore she finished speaking, her vision gradually became clearer as she stepped closer.The appearance of the man in the driver's seat suddenly came into view.The man's suit jacket was thrown casually into the passenger seat, underneath was a simple white shirt, and his dark tie was pulled slightly loose.The man's broad back was slightly tilted back, his beautiful fingers lightly grasped the steering wheel, his elbows were slightly bent on the edge of the lowered window, and he silently raised his eyelids.Why is it Xu Jisi?Chu Ying's voice was abrupt.His footsteps also stayed in place.Seeing that she was motionless, the man tilted his head slowly, raised his eyebrows slightly, and seemed to say hello to her: "Miss Chu, what a coincidence."Chu Ying:Who is it?Shouldn't he have gone back long ago?Chu Ying's originally polite smile froze, and then she suddenly changed her face and seemed to retract it. She turned into a expressionless look and turned around to leave.Unexpectedly, just after taking two steps, the horn behind him rang again.Someone passed by and stopped to look this way, his eyes gradually falling from the car to her accurately.His posture was so obvious that anyone could probably tell that the person he was waiting for was her.Chu Ying unconsciously stiffened slightly.The man slowly stepped on the accelerator, and the car drove half a meter away, and finally stopped beside her.It's more obvious.Xu Jisi peeked out half of Qingjun's face, and the mottled tree shadows swayed across his eyes, making it difficult to see his emotions even though they were half-covered.I can just hear his voice sounding like the autumn wind blowing now, with a hint of laziness in the coldness: Let's talk.Chu Ying was quiet for a moment and then slowly raised her eyes. Mr. Xu and I probably had nothing to talk about.Xu Jisi's dark eyes were deep, and the girl's words when she left a few hours ago flashed in his mind, and he moved his lips slightly for a moment.He lowered his eyes to look at her and paused slightly: "Miss Chu seems to have some misunderstanding about me."He was very concerned about what she said.He hadn't even cared so much about other people's words for a long time.After leaving in the afternoon, while busy at work, these words would suddenly linger in my mind at a certain moment.He wouldn't waste time in meaningless self-entanglement, so he came back.What do you mean by thinking she is still so easy to deceive?Let's not talk about how unclear the meaning of this word is.When did he lie to her?His eyes passed over Chu Ying's relaxed expression. Xu Jisi suppressed the emotion in his eyes and answered slowly:I don't want my reputation to be ruined without knowing why.

Chapter 16 RememberingMiss Chu, take me in out of kindness16Chu Ying got in the car anyway.It was the evening rush hour, and Xu Jisi's car was parked on the side of the road where cars were passing by. It was unknown when it would cause a traffic jam.In addition, there were many pedestrians after get off work, so after stopping for a while, Chu Ying could notice more eyes drifting towards her.How could Xu Jisi act like a normal person every time, even mentioning things casually but not looking down?This is not a threatChu Ying gritted her teeth and opened the car door angrily.Xu Jisi tilted his head, pointed his eyes at the co-pilot to put on the coat he had taken off, and lazily said: Please take it off, Miss Chu.Chu Ying almost wanted to complain to him about whether she was helpless, but reason pulled her impulse away, and she endured it for two seconds. Finally, before the honking of cars was about to sound from behind, she bent down and reached in, picked it up and sat down. It was said that it was folded violently and casually between the arms, without any regard for how this valuable suit would wrinkle.Xu didn't think about it but didn't care. On the contrary, she curled her lips as if in a good mood. She lowered the window while fastening her seat belt and drove the car slowly.The man's suit jacket hung between his arms, and the familiar aloes from the owner's body invaded his nose unreasonably. Chu Ying's face was sullen, and she deliberately tilted her head. Her eyes fell on the car window, but she saw him making a detour. Driving to the river.Some thoughts popped up in her heart, Chu Ying bit her lower lip lightly, but still couldn't hold it back: Where are you taking me?send you home.Chu Ying pursed her lips tightly, I don't need you to take me home.What on earth is Xu Jisi going crazy about?I made a special trip to be her driver.Chu Ying took a deep breath: What do you want to talk about?The neon-reflecting river surface was blown by the wind, and the rows of high-rise buildings and the greenery on the riverside quickly receded. Xu Ji thought for a while without making a sound, and the rearview mirror reflected Chu Ying's complex expression in his peripheral vision. It was beautiful. His eyebrows frowned slightly.After a long while, Xu Jisi glanced at her and asked nonsensically: Have I lied to you?Chu Ying paused and frowned even more tightly: What?You said I thought you were easy to cheatXu Jisi's voice was slightly hoarse: When did I ever lie to you?The car suddenly became quiet.There was only the sound of wind in my ears.The curve of the corners of Chu Ying's lips straightened.At his words, his heart felt like it was being tightened by vines and then dropped suddenly.As the car drove across the long bridge, until the road conditions in her field of vision gradually became familiar, Chu Ying finally found her voice.Mr. Xu really did. Her fingers that were tightly gripping the seat belt slowly loosened her grip. She raised her eyes and seemed to pull her lower lip. How noble a person forgets things.Xu Jisi frowned and was about to ask: YouThe phone's default incoming call ringtone rings at this moment.The man paused, lowered his neck and glanced at the notes dancing on the screen.His eyes flicked over the girl beside him, and his slender fingers slightly bent and stroked.The call was hung up.Xu Jisi's thin lips opened slightly, but he didn't make a sound.The next moment, the phone lights up again.

Young Master Xu lowered his eyes, his expression

filled with impatience, and he tried to move his finger to the left again.It's hard for Mr. Xu to be my driver when he has so many things to do.The girl beside her had a clearly calm voice, but her meaning was unclear.Xu Jisi raised his eyes and saw the girl's eyes were very calm: If I can't listen, just put me on the roadside.He could sense Chu Ying's sudden change in mood and attitude.Only others could figure out Young Master Xu's mood. Xu Jisi never thought that one day he would be so sensitive to other people's moods.There happened to be a red light ahead, so he eased off the accelerator and slowly stopped the car.He raised his gaze slightly and fell into the girl's calm black eyes.The incoming call on the phone is still bouncing one after another.Xu Jisi stared at her for two seconds, lowered his eyes and answered the phone under her gaze.A girl's voice came faintly from the microphone, but I couldn't make out what exactly she said.Probably because she talked too much today, the autumn wind was a bit cold, which made the itch in her throat surge up again. It was dry and slightly bitter. Chu Ying pressed her throat and looked away.In the corner of his eye, Xu Ji thought that there was no emotion on Qingjun's face. Only his fingers that kept tapping on the edge of the steering wheel revealed a hint of weariness.The words on the other end seemed very dense. Xu Jisi just listened. Half a minute passed before he replied coldly: Are you done?After two seconds of silence, without knowing what was said, the man suddenly raised his eyelashes and glanced at Chu Ying.The red light suddenly turned green.Sensing his gaze, Chu Ying turned her head slightly.I happened to see the man pull the handbrake and said yes.Their eyes briefly collided, and she saw the man staring straight at her as if he wanted to prove something, and replied lazily and neatly: There are more important things.After finishing his words, Xu Jisi didn't seem to want to wait for the other party to come back to his senses. Xu Jisi hung up with a perfunctory sentence, and hung up the phone with a slender finger.Chu Ying was left looking blankly, following the cell phone that was casually thrown aside and turned black.The screen reflected his stunned look for a moment.When she reacted again, Xu Jisi had already crossed the intersection, entered Jiananhui in a familiar way, and sent her downstairs.The car stopped slowly. Chu Ying blinked and focused her eyes on the man in the driver's seat again.Noticing her gaze, the man glanced at her suddenly.The dark and deep pupils fell into his eyes, and the scene in the dream suddenly appeared in his mind without warning.Chu Ying froze, and then remembered Xu Jisi's behavior last night. She loosened her fingers and hurriedly unbuckled her seat belt. She hurriedly opened the car door for fear that her dream would come true or old memories would reappear and she would be chased.Stepping out of the car, Chu Ying nimbly walked around the car door and closed it, inadvertently breathing a sigh of relief.When she turned to leave, she thought of something again.

The girl bent slightly, put her head forward, and said thank you as if she was in a hurry.She completely forgot that the reason she got in the car in the first place was because Xu Jisi wanted to have a chat.The man's eyes flashed across her face, and when he saw her standing up straight, he couldn't wait to leave. His eyes slowly moved down, landing on her slender arms, and he raised his eyebrows slightly, half-smiling.The meaning of this glance was really unclear. Chu Ying paused unconsciously and lowered her head.The next moment, Crimson suddenly fainted on her earlobes.The floppy suit was hung messily in one arm. She got out of the car in such a hurry that she even forgot to put her clothes down.So embarrassingThe suit, which was not heavy, seemed to have gained ten pounds at this moment. Chu Ying felt that her whole arm was numb. She stiffly moved through the car window and handed the clothes inside.Xu Jisi raised his chin slightly: Just throw it away.Chu Ying suddenly breathed a sigh of relief. As if throwing a hot potato, she threw her suit in, then turned around and left.Her steps changed from small to long, and even turned into a trot before entering the building. If she could teleport, she wished she could disappear on the spot.It wasn't until she couldn't see the car anymore when she turned around that Chu Ying raised her hand to slow down her breathing.The elevator stopped on the tenth floor. Chu Ying pressed the button and the elevator began to operate. During the short wait, she unconsciously raised her hand to rub her earlobes, and then she realized how hot her ears were.In her mind, she couldn't help but recall the scenes of Xu Jisi in recent days, how many times she had been caught in an embarrassing situation by him.She just wanted to maintain her stable life at the moment.As soon as Xu Jisi appeared, even a peaceful sleep became a luxury for her.Chu Ying felt that her temples began to throb again.Shaking her head, Chu Ying breathed a sigh of relief, and the elevator door opened in time.Chu Ying took two steps inside and was about to turn around to press the floor.Footsteps suddenly came from behind.Chu Ying tilted her head, thinking she was a neighbor on the same floor, and took two steps in to make room.In the peripheral vision, a pair of long legs were walking leisurely, wearing exquisite and shiny leather shoes. The view was slightly upward, and the crisp white shirt was tucked into the straight suit pants, outlining the narrow waist, and it looked vaguely familiar.Not quite right.Chu Ying blinked and turned her head sharply.He was caught off guard and met the man's lazily lowered eyelids.Chu Ying could hardly react and opened her eyes blankly: Why did you come in?Even Party A can't go so far. She didn't even invite him. How could he follow her on his own?There's surveillance here, don't be tooMiss Chu, Xu Jisi seems to be smiling, what do you think I will do to you?Chu Ying opened her lips, but before she even uttered a syllable, she saw him stretch out his long and well-jointed fingers and press a floor key accurately.Be on the same level as her.When she was stunned as to how he knew the floor of her home, she heard the man's clear voice concealing a bit of a smile, lightly touching his thin lips, and opening his mouth lazily:I just go back to my home.

Chu Ying never imagined that she and Xu Jisi would now have such a relationship that they could not see each other when they raised their heads and looked down.So close that maybe she could just close the door and hear the sound on the other side.How could Xu Jisi live next door to her by such a coincidence?Until she took the noodles with clear soup out of the pot and sat down at the table, Chu Ying was still in a daze, as if she didn't realize what a series of magical events had happened today.She absent-mindedly rolled out two mouthfuls of noodles, but before taking them into her mouth, her mind flashed back to Xu Jisi's familiarity with the road conditions when he sent her downstairs for the first time yesterday. Chu Ying finally recalled some fact that she had always ignored.Jiananhui has access control, you can't get in without swiping your faceTwice today, she forgot about it and he drove right in.What a coincidence.Chu Ying blinked blankly. She was silent for an unknown period of time. After a while, she suddenly heard the doorbell ringing again.Chu Ying subconsciously stood up and wanted to open the door, but then remembered that she had just moved here, and it was impossible for anyone to come to her. Her footsteps stopped at the entrance, she paused, and subconsciously turned her head.The next moment, the screen at the entrance suddenly lit up, and a face suddenly came closer.Desolate and distant, the turned-down collar around his slender neck was clean, and he had taken off his tie at some point.A trace of seriousness was missing, and a hint of the youthful feeling of the past seemed to emerge in a trance.It's Xu Jisi.Chu Ying froze.No matter who it is, this is probably the angle of death.But this man's face is so good, even if the man's jawline is close to the surveillance camera, it can be seen that he looks handsome.He just pressed it once and then waited patiently, as if he knew she heard her.What is he here for?Chu Ying came back to her senses, her heart tightened, and she hesitated for a while between pretending to die and committing suicide.Then I saw the man seemed to notice something through the cold electrons, and suddenly raised his eyes.Something flashed through his dark eyes, and he moved suddenly, looking down at his phone.His slender fingers touched the screen a few times and then pressed it off at will.The phone suddenly lit up, Chu Ying twitched her fingers and suddenly looked away.A message pops up at the top of the screen.Miss Chu, take me in out of kindnessChu Ying was stunned for a moment.Who takes in whom?Doesn't he live next door?Doubts arose in my mind for a moment, but when I realized what was happening, her message had already been sent.

It's a cold question mark.Young Master Xu has probably never been questioned like this in his life.Chu Ying slowly blinked her eyes and was suddenly startled into a cold sweat by her uncontrollable behavior.She subconsciously raised her head to look at the screen, and sure enough she saw that the man had his head slightly lowered, probably reading her message. The broken hair on his forehead was scattered around his eyebrows, casting a shadow, making it impossible to read his emotions.It's over.It's over, it's over.If she keeps pretending to be dead, she can later explain that she really didn't hear or see.If I reply to the news this time, won't it give someone a clue?She stared at the screen almost anxiously, her fingers staying in the air for a while, trying to find a reason to make up for her previous reply.Sorry, I bumped into it accidentally just nowSorry, I haven't finished typing yet and accidentally posted it.After thousands of responses, it seemed that no matter what the reply was, it seemed deliberate.Chu Ying bit her lip gently, and the thought of breaking the jar came into her mind.Anyway, we were almost at the point of breaking up at the company in the afternoon.Is it really necessary to maintain that superficial relationship?Just thinking so.Quite indifferentThe man sent another message.Chu Ying froze and read it twice, and somehow seemed to read a hint of humor in it.Feeling annoyance for no reason, Chu Ying turned around and turned off her phone without intending to answer it again.The next second, the phone lit up again.I just moved in today and haven't bought any dishes yet. I wonder if Miss Chu would like to take me in for dinner.Just be clear about it.

Chapter 17 RememberingWhat is public and what is private17What does it mean to just move in?What does it mean to take him in for dinner?Xu Jisi also used her as a shelterDignified young master, it's just dinner, there's no place to eat itDo I have to come to her house?What on earth does he want to do?Chu Ying's mind was confused, and her eyes fell on the last two words of the message repeatedly.Two clear things.This was the first time in a while that he had mentioned this matter to her head-on.It was obviously the result she wanted most, but when he really brought it up, she felt a little bit of evasion.There were some words she couldn't say.The girl was worried about something in her heart, and she couldn't express any of the conflicting thoughts she had had during this period of time.Xu Jisi asked her what she was afraid of, and she actually had an answer.Not only was she afraid that he would disrupt her life, she was also paradoxically afraid of many things.for exampleAfraid that he will be different from the past, and also afraid that he will be the same as before.Afraid that he is really special to her, and also afraid that he treats her the same as everyone else.She told herself countless times to be open-minded and forget.But no one told her that a teenage girl's heartbeat could get out of hand like this.It's like five years of not seeing each other can't suppress the intensifying heartbeat when we meet again.She did overestimate herself.She couldn't guarantee that she wouldn't make the same mistake again when she faced him.So she kept running away.It might have been okay before, but nowThe situation obviously cannot be solved by her escaping.Chu Ying lowered her eyes lightly, and her eyes fell on the dark eyes of the person on the screen.He was sure that she would open the door when she saw these words. His long eyelashes were slightly raised, as if he looked at her through the cold electron, Chu Ying moved her fingers.Two minutes later.The door lock clicked.The straight long legs of the man outside the door were the first to catch her lowered eyes.Chu Ying opened the door very slowly.Xu Jisi's deserted face seemed to soften for a moment, and then slightly raised the corners of his lips.He stepped in the door, took two steps inside, and said lazily: "I'm taking the liberty of visiting."Chu Ying turned around and whispered in a low voice: I knew it was presumptuous to come here.She couldn't see that he was being presumptuous.After a pause, the man raised his eyebrows, but didn't hear clearly: "What?"Chu Ying hurriedly shut her mouth, without saying anything to greet him. She took two steps towards the living room, her eyes fell on her bowl of noodles on the table, which was almost lumpy, and then she remembered that she didn't do anything today.Suddenly feeling a little embarrassed, Chu Ying opened her mouth: Well, I actually don't have much to eat at home.The man walked through the door and looked around calmly. Hearing the sound, his eyes fell on the table not far away.The room was deserted, probably because they had just moved in, and it looked lifeless. Only the faint aroma of noodles came from the slightly steaming pot on the opposite side of the island.It smells light.He withdrew his gaze, loosened his cuffs, and chatted casually like friends: Cooked noodlesChu Ying walked around the island, paused while holding the bowl, hummed, and then raised her head: "You may not be used to it." I'm not very good at it, otherwise you'd better go outThe man's expression did not change and he quickly answered: I quite like eating noodles.Then he looked at the shoe cabinet on one side. After a quick glance around, he casually asked: Are there any men's slippers?Ah, Chu Ying came to her senses, you can come in directly.She had just moved here, and she didn't expect someone to come to her door so soon. She didn't even prepare to take off her shoes, let alone men's slippers.Xu Jisi glanced at her thoughtfully, and then took two steps in. The noodles on the black and gray marble dining table came into view. The bowl was as big as a palm, and the wide white noodles were so plain that even the oil could not be seen. , only a few green vegetables add color.Unconsciously, he frowned slightly, Xu Jisi said in a clear voice: You eat this every dayChu Ying paused, thinking that he was disgusted with her, as if she was deliberately treating him badly.She didn't force him to eat this.The girl pursed her lips and put down the bowl: "So I said, it's better for you to go out to eat."Xu Jisi didn't seem to hear the implication of her words. He already sat down opposite her like a master and asked again: Are you losing weight?Before she could say anything, he looked at her again and paused: No need.There is no fat anywhere on my body. I am as thin as a bamboo pole. I look like I will fall over if I blow it. There is nothing to lose.Chu Ying didn't know why he kept changing the topic while reading the article. Yi Wu'er's ears were filled with confusion. When this happened, she didn't know how to respond. She wanted to say that she didn't want to lose weight, but she was just lazy, and she felt that with the two of them, she didn't know how to respond. There is no need to explain too much about the current relationship.In the end, I could only say dryly and immerse myself in serving him some noodles.The noodles she had just ordered were a bit too much, just enough for another bowl. Chu Ying took a pair of chopsticks, fished them out, and poured some soup into them.She was subconsciously about to add more spice, but suddenly paused, raised her head and asked hesitantly:Do you eat spicy food?Xu Ji thought for a moment and tapped his fingers on the edge of the table. His voice was very light:Don't you know whether I eat spicy food or not?The secret relationship that she wanted to hide was instantly nowhere to be seen under his indifferent reply. In stark contrast, the quiet lake in her heart was stirred up into thousands of waves.Chu Ying shook her fingers, and poured a handful of the white crystals in her hand.

Her mind went blank, and she only relied on instinct to grab a spoon and fish out a spoonful.After regaining consciousness for a moment, he looked up and glanced up again as if he was guilty.Xu Jisi's eyes fell on the coat rack not far away at some point.Chu Ying also looked over there and saw a tie hanging on it.The girl blinked and remembered that Wen Zaichen took it off two days ago when he felt uncomfortable when he was helping her move, and forgot to take it with him when he left.I've been busy these past two days, so I haven't been able to meet up.Miss Chu has a good rapport with the opposite sex.Xu Jisi lowered his eyes and suddenly spoke in a confused manner.Chu Ying said ah, and then subconsciously said: Not really.Not very good with you.Xu Jisi:Seemingly laughing at her words, the man twitched the corners of his lips, tilted his broad back slightly, and narrowed his dark eyes: Miss Chu is indeed eloquent.Growing up, people praised her for being sensible and well-spoken. For others, she wouldn't find it strange.But when the words came out of Xu Jisi's mouth at this moment, the taste obviously changed.Weird and strange.After all, she was the first to speak quickly. Xu Jisi had probably never heard such a blatant avoidance. Chu Ying pretended not to hear, coughed lightly, mixed the noodles, and put them in front of him.Here, you eat it.He spoke very fast, and it sounded like he was trying to get out of here after eating.Xu Jisi raised his eyebrows slightly and slowly rolled up his sleeves first.Those who didn't know thought they were going to eat some high-end Western food.Chu Ying curled her lips inconspicuously and lowered her head to stir the noodles.After all this fussing, the noodles in her bowl almost turned into a lump.She didn't know if she was hiding something in her heart, but she suddenly lost her appetite, so she secretly raised her eyes to glance at him.Opposite him, the man rolled up his sleeves to reveal his cold white forearms, his raised wrist bones were neat and smooth, and he had just picked up the chopsticks.As if aware of her gaze, Xu Jisi paused slightly and his eyes fell on her bowl.Seeing that her bowl of noodles was so lumpy that it could stand upright even if you inserted a chopstick into it, Xu Jisi suddenly said: Get another bowl.The pot is gone. Chu Ying poked her face and responded honestly.Xu Jisi's low voice seemed to be particularly patient today: I mean, exchange a bowl with me.Chu Ying reacted for a while, almost thinking that she heard wrongly.It's okay to let the eldest young master eat this clear soup with little water.I still want to change her naughty faceChu Ying shook her head repeatedly, but she was afraid that he would be stubborn with her in a place like this, so she simply stood up:Forget it, I'll put it back in and mix it.Seeing how evasive she was, Xu Jisi followed her and poured the noodles back into the pot, frowning slightly.After staring for a long time, he slowly lowered his eyes and picked up the chopsticks.There was a lot of soup left in the pot just now, and Chu Ying deliberately delayed it for a while before filling another bowl.When he walked to the table carrying the noodles, he happened to see Xu Jisi picking up his chopsticks and taking a bite.Chu Ying suddenly felt a little dazed.The scene was so natural that the two of them were just like any pair of ordinary friends.In the morning, she would never have imagined that they could sit at the same table and eat so calmly.Chu Ying was distracted, and her eyes fell on Xu Jisi's face.The next moment, he saw a slight frown on his eyebrows.The jaw that was chewing suddenly paused.Chu Ying was brought back to her senses by this subtle look and also followed suit.But in the blink of an eye, his expression quickly returned to its original state, and he slowly started chewing again.Chu Ying gently put the bowl on the table, sat down, and looked at him hesitantly.The sight was so obvious that Xu Jisi swallowed it naturally and raised his eyelids. He couldn't see anything wrong. Those who didn't know thought that the moment just happened was an illusion.Chu Ying suddenly remembered the large amount of salt she had accidentally shaken into just now.Although she picked it out in time, she could not ensure that it was mixed thoroughly.Chu Ying blinked: Isn't it a bit too much?Before he could say the word "salty", he saw Xu Jisi swallowing his mouth again. The expression on his face remained unchanged and his tone was lazy: What?After a pause of about two or three seconds, the girl held it back again: It's nothing.With his tone, if she asked more questions, it would seem like she was caring too much.The eldest young master has a very tricky taste. If it is really unpalatable, he will not forcefully eat it.Besides, she wished he would stop eating and leave quickly.Chu Ying lowered her head in disinterest, picked out a green vegetable from the bowl and chewed it twice.The scene became quiet again for a while.Xu Jisi didn't know what he was thinking.The first bite hit my mouth with a lump of salt, and a salty and bitter taste filled my mouth almost immediately.But his first reaction was to swallow it.Otherwise, he could have imagined what Chu Ying would look like or what he would say.I didn't force you to eat, I told you to go out to eat. Why did my little ruined temple attract the mouth of your young master Xu, and so on.80% of the time he will sag his lower lip to chase away guests.After all, her resistance to him was almost written on her face.Xu Jisi's dark eyes slightly raised, and his gaze fell involuntarily on the girl opposite.She ate gracefully and silently, her long curly eyelashes drooping quietly, and she was holding a piece of green vegetables, biting it into her mouth bit by bit like a rabbit, her pale pink lips were moistened by the soup.Suddenly he was reminded of that time in the shed in the afternoon, when she was so flustered that she didn't even open the water glass. Later, she finally opened it with great difficulty and drank in a hurry.He doesn't like to speculate on other people's thoughts.There was never any need to figure out his identity.But when facing Chu Ying, he couldn't help but think about and analyze her behavior.For example, on the day they reunited, why did she pretend not to know him.He thought at the time that she really didn't remember who he was.He wasn't a very narcissistic person, and he didn't think that the short few months he spent with her could leave an indelible impression on her, so it was normal for him not to think about it.But when she ran away so deliberately, he realized that she remembered.She was deliberately avoiding him.This realization suddenly ignited the annoyance in his heart.Wasn't he the one who was rejected in the first place?Xu Jisi lowered his eyebrows and half-draped eyelashes to hide the emotions in his eyes.The silence lasted for a long time.Chu Ying poked at the bowl and chopsticks and ate a few noodles absentmindedly. After a while, she felt that the atmosphere was so weird that she felt a little uncomfortable all over. She quietly raised her eyes, but couldn't help but speak first: "You just said, Just moved in, what do you mean?She clearly saw that he was very familiar with the road conditions.Xu Jisi held the chopsticks with slender fingers. He paused slightly when he heard the voice, and looked into her clear black eyes: I bought this at the beginning of the year.He was busy before and only occasionally stopped by to sleep. After a pause, he added that he had been free for the past two days and planned to move here.Chu Ying:It's casual and convenient. Either use it for a party or use it as a hotel.Do the rich second generation treat buying a house as buying groceries?I really want to fight the rich second generation.The corners of Chu Ying's lips twitched slightly, and within a few seconds, she suddenly remembered something.Since Xu Jisi has so many properties under his name, why did he move here?This timing is too delicate.Chu Ying couldn't help but think too much.But she couldn't ask.Is it possible to ask, did you move here because of me?This is not a joke.Chu Ying felt that her head began to swell and hurt again.Originally I was just Party A and Party B in the company, but now I live across the street.Can he really be clear about what he said?As if she could think of the torture in the future, Chu Ying's mind heated up and she called out his name: Xu Jisi.There was no emotion on the man's face, only his Adam's apple moved slightly, and he responded with a voice from his nasal cavity: HmmYou made it clearShe paused, and she could clearly feel that the line of sight across from her was slightly dim after she said these words.Facing the man's cold gaze, she took a deep breath and added the second half of the sentence: "Is it also included in official business?"After half a second, she gritted her teeth again, thinking that she had already said everything, so why not just say it clearly:What I mean is that the project in your hand is not inferior to mine. There is no need to bother you to check it in person.No matter how dull she was, she noticed his deliberateness.He mentioned specious words again and again in front of everyone, and he seemed to want everyone to know that they had something in their past.She didn't dare to think carefully about the logic behind Xu Jisi's actions.It was impossible for her to abandon her career or leave Lizhou to avoid him. The cost would be too great, and she still had to live.Since it was already a mutual relationship, she hoped they could reach a consensus.Just pretend they don't know each other.Everyone should return to their own lives.She didn't know what had gone crazy for him recently, maybe the eldest young master had the same whim as in the past.She couldn't guess what Xu Jisi wanted to do next, but she didn't have the energy to play any more drama with him about reuniting after a long separation.Chu Ying pursed her lips tightly, clasped her fingers tightly on the edge of the chair, and didn't dare to look at him again after she finished speaking.There was silence for a while.What is public and what is privateXu Jisi finally raised his eyelids and did not answer her. Instead, he suddenly asked in a calm tone: "As an investor, I appear in your company to follow up on the project. Is it a public or private matter?"Chu Ying blinked and paused.When I raised my eyes again, I was caught off guard and fell into his dark, silent pupils. Like the snow falling off the bed, his expression was very calm, and the smile faded from his face, which made people feel as if the surroundings were getting colder for no reason.Chu Ying's fingers holding the chopsticks tightened unconsciously, and she was sensitively aware of Xu Jisi's sudden change in attitude at this moment, which made her a little unaccustomed.Very strange.But if you think about it carefully, you feel that he is like this.Before she could catch the thought that came to her mind, the soft sound of the silverware touching the ceramic bowl seemed to suddenly amplify several times at this moment. She came back to her senses and saw Xu Jisi slowly putting down his chopsticks.The man's eyebrows were very light, and his smooth jawline was even more sharp under his expression. He stared at her for a few seconds before speaking calmly, with a cold tone:Since I'm a man, there's no reason for me to decide based on my mood. If I can decide based on personal feelings, it's not fair.Not only do you want me to be able to distinguish between public and private, but you also want me to use my private life to abolish public service.He wasn't angry or annoyed. He paused and raised his eyebrows slightly, as if he was amused:Chu Ying, do you think I have a split personality?

Chapter 18 Rememberingconfident18Chu Ying was stunned for a moment, feeling that the cold gaze in front of her suddenly made her feel hot everywhere.Only then did she realize how unreasonable her words were.If you want to be clear about the differences, you have to distinguish between public and private affairs.If she used this to try to get him to stay away, it would mean she owed him a favor.After all, as an investor, it is natural for him to keep an eye on the project. Otherwise, if something goes wrong, he will be the only one who really loses profits.What qualifications does she have to ask him to take such risks?Because that past may not be pleasant to the other partyTo say the least, there is no reason for Party B to negotiate with Party A.If it were Ji Ran, she wouldn't dare to make such a request.The moment this thought flashed through her mind, Chu Ying's breath suddenly froze, and then she suddenly discovered a terrifying fact that she didn't want to admit.Maybe Xu Jisi's recent behavior gave her some illusion, or maybe her recent state really affected her judgment.The underlying logic behind her daring to say these words to Xu Jisi was precisely that she had included him in the safety line of defense in her heart.There was such a hint of confidence.Chu Ying froze, and before the thought of shame arose for a few seconds, her breathing became disordered for a moment.She could even feel her blood being invaded by the coldness that crawled down her tailbone.My fingertips felt a bit cold.Xu Jisi's gaze still fell on her, Chu Ying slowly moved her fingers and her tone was slightly stiff: IChu Ying opened her lips and made a sound, but her brain was still confused. She subconsciously made a short sound under the gaze, and then froze again.at this time.The chair swayed slightly, and the man seemed to straighten up slightly.However, you are right about one thing.Xu Jisi rolled his eyes and calmly broke the short deadlock: I am indeed very busy and have many projects at hand, and I may not be able to keep an eye on them every day.so.He paused slightly and his tone was very calm.You got your wish.

Chu Ying blinked her eyelashes lightly and was stunned for a moment.His clear pupils subconsciously raised slightly, and when he saw that the man was lagging behind in speaking, he calmly and naturally took out a piece of paper and wiped his mouth.A vibrating sound suddenly sounded in the silence.Xu Ji thought for a moment, then looked around and saw Chu Ying's mobile phone placed casually on the table lit up.Note: Brother.Something flashed through his mind. The man's long eyelashes were half-draped, his vision was obscured, and there was no obvious attitude on his clear face.Chu Ying seemed to react for a while, and subconsciously took the phone with her slender fingers. She quickly remembered that there was someone in front of her, and raised her eyelashes again, wanting to say something.Before I could say anything.The man met her gaze, paused slightly and then raised his chin slightly.It seems that Miss Chu is also busy, so I won't disturb you further.Xu Jisi stood up and looked down at her. His voice was clear and clear, and he could not hear much emotion. He seemed as distant as ever:Thank you, Miss Chu, for hosting me.By the time she came to her senses, the click of the door lock had already sounded in the empty living room.It became deserted again in an instant.It seemed like no one had been there.Chu Ying glanced at the closed door blankly, curled her fingers, and her chest felt somehow empty and a little cold.She blinked.The phone was still vibrating, which drew her attention back. The girl lowered her head slightly and glanced at the call.She suppressed her emotions, calmed her voice, and answered the phone.eatingWen Zaichen's clear voice reached his ears through the mobile phone.Chu Ying glanced at the noodles that she had not eaten two bites of, and responded vaguely: Well, I just finished eating.Is there a problemThe person on the other end was probably driving, and I could vaguely hear the whistling wind and the occasional honking of the car. After hearing her words, her tone was slightly raised: I can't call you if nothing happens.This person always has to argue with her.I knew she didn't mean it.Chu Ying didn't answer his words, knowing that he must have something to say when he called, so she sighed: Don't beat around the bush, just say it.I don't know if he noticed the fatigue in her tone, but Wen Zaichen paused and stopped talking to her.It's nothing big, I just might have an event later and asked if you are free.Chu Ying blinked and unconsciously rubbed the edge of the dining table with her fingers: Is it appropriate to take me with you to social events?As a host here, I have to bring a 'family member' to fill the role. Is there anyone more suitable than you?Chu Ying hesitated for a few seconds:But I have never participated in this kind of thing. What should I do if I cause trouble for you?Just keep your head down and eat. Wen Zaichen said without hesitation, "With me here, you don't have to do anything."Chu Ying was amused by him: OK, then I'll treat it as a free meal.Enough for you. The other end also laughed.Although Wen Zaichen usually looked at him as a fool, Chu Ying had unconditional trust in him.It was probably the most difficult period that he accompanied him through. In Chu Ying's heart, Wen Zaichen was no different from his biological brother.We chatted a few more words along the way, mostly around the recent life. Wen Zaichen basically said it, and Chu Ying occasionally echoed it.Wen Zaichen was complaining to her about the fact that the newly recruited assistant did not have a driver's license. If the previous assistant had not gotten married and he was given a honeymoon leave with a wave of his hand, and the new assistant was still getting used to it, he would not have been so busy recently that he had no time to see her.Tell me, how can a boss serve his assistant as a driver?Wen Zaichen still gritted his teeth when he thought about it now: We stared at each other in the car for a long time before he told me that I didn't have a driver's license. I was in a hurry that day and I got six points for running a red light.After chatting for a long time, he suddenly found that Chu Ying had lost his voice for some time. Wen Zaichen paused and asked her what was wrong.Someone's face appeared in her mind for no reason, and she unconsciously became distracted again.No boss acts as a driver for his assistant, and no

Party A acts as a driver for Party B.Xu Jisi's cold and indifferent voice before leaving flashed across her mind, and confusion spread in her heart without warning, as if she suddenly fell from the clouds. After a moment of weightlessness, her figure swayed slightly, and her pupils focused on her body. Empty seats in front.Chu Ying calmed down for a while before she suppressed the soreness in her throat and whispered that it was okay.Wen Zaichen felt that something was wrong with her today, and her voice seemed to be hoarse. Worry came to his mind. He paused and the car slowed down: "You're not feeling well?"I just talked too much and became a bit dumb. I just need to drink more water.Chu Ying could hide it.There was silence for a second, as if to judge the authenticity of this statement, Chu Ying picked her fingers uneasily, and accidentally glanced at the tie hanging on the coat rack not far away.Afraid that he would react if he was delayed for a second and ask questions, Chu Ying hurriedly changed the subject: By the way, your tie is still at my house.After a pause, Wen Zaichen seemed to recall something like this: I almost forgot about it.That's not the case, he said casually, I'll pick you up in a few days and see you later.Chu Ying responded repeatedly and was just about to end the topic. Unexpectedly, Wen Zaichen was not fooled and asked again: Are you really?Are you okay? I didn't even have time to say the three words.are you drivingChu Ying suddenly asked.Wen Zaichen replied, and just as he was about to say something, he heard the girl reply very quickly, with an extremely serious tone: Two points for answering the phone while driving. If you are photographed again, all your points will be deducted.Wen Zaichen:Chu Ying squeezed the phone tightly, fearing that he would not realize the impact of this, and continued to add: You and your assistant can't drive, what will you do with your work during this time?You are really good at talking.She heard the person on the other end grinding his teeth, and finally the words she wanted to hear came out.OK, hang up.Chu Ying's heart fell silent as she hung up the phone.It took her a while to get used to the silence.What she told Wen Zaichen was not a lie. She did use her voice a little too much today. Just thinking about it, she felt a soreness in her throat.There was no water at home, so Chu Ying slowly moved to the island, took out an electric kettle from the cabinet, and boiled a temporary pot of water.She walked slowly to the balcony, leaned forward and half leaned on the railing, watching the night slowly fall.His eyes wandered, and then unconsciously drifted to the balcony next door.It was empty there, with no lights on, and no sign of life, as if he had never gone back.But it was none of her business where he went.In a way, she should be congratulating herself.Isn't this the result she wants?ButShe didn't seem happy either.Chu Ying suppressed her empty mood and slowly looked away.

After that day, Xu Jisi did not appear in Lingting again.At first she was worried that she would bump into

Xu Jisi when she went home, but after paying attention for two days, she didn't even see Xu Jisi's car downstairs.He seemed to have really kept the promise they made that day.From business to private, he really never appeared in front of her again.Her life seemed to have returned to its former peace, but occasionally when she returned home, her eyes would touch the opposite door and she would be distracted for a moment.So, he must be lying to her if he talks about moving here.Perhaps it was teasing on a whim, or revenge in a bad taste. Chu Ying stared at the door that had never been opened before, as if she saw that the man's heart had never been open to her.The progress of "Wild Tangzhi" is also very fast, and it was recorded in just two weeks, no more, no less.The rest is post-production work. If it fails to be submitted for review, the lines will be modified and they will make up the recording.The entire National Day was being rushed, and the day it ended happened to be the last day of the National Day. In order to reward everyone, Ling Tingyang treated everyone to Haidilao. It was about eight o'clock when he came out.In fact, it was not too early, but everyone obviously still had some unfinished ideas. I don't know who first proposed to go to KTV to sing all night, and everyone expressed their support.Chu Ying originally didn't want to participate, but she was teased again, saying how could the heroine be absent, let alone her first film and television heroine, so she shouldn't commemorate this.There were echoes in his ears. Chu Ying suddenly became the center of attention, so she could only accept it.There happened to be a restaurant upstairs in the shopping mall next to it. Ling Tingyang never treated his employees badly and did what he was told. He directly opened a large luxurious private room and asked everyone if they wanted to drink.Why don't you drink? I didn't have a day off on National Day. It's finally over. I can't have fun.We won't get drunk today and won't return homeThe crowd was extremely enthusiastic, and they all talked about it, but they unanimously came up with a choice. Ling Tingyang ordered two more boxes of beer.In the acquaintance game, everyone let themselves go, some sang and sang, some played guessing and drank, and some joined the table to play poker or board games.Chu Ying was played with by Luo Hui. The light ball above her head was flashing with colorful lights, and the noise in her ears was intertwined with the singing coming from the loudspeaker. It made her eardrums tremble and her temples swelled tightly.Everyone was having a great time, and at first they poured wine into cups to drink, but later they became too lazy to pour wine again, and everyone had a bottle of wine in their hands. When Chu Ying realized what she was doing, someone had already stuffed a bottle into her hand.Ling Ting was like her second home, which gave her a sense of belonging. It was rare that everyone was here and in high spirits. Chu Ying couldn't help but take a few sips.The air conditioner was turned on very low, but the feeling of heat still rose from my neck.The air was filled with the intoxicating smell of wine and sweet fruit, and her ears were filled with laughter and curses. As they drank and drank, Chu Ying sat in a dark corner, with blue and red lights flashing across her face from time to time. She had not drunk any wine. After a few sips, I felt as if I was drunk, and my ears were covered with an inconspicuous red color.Her hands were still cold, so she stretched out her hand and put it against her face, feeling a little hot.Her chest felt tight, her breathing became a little heavy, and she really couldn't hold on. Chu Ying signaled to the people beside her that she wanted to go out to catch her breath, and quietly left the private room and went downstairs.The stars were high outside. Chu Ying took her phone and checked the time. It was already early ten o'clock.Chu Ying came down from the elevator at the back door of the mall. There was no one there. She found a random step and sat down. Chu Ying rubbed the back of her neck. When she lowered her eyes, she saw the breathing light on her phone turned on. When she opened it, she found a message from Luo Hui, asking where she was.Chu Ying was about to reply to the message when the click of high heels suddenly sounded clearly in the lonely night, interrupting her movements.With her long eyelashes trembling slightly, Chu Ying raised her eyes and caught a glimpse of a woman running past her. A gust of wind swept through her, and the strong smell of alcohol dispersed in the air and slowly entered her breath.The woman was wearing thin clothing, a short suspender belt and a hip-covering skirt, with only a cardigan on top, which had fallen down a bit because of the running motion.Chu Ying flexed her knuckles slightly, raised her fingers slightly, and looked in the direction where the woman was running. She saw a tall and tall figure leaning against the car with her long legs slightly bent under the quiet dusk.The night wind was so chill that his hair was cold. The man was leaning sideways, and the branches and leaves of the street trees nearby were rustling in the wind. They swayed past his face from time to time, blocking part of Chu Ying's sight.She didn't see the man's appearance clearly, but she could only see the gray windbreaker he was wearing swaying gently in the evening breeze, occasionally revealing a strong and smooth waist covered by a casual black inner layer.He probably had his eyes lowered and his fingers were typing on the screen. Suddenly his attention was attracted by the approaching footsteps, and the man slowly raised his tall and tight body.The woman's face was red and her steps seemed a bit chaotic. She didn't open her lips until she was running closer. Her voice was crying and her nasal voice was heavy:You finally came.His steps slowed down as he approached the man.She didn't know if her brain had been invaded by alcohol. She slowly raised her head and stared at the man standing there who seemed to be unresponsive for a few seconds. She suddenly swayed slightly and almost lost her balance.Chu Ying watched the whole process, wondering if she was going to jump into that person's arms as if watching the excitement.The next moment, it was exactly as she expected.The woman's straight and slender calves suddenly softened.The graceful and soft figure leaned forward.Just before she was about to throw herself into that man's arms.Chu Ying heard the woman's very low, drunken voice, as if trying to catch something, and repeated it again:You finally cameShe almost whispered the man's name.Xu Jisi.Chu Ying suddenly froze.

Chapter 19 RememberingMr. Xu, please respect yourself.19On a quiet night, the sound of the wind can be heard clearly.Chu Ying stood there blankly, her dark eyes slowly falling on the two almost overlapping figures in the distance, and a picture passed in front of her eyes without any reason.It was an ordinary morning with the dawn gradually breaking out.Fish belly white cuts through the sky. The strange girl is wearing a beautiful and exquisite long dress. Her long slightly curly hair is scattered on her shoulders, with a burgundy bow tied in her hair, like a little princess living among the people.Standing next to the girl was a young man with a clear profile and clear outlines. His brows were bland under his broken hair, and his cold and dignified aura was incompatible with the low and dilapidated tile-roofed house.But Chu Ying couldn't be more familiar with it.She always thought about how special Xu Jisi was in Wuning Town.With a slim and tall figure, a distinguished and distant temperament, and a naturally arrogant demeanor, some discomfort in life will be revealed inadvertently.It's as if it's from another world.Only a hundred meters away, she stood under a lush and evergreen old tree. The thick trunk covered her delicate figure, and the shadow of the lush branches and leaves seemed to envelope her whole body.Like a voyeur who cannot see the light.She saw the girl's delicate white hand wrapped around the young man's arm, shaking his forearm coquettishly, but the lonely young man who always rejected people thousands of miles away seemed to just frown helplessly.Behind them was an old and mottled gray tile-roofed house, but beside them stood a man in a suit that Chu Ying had only seen on TV. The man lowered his head slightly and looked humble. He could vaguely hear calling him "Master," And they seem to be used to it.At this moment, she seemed to be the one who was out of place.The wind suddenly blew.The lush branches and leaves rustle.A gust of breeze blew up the girl's cheap new skirt.Her hair was a little messy, and the soft long hair at her temples was blown by the wind and stuck to her cheeks. The long black hair made her face look even paler, her watery black eyes were devoid of light, and even her lips had lost their color.Chu Ying just stood there, watching the man in the suit carry the luggage from the young man's side, and watching the girl pull him intimately and walk out. She couldn't see her features clearly, but she could see her smile.At that time, the sun was rising in the sky and the clouds were dispersing. It was undoubtedly a good weather to clear the clouds and see the sun.Xu Jisi left.I do not know how long it has been.It wasn't until the three figures completely disappeared from sight that she approached them with an almost stiff pace, like a zombie.The old-fashioned glass window of the tile-roofed house opens outwards, revealing a corner of the solid wood desk.The sun was pouring in, and the room was so empty that you could see the fine dust in the air.The trance was no different from when he arrived a few months ago.It's like he never came.The cold wind of the autumn night penetrated into the cuffs of her sleeves. Chu Ying blinked slowly, and her dark black eyes gradually regained focus.The slender arms were folded at his sides, and the few sips of wine he had just taken seemed to have finally taken effect at this moment. The alcohol merged into his blood, and his limbs were paralyzed.My fingertips were numb from the cold, and breathing seemed to hurt.The moonlight seemed to make the streets even more lonely and colder at night.Unable to watch it any longer, Chu Ying stood up in a panic and tried to escape.The upright figure beside the car raised his eyes as if he noticed something at this moment.Xu Jisi recognized the figure who stood up unsteadily almost at a glance.His heart suddenly sank, and he subconsciously wanted to speak out, but the next moment he was pulled back to consciousness by the heavy smell of alcohol on the woman in front of him.Not only the smell of alcohol, but also the smell of sweet perfume from nowhere, Xu Jisi frowned.The moment she was almost close to him, he lowered his voice and his cold voice contained a warning: Liang Yuqing.The woman's body froze almost imperceptibly, but she still gritted her teeth in the next second. As if she didn't hear him, she reached out drunkenly to wrap her arms around his neck.Liang Yuqing, I'm here to give your brother face.The tone of the statement was very cold, without any emotion at all. He lowered his eyes slowly, and his gaze fell on her hand that was about to touch his chest with a cold look.When they met, Liang Xuqing would no longer have such dignity.Liang Yuqing's hands froze in the air, and her pretended drunken expression completely collapsed. She bit her lip lightly, and tears instantly welled up in her pupils.Xu Jisi didn't pay attention at all. He subconsciously looked past the woman in front of him and looked at the thin and staggering figure not far away.Lowering his eyes, he almost synchronously moved his legs, passing by Liang Yuqing's side. He paused suddenly, his eyes quickly swept over her thin clothes, he frowned slightly, paused, and said: "You get in the car first."Then, without waiting for her to react, he strode towards that figure.Liang Yuqing stared blankly at him passing by her, turned around in a panic and stretched out her hand, trying to grab his arm: Where are you going?But the man walked too fast, and her hand just barely brushed his cuff in the end.Her hands fell down in a daze, with tears lingering in the corners of her eyes. Liang Yuqing slowly came back to her senses, raised her eyes slightly, and caught up with the man's broad back.She stared at him unblinkingly for a few seconds until he disappeared from sight, and then she suddenly realized something was wrong.His direction is clearly purposeful.It seemed like he was chasing someone.The scene just now flashed through his mind like a slow replay. Liang Yuqing's expression paused, and she was not sure whether the skirt he just scanned at the corner was an illusion.where is he goingWho did you see?The woman stood there, constantly analyzing every scene in her memory, and suddenly seemed to capture some details. She froze in place, and her eyes slowly moved to the steps.When she came out just now, there seemed to be a woman in a skirt sitting on the steps next to her.womanLiang Yuqing froze when she realized something later.Why would a woman appear next to Xu Jisi?No one in the circle knew that Xu Ji had a tendency to avoid flirting with women. If he had come out to show off, everyone would have gone crazy.She was even certain that she was the member of the opposite sex who appeared around Xu Jisi the most.Liang Yuqing gritted her teeth tightly, not wanting to believe it, but also afraid that it was really happening. After a long while, she took out her mobile phone with red eyes, found a number, and sent a text message.

Her heart was as messy as her feet, and Chu Ying didn't know why she became so embarrassed again.At the corner was the elevator, which showed that it was on the sixth floor. The girl stood in front of the door, breathing calmly and pressing the buttons with her fingers.The dull sound of footsteps touching the tile floor suddenly sounded. Chu Ying's breath froze, and an idea that she didn't want to believe came into her mind.As if being heard by the God of Destiny.That familiar low voice entered the ear canal unexpectedly.Chu Ying.My heart skipped a beat in response to this call, and an unspeakable feeling of grievance came to my mind for no reason.His eyes filled with heat almost instantly.Chu Ying lowered her head instinctively, and the broken hair on her temples fell on her face, covering her expression.The sound of the friction of clothing made her realize that the person was behind her, but she didn't dare to look back.The descending floor number jumps slowly.During the long wait, the footsteps approaching behind me seemed to slow down.Any slight movement would be amplified several times in her cochlea at this moment, but she could still feel that the sound of her heartbeat clearly drowned out all sounds when he was close to her.Chu Ying's nerves were tense, and she clenched her hands unconsciously, so hard that her nails almost dug into her palms, and the pain was felt in her brain.Chu Ying.He called her again, his cold tone seemed to have some unknown ups and downs. Xu Jisi's eyes fell on her side and he frowned slightly.Just about to raise his hand.A short sharp cry sounded, and Chu Ying came back to her senses in an instant, and was about to walk in hastily.The next moment, someone grabbed the slender white wrist.Chu Ying's heart suddenly skipped a beat, and her steps froze in place.She could feel the intense gaze that was staring at her, mixed with scrutiny.The man's big palm was dry and warm, and the thin and slender finger bones covered her wrists that were cold by the wind. The two extremes of cold and heat almost made her heart feel hot along with the slender wrists being held.Chu Ying bit her inner lip, and a suppressed tremor could be heard in her voice:Mr. Xu, please respect yourself.Xu Jisi was stunned for a moment, as if he didn't realize what he was doing. A trace of confusion flashed across his pupils, and his fingers unconsciously loosened slightly.Just this.As if she had found a flaw, Chu Ying struggled a little and broke free from his restraints.When Xu Jisi came to his senses again, the elevator door had slowly closed in front of him.

After waiting for a long time, Chu Ying didn't reply. The dynamic music in the private room shook her eardrums. Luo Hui sighed silently, turned her head to face the boy with expectant eyes, and was thinking about how to organize her words.As soon as he raised his eyes, he saw that the door of the private room was slowly pushed open by a slender figure.Luo Hui happened to be sitting next to the door. She recognized Chu Ying at a glance and quickly waved her hand: Hey, YingyingChu Ying's thoughts were wandering and she was called back by this sound. The girl slowly came back to her senses, raised her long eyelashes, and focused her eyes to one side, meeting Luo Hui's eyes.Sister HuihuiLuo Hui stood up to greet her. The private room was dark, and she didn't notice anything wrong with Chu Ying's face. She leaned into her ear and whispered, "Where were you just now?"It was a bit boring, so I went out to catch some wind.Chu Ying's voice was soft, and she suddenly raised her eyes as if aware of something, and met a pair of bright black eyes.It was a boy, his face was not familiar to her, he was tall and thin, and he was wearing a black sweatshirt. When he saw her, his eyebrows and the corners of his lips were raised at the same time, and he looked obviously happy.Chu Ying blinked slowly.Luo Hui groaned and turned her head to see her staring not far away. She followed her gaze and then remembered something:By the way, this new guy has been looking for you just now. I wonder if you have seen him before.Luo Hui took it upon herself to introduce her: I am your little fanboy. He really likes you, he's totally 'star chasing' hereChu Ying was stunned for a moment and glanced at him. Before she could extract his face from her memory, she saw that the other party had tentatively walked up to her.Luo Hui patted her shoulder knowingly and lowered her voice: "Then you can chat and I won't disturb you."Then he walked past her, made a cheering gesture to the boy, and walked away with a smile.Chu Ying hadn't recovered yet. The boy was probably encouraged by Luo Hui. He took a deep breath and took a step closer to her. His tone was nervous, but there was also a trace of expectation:Sister Yingying, do you still remember who I am?RememberThere was an inexplicable intimacy in his tone, and when he called her, it was as natural as if they were familiar with each other. Chu Ying was slightly startled, her eyes swept over him, trying to search for some information about this face in her mind.She actually had the impression that Ling Ting did recruit a potential newcomer last month.However, she usually went into the shed after arriving at the company. Except for meals, she almost stayed there for the whole day. She really didn't have a deep memory of him. She just heard someone mention it before. He was still a college student, and his name was about Yes, but I don't remember either.But what he said meant that the two of them might have met in the company.Maybe they met during a busy moment, she forgot.His tone was full of expectations. Chu Ying was afraid that speaking too directly would hurt people's hearts. She quickly sorted out the words in her mind, and after a few seconds she responded in a evasive manner:Well, I have an impression of you. I heard that you are still a college student.It was obvious that his words were unexpected. The boy looked disappointed for a moment, then quickly adjusted himself, raised a smile and scratched his head:Sister Yingying, it's normal if she doesn't remember. My name is Zhou Zimu.You are still my senior sister. he added.Senior sister Chu Ying's brain turned around: You are also from Lychee.There are basically no dedicated dubbing majors in colleges and universities. In fact, very few people working in the dubbing industry are born in professional courses. And among the very few college students, they are basically majoring in broadcasting, hosting or acting.Lychee University is not an art school, nor does it have related majors. Even Ling Tingyang came here because he was invited by the dubbing club.The dubbing industry is already a niche, and it is rare to work in the same company. It is really surprising that they are both from the same school when they are both non-majors.Seeing her surprised expression, Zhou Zimu said shyly:Yes, I'm in my sophomore year.When I first entered school last year, you gave me a bottle of water during military training.He finally mentioned the connection between the two.Chu Ying tilted her head and thought about it for a while. Then she remembered that she seemed to have participated in such a fun last year.At that time, it seemed that my roommate had fallen out of love. The air pressure in the dormitory was low for several days. It wasn't until the roommate saw someone on the school confessional wall saying that there were so many handsome boys among the freshmen that she cheered up again and dragged her to buy one. After piling up snacks and water and observing for a while, I finally picked a class with so-called handsome guys.The roommates expressed great enthusiasm and interest in this regard.After a brief chat with the instructor and explaining that he was a volunteer, the instructor looked at the students and blew a whistle to indicate a break.The roommates came forward to distribute water one by one. Chu Ying saw that she quickly blended into the crowd and chatted with everyone. It was not appropriate for her to just stand aside. After much deliberation, she still took a bottle of water and looked around. , and took it to the boy closest to her.Unexpectedly, it was such a coincidence that it was Zhou Zimu.I wanted to ask you for your contact information, but you refused.The two of them chatted and sat down nearby. When he said this, his cheeks turned red: I was a little sad to be rejected. I never thought that I could become colleagues with my senior sister today.Chu Ying's black eyes blinked slightly, feeling that he seemed to be hinting at something else.But his expression was truly sincere, and it felt like he was just expressing emotion.Suppressing the speculation that came up in her heart, she smiled calmly and said that it was quite destined. She also politely said something about welcoming him to Lingting and treating Lingting as his family.Zhou Zimu nodded, his eyes passing over her vaguely, and then quickly looking away when she raised her eyes. Some thoughts came to her heart, and Chu Ying subconsciously distanced herself from him.For a moment, she didn't know what else to talk about. Chu Ying's eyes stopped at the MV that was playing on the screen. Luo Hui happened to be singing. She listened to a few words carefully, met Luo Hui's eyes, and raised a smile on her lips. In the noisy private room, someone raised her voice and praised her for singing well.When he tilted his head inadvertently, he saw from the corner of his eye that Zhou Zimu was obviously nervous, as if he was doing some mental construction, and he seemed to be talking to himself without knowing what to say.Chu Ying paused and had an intuition of what he wanted to say to her next.Suddenly alert in her heart, Chu Ying opened her lips, trying to find an excuse to get up and change positions.However, Zhou Zimu happened to raise his eyes at this moment, as if he had finished accumulating energy, and spoke very quickly:Sister Yingying, can I add your contact information now?There seemed to be a faint creaking sound in the short time after he called her name, but Chu Ying's attention was quickly drawn away by the second half of his words. She was startled, raised her eyes, and faced the boy. He didn't dare to look directly into her eyes.He didn't even notice when the noisy private room quieted down.The human voice became softer and softer, and finally only the melody without lyrics was left on the screen and continued.Until Luo Hui hesitated, these strange sounds sounded through the microphone and lingered in the private room.Mr. Xu

Chapter 20 Rememberno one can resist20Chu Ying's body suddenly stiffened.What she wanted to say just now was completely forgotten at this moment. She saw Zhou Zimu raise his head at this sound, and almost everyone's eyes passed through her side and fell on the door less than one meter away from her.The first person to react was Ling Tingyang, who was leaning in the corner and smiling at a group of people playing truth or dare.Surprise flashed in his eyes, and then he quickly walked through the group of people and walked forward: Mr. Xu.He paused, turned to look at everyone, and then turned back to explain to him: We just finished matching today, and we are doing team building. youBefore he finished speaking, Xu Jisi answered in a calm tone: Oh, we went to the wrong place.The atmosphere was silent for two seconds.There were people in the private room who seemed to be unable to hold themselves back any longer, whispering quietly.He said he was on the wrong track, but had no intention of leaving. He made it clear that he was waiting for him to keep someone. Ling Tingyang didn't know what Xu Jisi was causing, but after a slight pause, he still extended an invitation to him decently. :Since we are so destined, I wonder if I would have the honor to invite you togetherHis words were extremely high in emotional intelligence and gave him enough face.In fact, it's all just talk.He had heard that Xu Jisi did not like to participate in such occasions, not to mention that they were not of the same class as him, and it was impossible for Xu Jisi to really play with them.He just thought that maybe he wanted to have a formal sense of presence.After all, the eldest young master should have this awareness. They are not from the same world. If he is here, he will only be out of place. His presence will make everyone more helpless.But surprisingly, he agreed.The eyebrows were slightly raised, and the tone was natural and taken for granted, as if she was waiting for this sentence from him.Ling Tingyang hesitated and raised her eyes to look at him, only to see that his eyes swept somewhere indistinctly, and then his eyes dimmed.He came to his senses and glanced in his direction.At first glance, he noticed the extremely prominent and delicate back.Among the people, she was the only one who was carrying them, as if she didn't know what was happening behind her.All the irrationality was instantly explained at this moment.Ling Tingyang came to his senses quickly. After reacting, he pressed his temples with a headache.After chatting with Chu Ying that day, he had indeed not seen Xu Jisi for many days. Xu Jisi was not here, and Chu Ying's condition was indeed back to normal, otherwise he would not have been able to complete it within the scheduled two weeks.He thought they should have reached some agreement.But now it seems that this is not the case.Ling Tingyang was not sure whether the invitation he just made was the right choice.Before he could think about it, Xu Jisi had already walked around him and walked in.He seemed to be looking around casually for a week, and he didn't feel anything inappropriate when he met the gazes of everyone. His clear voice had a hint of casualness: You guys are playing, don't pay attention to me.There were more than a dozen people, some who had seen him and some who had not. Some people bumped the people next to them with their arms and whispered who they were, while others secretly took out their mobile phones to take pictures.But overall, after his words, although there were some more low-key conversations, everyone was obviously still a little reluctant to let go.As if he didn't expect his words to be useless, Xu Jisi raised his eyebrows slightly, turned his head and met Ling Tingyang's gaze.Quickly understanding what he meant, Ling Tingyang sighed inwardly, but walked forward, waved to everyone, and joked: During off hours, there is no boss or Party A, so don't be nervous.Ling Tingyang and most of his employees were friends, and they could joke with each other. As soon as he said this, everyone was confident.Seeing that everyone was visibly relieved, Ling Tingyang said a few good words without blushing and saying that Xu Jisi had a fun-loving temper and was about the same age as everyone else, and then called Luo Hui to warm up the place again. Then slowly the commotion started again.Ling Tingyang turned around and asked: Mr. Xu, what would you like to drink?Xu Jisi paused for a moment, and was about to say no, when he saw a boy appear next to him. He must have been bewitched by Ling Tingyang's words just now, so he actually came forward and invited him warmly:Mr. Xu, do you want to play dice with us?Xu Jisi turned his face and saw the boy raising the dice cup in his hand:Talk nonsense and drink if you lose.Ling Tingyang paused. When he saw that the man didn't reply for a while, his eyebrows jumped and he was about to speak.But Xu Jisi looked away and the corners of his lips lazily raised: Okay.He tilted his head slightly and glanced at Ling Tingyang, but he couldn't tell what he meant in his tone: Your employees are quite enthusiastic.There were obviously a few people waiting for them in front, and they would sneak glances at them from time to time, probably waiting for action here.Ling Tingyang had just said a lot of nice things for him, so naturally he had to cooperate. Xu Ji didn't think about Ling Tingyang's reaction to him, so he just put one hand in his pocket and followed the boy leading him in front, looking for him together. He took a seat and sat down.Ling Tingyang was left stunned on the spot.Xu Jisi really blended in naturally.As soon as he walked over, someone consciously made room for him. He nodded slightly, probably as a token of thanks. After sitting down, he rested his hands lazily on the edge of the table, his sharp-boned and cold-white fingers resting on the black dice. On the cup.In the dim light, only the screen directly in front of him cast a little light, which made the hand, which could even see the lightly raised cyan veins on the back of the hand, look cold and a little abstinent.He moved his wrist slightly, turned his head slightly, and looked at the boy who called him just now. His thin lips were slightly opened. He must have asked about some details of the rules. The boy hurriedly supplemented him. He nodded occasionally, but it was hard to tell whether he was paying attention. , with a hint of spontaneity.Probably because he seemed to have really lost his aura of keeping strangers away from him, the people next to him plucked up the courage to start chatting with him one after another.It was obviously just a casual conversation, and his reply was concise. He was still sitting and chatting. Somehow, there was an abrupt feeling of being dignified and cold about him.Even the girl next to him who answered the conversation generously and enthusiastically at first, her eyes fell on him for a moment, and she suddenly blushed after staring at him.Ling Tingyang felt that his head hurt even more.And by the door.Zhou Zimu finally came back to his senses and looked away from a short distance away. He didn't seem to notice anything was wrong with Chu Ying. He turned around and asked hesitantly: Is this Mr. Xu the investor of Sister Yingying's drama?He hasn't graduated yet, and usually only comes to Lingting on weekends or when he doesn't have classes. He happened to not be there during the two days Xu Jisi came. He only saw other people talking about this in the group, and now he is right Number.Chu Ying slowly straightened up her stiff body, her mind still blank, her black eyes turning slightly as if without any purpose, landing on the elegant back over there.Sister YingyingThe sound in my ear came closer.Chu Ying moved slightly, but didn't turn around.

The next moment, she didn't know if she noticed the line of sight here. The figure turned sideways without warning, her neck turned slightly, and then a pair of deep black eyes met her accurately. Her misty sight.After freezing for a second, Chu Ying's pupils suddenly focused.Then he turned his head in panic.His forehead hit someone's nose.Zhou Zimu gasped in pain subconsciously.Chu Ying suddenly raised her eyes and saw the boy leaning back slightly, raising his hand to cover his nose.Only then did she realize how close Zhou Zimu had been to her just now.Chu Ying moved back instinctively, paused, and said with a little guilt in her gentle voice: I'm sorry, are you okay?fine.Zhou Zimu rubbed his nose and raised his eyes to meet the girl's worried gaze.Chu Ying's eyes were always pure and clean without a trace of impurities. In addition, the ends of her eyes drooped slightly, which made the gentle and gentle feeling even more obvious. Her face was so close that he could almost see her long curly eyelashes clearly. The tiny fluff, even closer, seems to be able to sense her gentle and gentle breathingZhou Zimu's heart suddenly dropped for half a beat.The thoughts that were filling his heart were about to overflow. He opened his lips and almost blurted out something, but the next moment he heard Chu Ying's voice, which suddenly brought him back to his senses.Sorry, really sorry, I didn't mean toHer tone suddenly sounded panicked for some reason, and her eyes fell under his nose. As she spoke, she hurriedly pulled out a few pieces of paper from the side and put them into his hands: You, please wipe it quickly.Zhou Zimu calmed down for a while, and just when he was about to look down at the tissue in his hand, he saw a little red dripping on the tissue.The red dot quickly faded away. Seeing that he was motionless, the girl hurriedly took out another piece of paper and put it into his heart.You can faintly smell the fragrance of gardenia.It's the smell of Chu Ying's hands.Hurry up and cover yourselfClearly aware that the thin tissue in her hand was quickly soaked, Chu Ying was really panicked.Why did he hit someone and cause a nosebleed?Zhou Zimu finally realized what had happened, his cheeks turned red instantly, he pursed his lips and wanted to speak, but the blood couldn't stop flowing down his middle.Stop talking now. The light was too dim and you couldn't see his expression. Chu Ying took a deep breath and calmed down quickly. I'll accompany you to the bathroom first and you can wash up.If he hadn't had a nosebleed at the moment and Chu Ying offered to accompany him, he would have gladly accepted it.but.It's really embarrassing to have a nosebleed in front of the girl you like.Regardless of his impression, he must be very ugly and embarrassed now.Besides, this was only their second meeting.Zhou Zimu suppressed the despair in his heart and hurriedly waved his hands, his voice muffled because he covered his nose with paper: It's okay, it's okay, I can just go by myself, thank you Sister Yingying.He stood up and crossed her side. Chu Ying was still a little worried. As soon as she took a step forward, the boy pressed her shoulders down again: "It's really not necessary. I can do it myself."Then I saw Zhou Zimu walking out of the private room very fast, almost as if he was escaping.Compared with the various collisions or sudden voices from the games playing around, the movement here was not big, and no one even noticed that Zhou Zimu went out.Chu Ying packed up the tissues next to her and threw them away in the trash can. When she raised her head, her eyes looked somewhere uncontrollably.The man had withdrawn his gaze. He was really playing with them cooperatively. He was sitting leisurely with one leg upright and the other bent. He hooked the dice cup with one hand and slightly flexed his long fingers. He squeezed the dice cup tightly with smooth and neat movements. He brushed the dice on the table, then raised his elbow slightly.The cuffs slid down slightly, revealing half of his tight and sharp forearms. Without stopping, he swayed the dice cup in the air for a few times, and with a beautiful finish, he put it back on the table with his backhand.He didn't even move his head.A set of movements went smoothly, but within a few seconds, the wood and glass made a crisp collision sound. The people at the table were stunned for a while before they came to their senses, and then they burst into exclamations.She stared at him blankly and heard someone whistle, saying that she didn't expect Mr. Xu to hide his secrets. She also saw someone blushing involuntarily and speaking so handsomely.Not showing off his skills, his Qingjun face was still dull, and the curvature of the corners of his lips had not changed. However, after just one glance, the person who felt deserted came to his face, but he smoothly performed a set of actions that were completely different from him. The contradiction was vividly displayed on him. It was this contrast that surprised everyone. point.Within a few minutes, he was completely involved with this group of people.The newly exposed hand was not too difficult, but it was enough to bring the relationship with several boys closer, and it was also enough to make the hearts of the girls present quicken, or even make them fall into despair.As if he realized something, his heart stopped uncontrollably for a moment, and then he felt some emotion suddenly spreading in his heart, making it feel astringent.Chu Ying slowly blinked her sour eyes and suddenly understood at this moment.In the past, no one dared to approach him because he had always been subjective and kept people away thousands of miles away.But when he took the initiative to take off that tough shell and released the signal that he was approachable, there was no doubt that no one could resist.no matter who.Without exception.He was never her choice alone.

Chapter 21 Rememberingonly youtwenty onel thought Xu Jisi's arrival would cool down the place, but unexpectedly, the atmosphere in the second half reached a climax with his participation. He really had the fun-loving temper that Ling Tingyang said. If Ji Ran was allowed to come to the scene, Seeing this scene, I would probably knock myself out.When did Young Master Xu show you face like this?The movement in that circle was really loud, and from time to time there would be cheers and voices urging people to drink. Later, people on the side were attracted to the scene, dropped the cards in their hands, and crowded forward as if to join in the fun.There is no doubt that Xu Jisi has become the focus at this moment.Yes, a person like him can easily become the one that attracts everyone's attention no matter where he is.Being sought after by others and being admired by all the stars is his daily routine.Everyone was talking, and the chatter was never closed again. Among the chatter, their actions became more and more open. She even saw someone boldly handing a full wine glass to Xu Jisi.In a daze, the man seemed to be leaning forward while pushing the lamp, and his eyes intersected with hers for a moment. When she was stunned, it seemed as if she had just glanced at him accidentally, and then looked away again the next moment.She saw a cold but less distant smile on his lips.He took the wine.

After three rounds of drinking, Zhou Zimu came back once. As soon as he sat down, he was called away again by a crying phone call from his roommate.Zhou Zimu was obviously reluctant, but he couldn't bear it and cried so hard that he still valued friendship. While the boy scolded him for losing his love, he had to say goodbye to Chu Ying and leave early.Before leaving, she remembered not to ask for Chu Ying's contact information. The situation was urgent. Seeing that he stood up with hesitation in his eyes and didn't know whether to hand over his phone, Chu Ying sighed and said proactively: Is there any problem with the dubbing? You can contact me at any time and just add me in the group.Zhou Zimu's eyes lit up, he nodded repeatedly, and the depressed mood just now was gone. He told Ling Tingyang the reason again, and then he was willing to leave.As it approached twelve o'clock, everyone who had said they would stay up all night was almost exhausted.Luo Hui took the lead in drunkenly waving her hands and pushing away the wine bottle handed to her: No more, no moreHalf drunk and half awake, I took out my phone and looked at it again, and saw a dozen missed calls and dozens of text messages from my boyfriend.Some consciousness returned to her chaotic brain. She glanced at the messages. Most of them asked her when she would come home. The latest message asked her where she was.Luo Hui's head was dizzy and she sent him a message, then she stood up staggeringly: I have to go back first.As soon as this sound came out, some people got up one after another and said they wanted to go home.Ling Tingyang also drank some wine, but his mind was still clear. Seeing that most of the people were drunk and it was impossible to really spend the night here, he got up and organized, counted the number of people who were leaving, and planned to call a taxi for everyone.Only a few people were shouting loudly about where they were. They agreed to be high until dawn, but Ling Tingyang slapped him on the back of the head and said that you were the one who drank the most.Someone asked if they wanted to go to the bathroom, and soon there were three or two groups of people. The door opened and closed automatically. In the suddenly quiet private room, Chu Ying rubbed her temples, and she didn't know when she sat in the corner. The whole person was nestled in it, and his eyes were half-closed as if he was still very sleepy.She doesn't like to drink. She only drinks some occasionally when she has insomnia. It physically numbs her brain and makes it easier to fall asleep.But just now, the dim lights above her head were flashing, the voices were noisy in her ears, the clinking of glasses as you came and I, and the sometimes exciting and sometimes soothing melody from the speakers. I don't know which part caused it. By the time she came to her senses, she had already followed. Got half a bottle of wine.The noisy ambient sound actually became the best lullaby.Before I knew it, I felt sleepy and squinted for a while.Now that those noises were gone, she felt somewhat sober.Chu Ying stood up slowly, her mind was blank and her eyes were wandering around.It seems that the figure was not seen.Suddenly, a piece sank next to him.Chu Ying blinked absently and slowly turned her head.The familiar agarwood smelled faintly in her nose before she raised her eyes to see the man's face clearly.Chu Ying reacted slowly: Xu JisiUm.The man responded in a low voice, and then said: I will take you back.The deep voice naturally merged into her tired brain. Chu Ying didn't seem to notice anything was wrong. She tilted her head and said hesitantly: "Aren't you drinking?"After a pause, she didn't seem to expect that her first reaction would be this. The person in her ear seemed to smile: I only drink it after I lose. Do you think I will lose?Chu Ying subconsciously retorted: I clearly saw itHe clearly saw someone handing him a drink.Before she finished speaking, she suddenly realized something, and her brain finally returned to some sense at this moment. Before I even raised my eyes, I heard the man's teasing voice: He's paying attention to me.No one can ignore it.How could anyone not be attracted to him.Chu Ying didn't reply, but just lowered her head, her broken hair falling on her ears, her dark eyes half-closed, making her expression unclear.In silence.Lied to you.Xu Jisi looked down at her slightly, and when he saw her raising her eyes blankly after these words, she seemed to raise her lower lip, and said calmly: I fell down.

Chu Ying blinked. She didn't expect that he could not touch it under the eyes of so many people.No one can make me drink.His tone was natural and casual, like a statement.Not knowing what to reply, Chu Ying could only respond dryly.Xu didn't think about it and didn't care. He just asked: Go back now.Chu Ying slowly raised her head and looked around. The song on the screen was paused, and several people collapsed on the sofa. Ling Tingyang was helplessly waking them up one by one, asking for their address or the contact information of their friends. It was obvious that they were overwhelmed.As if she suddenly remembered something, Chu Ying tightened her fingers on her side. Without answering directly, she asked coldly: "You have been here for so long, what will others do?"Xu Jisi frowned for a moment: Who?The girl just now, Chu Ying turned her head unnaturally, and her eyes fell aimlessly on a few wine bottles lying on the ground at the corner of the table. She paused and added, isn't she drunk? Why didn't you give it to her?He came in not long after she came up. It only took a few minutes. It was impossible to arrange the person.He even stayed here for more than an hour.She could tell that the girl must have liked him.Did he just leave her there?Just like when I left her behindWithout any warning, her heart felt like it was being pressed down hard by some big stone. Chu Ying muffled her voice and said in a somewhat confused tone: You can't do this.She didn't know what his reason was for catching up today.But there is no doubt that his behavior is trampling on another girl's feelings.After Xu Jisi reacted for a while, he recognized from her words that the person she was talking about was Liang Yuqing.But what do you mean you can't do this?Her logic is that whenever a girl gets drunk, he has to take her home.Xu Jisi lowered his eyes and looked at her a little amused: Am I free enough to be a driver for anyone all day long?

Chu Ying's fingers under her long sleeves slightly bent: Then sheXu Jisi rarely explained: I asked others to send her back.She's my friend's sister.He paused, thinking of Liang Xuqing's helpless tone when she called, saying that she had broken up, and drunkenly sent him a message saying that she must see him. If he hadn't been a friend for many years, he wouldn't have given this face.It was hard to tell Chu Ying these words, so Xu Jisi simply skipped the introduction: "I'm not familiar with him, and I don't have the obligation."His tone was calm but decisive. She didn't expect Xu Jisi to explain this to her. Chu Ying was stunned for a moment, and soon realized that she had just misunderstood. An indescribable embarrassment came to her heart, and her neck felt inexplicably hot. It felt hot, and then felt inexplicably soothed, and my heart, which had been dull for several hours, suddenly jumped up again.But soon, she was pulled by reason again: But she likes you very much.Xu Jisi's eyes suddenly paused. There was a surge in his eyes for a moment, and then suddenly suppressed. He slowly raised his eyelids to look at her, and his tone was a little unclear: If you like me, you have to give it to someone.That was not what I meantChu Ying didn't know how to explain to him that this was not a question of whether to send it or not. She opened her lips and went through what she wanted to say several times in her mind before she finally said a blunt sentence: If you don't like it, you should Make it clear to her early.Instead of saying nothing and letting the other person think it's possible, only to find out in the end that it was just a dream.There was silence for a long time after the words fell.After getting no response for a long time, Chu Ying realized what she had just said, her heart beat fast, and she glanced at him in panic.It happened to meet his dark pupils under his long eyelashes.He didn't speak for a while. Chu Ying bit her lip lightly. She didn't know how to fix it for a moment. When she was about to look away, she heard him smiling: In your eyes, this is who I am.How do you know I didn't refuse?There are some things I know better than anyone else.Chu Ying blinked blankly, hearing that his voice was a little deeper, and her lowered eyes flashed slightly: I will not spend time and energy on unimportant people, and I have no habit of being a driver for others, let alone again and again. Take the initiative again and again.He didn't pause, almost explicitly.You should know that there is only one of you.His heart was beating faster and faster uncontrollably, and it was as if the only thing left in his ears was the frequency of her heartbeat. He stared at her unblinkingly, as if he wanted to take in every microexpression of hers. Chu Ying stiffened her body. , barely daring to look at him directly, curling up his fingers, and after a long time he moved his lips, his voice as thin as a cat meowing: It's too troublesome.She abruptly skipped the topic.Xu Ji thought for a moment, but didn't press too hard. He just raised his eyebrows and said, "On the way, what's the trouble?"Aren't you Chu Ying? She suddenly stopped talking, paused, and changed her question. Are you still living there?Why can't you live?Xu Jisi asked back, as if he was wondering why she asked this question. After a pause, he probably had some guess in his heart. His cold voice was teasing and he drawled. He was busy these days. , I slept in the company.You think I'm lying to youNo.She turned her face and answered very quickly.Xu Jisi chuckled: OK, I thought I was taking the blame again.What is anotherChu Ying felt her earlobes burning.Xu Jisi threw the car keys into the palm of his hand, stood up, and looked down at her: I wonder if I will have this opportunity to send Miss Chu home.The girl touched the tip of her nose, paused, and then slowly followed: By the way.Xu Jisi raised the corners of his lips slightly, hooked his slender fingers through the buckle, and the keys falling between his fingers collided, making a crisp dinging sound.She blinked and heard the man's clear voice, which seemed to be filled with joy:My pleasure.

Chapter 22 RememberingAren't I chasing you?Ling Tingyang was busy, and Chu Ying didn't bother him. She just sent him a message on her mobile phone to say that she was leaving first, and followed Xu Jisi downstairs.The man was very tall, with a slender figure and a broad back. His white shirt was just the right amount of looseness, but his tight muscles could still be seen. He walked calmly in front, and Chu Ying slowly followed behind him. When he came out, he was just right. I saw a car parked on the side of the road with its lights on. A man was supporting a familiar drunk figure, and he was struggling to get the person into the passenger seat.After finally placing the person in place, the man let out a sigh of relief and sighed helplessly as to why he drank so much. When he turned around to go to the driver's seat, he saw a man with outstanding temperament behind him.It was too late now. This was the back entrance. The mall had closed early, so the elevator could go directly to the KTV upstairs. There were almost no people on the street. He glanced back and saw a girl with her head lowered behind him. It was judged that she was probably the same as him, and also came to pick up people.As soon as he raised his head, he happened to meet the man's eyes and said hello: Brother, come to pick up your girlfriend too.Chu Ying's steps stagnated and she almost tripped herself.She raised her eyes in panic, but could only see the broad back of the man in front of her, but could not see his expression. She bit the tip of her tongue lightly, wanting to deny it, but there was a hint of secret fear and expectation in her heart.Chu Ying opened her lips, and while her mind was in confusion, she heard the man in front of her said in a lazy voice: No.Chu Ying's figure stiffened slightly.The next moment, she saw him turn his head slightly and look at her with dark eyes. Then he turned his head again, raised his lips slightly towards the man, and added: "Not yet."

Chu Ying was at a loss all the way home.I don't know if he was giving her a chance to buffer, but Xu Jisi didn't take the initiative to chat except for saying something casual about the company atmosphere being pretty good. When he sent her to her door, he didn't know who had sent him the message in the middle of the night. After receiving a message, he seemed to want to tell her something, but in the end he didn't say anything. He only looked down at the phone and told her to go in.Her tone was so natural that it was unimaginable that a few hours ago she had had the thought that the two of them might really be done with it.She turned her head blankly, stepped over the threshold and took two steps in. She felt her heart swell again, and she wanted to ask something.She stopped suddenly and turned around suddenly.By coincidence, just as he was about to turn around, he heard the man calling her name.Chu Ying.The moment he turned back, his eyes suddenly collided.His dark eyes were unblinking, and the desolate eyebrows seemed to soften for a moment. Chu Ying's fingers tightened slightly. In her brief absence, she heard Xu Ji's clear voice softened, and there seemed to be a trace of curl between his lips and teeth. Tenderness that does not belong to him.Good night.

After taking a bath, Chu Ying's originally sleepy

consciousness became more and more awake for some reason. Chu Ying lay on the bed and couldn't fall asleep. The clear moonlight poured out of the window. She stared at it for a long time, but she felt that the moon tonight seemed like... It's not as distant and deserted as before, but it's a little gentle.A sentence that that person said today seemed to flash through my mind again.He was probably hinting at something.Whether it's the straightforward statement that it's only you, or the ambiguous statement before getting in the car, or even the almost affectionate good night outside the door.The man's cold voice seemed to ring in her ears again. The temperature in the room was not high, but Chu Ying felt like her whole body was heating up. She suddenly sat up and turned on the bedside lamp.The quilt slid down, revealing her not-thick pajamas. Chu Ying leaned against the bed screen and patted her face gently.The breathing light of the mobile phone beside the bed kept lighting up. Chu Ying took the mobile phone as if to divert her attention and saw that it was a message in the company group.Chu Ying clicked in, scrolled up, and saw that Ling Tingyang had sent a message half an hour ago, saying that all employees would have a day off tomorrow.Someone posted a voice message below, and when I opened it, it was the BGM of the punching and moving, and the tone was obviously drunk, shouting thank you Yang Ge, Yang Ge, Shoubi Nanshan.Ling Tingyang replied with a series of ellipses, and Chu Ying could imagine the expression on his face that showed a headache, and couldn't help but laugh out loud.There wasn't much news back later. It was probably because most people went back to sleep and didn't look at their phones. Chu Ying finished the row after a while and entered the circle of friends out of boredom.Most of them are photos of people flying here and there during the National Day holiday, mixed with some lamenting about having to go to work again, and some colleagues took photos of their trip to Haidilao and KTV, and the copywriting was a treat for the boss.Compared with most people's fixed 9-to-5 job, her daily life is actually much more flexible.There is no regularity in this job. I am just busy when I have a role to play. If I get busy, it may be like this project, and I won't have to take vacations.As for not having a role at handChu Ying thought about it and found that since she joined Ling Tingyang, Ling Tingyang had not left her idle for too long. Games, radio dramas, and even this TV series were scattered here and there, and she picked up a lot of them during her spare time in class. It has been only half a year since graduation, and it seems that she has never taken any long vacation.No wonder someone on the Internet spread rumors about whether she had saved Ling Tingyang's life.A newcomer, in just two years, she has produced more than a dozen works of various sizes. She has participated in almost half of the dozens of works produced by Ling Ting in the past two years, and most of them are named characters.Someone compiled these statistics and said that Ling Tingyang was trained with her as his heir. She probably knew that she did have some talent in dubbing, but it was still far from this level.There was a time when she doubted herself because of these comments. It was Ling Tingyang who told her: A good voice actor deserves more good works to be heard by more people.However, thanks to the resources that Ling Tingyang continued to give her, she had a small savings just after graduation, and her living expenses at school were not tight in the past. In terms of ability, she can also notice her progress in the past two years. .Chu Ying was lost in thought as she flipped through the pages. When she reached Ji Ran's Moments, she paused.The time happened to be around eight o'clock in the evening. He took screenshots of a few message records and sent the most original smiley face on WeChat. The caption was "Is there anyone who can make an appointment with this person?"Chu Ying blinked, her fingers paused in the air for a second, and then she clicked on the screenshot.The records were recorded from last year to this year, with intervals ranging from one to three months. They were all about him asking someone to be a host, someone's birthday, someone opening a bar, and whether he wanted to be a guest. .She had only seen the face of the person across from her once, but it was so deep in her mind that Chu Ying recognized it almost immediately. That person was Xu Jisi.The messages replied on the left are all cold, not going, not available, busy.The latest one is that he said that he was heartbroken and asked if he could come out and have a drink with him.Of course he didn't mean to drink two glasses of wine literally.Most likely it's a nightclub with blurry lights and beautiful women.Chu Ying tightened her fingers and scrolled down the screenshot. She saw that the man obviously knew his virtue very well, and the reply was still cold: I'm drunk, so I won't go.The last sentence was sarcastic again: How many times this week?Ji Ran obviously didn't give up and said it was true this time, and also said he wouldn't let you drink, not even watching me drink.The reply from the other side: I feel dizzy from alcohol, so don' t come to me tomorrow.Ji Ran:Ji Ran's speechlessness was obviously all in the ellipsis.Chu Ying's eyelashes trembled slightly, and without any warning, she recalled the slightly raised tone of the man when he accepted Ling Tingyang's invitation without hesitation, and the words he said when his colleague invited him to roll the dice and drink.His eyes fell on Ji Ranfa's caption again.He didn't seem like someone who would be willing to participate in such an occasion.But why did he agree?Some ideas seemed to pop out of my closed mind.He would catch up, he would accept the invitation, he would explain to her the meaningless words he said, and he would take the initiative again and again.Is it what she thinks?The moment this thought flashed through her mind, Chu Ying's mind went blank.She felt helpless for a moment. She stared blankly at the phone, her heart seemed to be pulled invisibly by a hand.What also appeared together was the corner between the roofs and under the eaves that we first met when we were young.As if overlapping with the past, she seemed to be standing in that autumn evening again.The lonely young man wants to rub shoulders with her.She remained motionless.Only the invisible heartbeat is still pounding as it is now.

Dreaming again.In the dream, she took the high-speed train to Lizhou for the first time four years ago. During the three-hour journey, she looked out the window.The high-speed train was speeding, and the scene outside receded quickly and blurred.She sat on the trolley of her small suitcase and looked at the scenery outside the window, from green paddy fields to rolling mountains and green forests, passing by sparkling lakes, and the low bungalows in the distance gradually climbed higher and higher into towering mountains. Buildings reaching into the sky, bustling and noisy streets crisscrossing each other, the vast and glitzy world seems to be all in sight.Later, I stood at an intersection in Lizhou, with pedestrians bustling and traffic flowing in and out. When the sky was getting dark, mottled light and shadows were reflected in my eyes. The lights on the roadside almost illuminated the sky like daylight, and the car lights flashed through my eyes incessantly. .That was the first time Chu Ying had a clear concept of the word prosperity.The thought that flashed through my mind was that there was only three hours difference between Wu Ning and the so-called world outside.I didn't even get enough sleep at this time.Suddenly, what came to mind was the emotionless young man again.He grew up in this environment.She seemed to have entered a world that did not belong to her.Various unaccustomed things in life followed one after another, and at this moment she realized Xu Jisi's experience in Wu Ning Town.No wonder he left.She thought so in her dream.

When I woke up, the sun was already shining brightly.Chu Ying didn't sleep well and her eyes were swollen.Fortunately, she didn't go to work today, so she had time to take care of herself.After washing, she applied a facial mask. While waiting, she looked at her phone.Zhu Ruoxuan's news was at the forefront. Just a few minutes ago, he asked her if she was free today.Chu Ying asked what was wrong, and soon got another message from her, saying that she wanted to return her earphones.This headset is actually not that important. But since she had a day off today, Zhu Ruoxuan happened to send her a message. Chu Ying thought about it and agreed.The two met at five o'clock in the evening. Chu Ying wanted to take the earphones and leave, but Zhu Ruoxuan called her out for the first time and said that she wanted to treat her to dinner, so he treated her as a thank you.It's like a compensation for the lack of words.Chu Ying raised her eyes and met Zhu Ruoxuan's hurriedly looking away.She was a person who usually had fun with everyone, but this time she was a little nervous and clenched her phone tightly.Whether it was because she was soft-hearted or had some other selfish motives, Chu Ying paused slightly and agreed.The meal was extremely awkward. Zhu Ruoxuan obviously wanted to find something to talk about, but found that she didn't know what Chu Ying's hobbies or interests were. After holding it in for a long time, she said that the food here was delicious.Chu Ying paused with her chopsticks and hummed softly.Until the meal is almost over.Chu Ying took out a tissue and wiped her mouth. The two sat face to face, not knowing what else to say.She glanced at the setting sun outside the window and thought it was getting late and they should go home.Zhu Ruoxuan raised her head stiffly, as if she finally remembered something and wanted to keep her.thatChu Ying paused slightly when she wanted to stand up, then looked up at her: What?Regarding what happened last time, Mr. Xu said about compensation, she paused, put her hand around the back of her neck and pinched it, "I don't have anything serious to do, so I won't go looking for it. You can say thank you again for me."Chu Ying blinked, her heartbeat seemed to stagnate, she subconsciously lowered her gaze and looked away: I'm not familiar with him either.Unexpectedly, Zhu Ruoxuan paused, with a strange expression and hesitant tone:Isn't he chasing you?

Chapter 23 Rememberingdraw clear boundariesA memory that she had deliberately forgotten since she woke up suddenly emerged. Chu Ying's fingers froze and she couldn't control her expression for a moment.Zhu Ruoxuan was sensitive to the ups and downs of her emotions at the moment.There was no shame or joy.There was nothing like the reaction she expected when her ambiguous relationship was exposed.Zhu Ruoxuan moved her fingers, and soon she thought of the obviously unusual atmosphere between the two last time. After a while, she realized that she might have thought too simplistically, and that there might be a deeper bond between them that she didn't know about. .However, the words had already been spoken, and trying to make up for it would seem deliberate, and it might even affect Chu Ying's mood even more.She never expected that the topic she finally thought of would make the atmosphere between them even more silent. Zhu Ruoxuan patted her head in annoyance.

Later, she didn't know how she said goodbye to Zhu Ruoxuan. When she came to her senses again, Chu Ying saw that she had returned to the downstairs of her home.Away from the noisy intersection, the community was very quiet. The sun was setting in the sky, and there were familiar scenery everywhere. Chu Ying blinked to calm down. Just as she was about to walk to the hall, her footsteps suddenly stopped.In the peripheral vision, an unfamiliar car parked on the side slightly out of place.Chu Ying looked back and stared, but she wasn't sure if it was parked by a certain owner who came back occasionally, so she didn't think much about it.It wasn't until five minutes later that she saw a familiar figure in front of her house that she suddenly froze.This time the man no longer wore that fancy shirt, but instead put on a decent leather jacket. He squatted in front of her house, holding an unlit cigarette in his mouth out of boredom.Some unpleasant scenes suddenly reappeared in her mind, and the man's sinister eyes and smelly breath seemed to be entangled again. Chu Ying shuddered and took two steps back almost subconsciously.The heels scraped against the tile floor, making a small but sharp sound.Chu Ying felt a chill in her heart, and when she raised her eyes in a panic, she saw the man raising his head as if he noticed the movement here.The moment she looked at him, Chu Ying felt that her blood was flowing backwards and her fingertips were cold. She backed away stiffly and almost tripped herself in panic. She held her hands tightly against the wall to stabilize her body.The man's eyes lit up, and in Chu Ying's eyes, he seemed to have discovered the prey that escaped last time.He suffered a bad loss last time, and now that he is here, he must want to take revenge.Chu Ying's fingers almost pinched into the palm of her hand and she turned around to run away.Unexpectedly, as soon as he turned his head, he was caught off guard and bumped into a warm chest.Chu YingThe gentle and delicate body was pulled into the man's arms. At the same time, the other person's cold and nervous voice sounded above her head. Chu Ying raised her head in confusion, and could feel the man's chest rising and falling rapidly, as if he was running over.The violent heartbeat was instantly soothed for no reason at this moment, and her breathing gradually calmed down. She blinked and looked into Xu Jisi's dark eyes.Both of them seemed to be stunned for a moment, and time was paused by Void's hand. It seemed to be quiet for a few seconds. After a long while, a tentative male voice sounded from not far away:Am I watching an idol drama?After coming back to her senses in an instant, she realized what an ambiguous posture she and Xu Jisi were in at the moment. Chu Ying lowered her eyes at a loss and stretched out her hand to touch the man's chest.Xu Ji thought for a moment and loosened his grip around the girl's waist.Only then did Chu Ying look a little embarrassed and straightened up.Xu Kaiyuan hadn't recovered from Chu Ying's reaction of avoiding him as if seeing some wild beast. He turned around and saw the two of them hugging each other. He was confused and didn't know what to react first. He stared blankly. After waiting for a while, he followed his instinct and turned his attention to the man in a suit and leather shoes with a cold temperament, and said in a puzzled tone:Brother, why are you here too?Xu Jisi took two steps forward and almost instantly lost his previous emotion. He raised his eyelids coldly and said in a deep voice:I haven't asked you why you are here.Xu Kaiyuan paused, then remembered Xu Jisi's threatening aura that day. Recalling his dishonest method of obtaining Chu Ying's address, he touched his nose guiltily, coughed lightly, and said lightly:Isn't that right? Do you want to apologize to your sister-in-law?His mind flashed back to Chu Ying's obviously panicked look and actions when he saw him just now, and he smiled again: It seemed that he had scared his sister-in-law again.sister in lawChu Ying's expression was stagnant for a moment before she could adjust, as if to confirm whether she heard correctly, she raised her eyes blankly.However, Xu Kaiyuan's coy expression showed no signs of teasing or joking, and he seemed to really think so.Maybe it was the previous conversation between the two at the police station that made him misunderstand something, and their unexpected close contact just now confirmed his suspicion.Chu Ying subconsciously wanted to clarify this misunderstanding before being embarrassedly denied.She tightened her cuffs, quickly glanced at the figure in front of her who had not yet moved, and opened her lips, about to speak.But he saw that the other person's footsteps moved and he spoke first, his tone as calm as ever.How did you get in?Xu Kaiyuan slowly put down the hand that touched his nose, and when he met his brother's clear eyes, he felt that his brother's tone seemed to have lost some coldness. He was stunned for a moment, and then said honestly:Forced in.His tone seemed to be a bit proud: If you don't let me drive, I will crash in. Anyway, I have plenty of money to compensate. The security guard at the door called, I reported my name, and they let me in.

The corners of Xu Jisi's lips twitched slightly, but he didn't feel that it was outrageous.What happened to Xu Kaiyuan was very reasonable.He remembered that the Ji family had invested in this property, and it was probably for the Xu family's sake.Xu Kaiyuan obviously didn't feel that there was anything wrong with what he did. He followed Xu Jisi with his eyes and thought of something: That's not right. Brother, how did you get in?He admits that his behavior is a bit bandit, but his brother is not like that.Within two seconds, he suddenly remembered that the two people appeared one after the other. After a pause, he suddenly seemed to realize something. Xu Kaiyuan's eyes widened again, and his eyes kept wandering around the two people:You guys, you won't live together anymore, right?NoWhat are you thinking about?At this moment, the two voices sounded together.As if he didn't expect Chu Ying to come back so quickly, Xu Jisi paused in his steps and looked back after he finished speaking.The girl's eyes were wide open, her expression was as panicked as if she had heard some ghost story, and her desire to draw a clear line with him was almost written directly on her face.The feeling of boredom came to his mind unconsciously again. Xu Jisi pressed his eyes, but there was no emotion on his face. He glanced at Xu Kaiyuan and sneered coldly: If you can find out the person's address, you don't know that I live across the street.He could guess what method Xu Kaiyuan used to obtain Chu Ying's home address, so his tone was naturally not good. But in Xu Kaiyuan's eyes, his brother's attitude had always been like this, so after receiving this information, his eyes only widened:WhatDon't wait for a flat floor with a good river view, live in this shabby placeIn the eyes of ordinary people, Jiananhui is already considered a high-end place, but for a rich second generation like Xu Kaiyuan, this place is really not high-end.Even Ling Tingyang's friend bought this just for fun with his friends.So when Xu Jisi said that he lived here, his first reaction was that he couldn't understand it.But in a flash, his eyes touched the girl beside him again, and he seemed to understand something.His brother is indeed his brother.In order to accompany my sister-in-law, I even had to downgrade my living environment.He couldn't help but feel a hint of admiration in his heart.Xu Kaiyuan knew very well what his daily standards of food, clothing, housing, transportation and entertainment were, and it was impossible for him to lower his standards for anyone.He now felt that the rumors he had heard a few years ago were somewhat credible.I heard that when his brother disappeared a few months ago, he went to a run-down town.He thought it was a joke when he heard about it.His brother has been a proud man since he was born. Everyone knows that Xu Jisi is the only heir to the Xu family.His uncle would never let his brother go to that kind of place.Xu Jisi couldn't possibly stay.But now, he felt that from the latter perspective alone, it was not impossible.But in the end, the uncle from above suppressed him and took ten thousand steps back, saying that even if he wanted to go, he couldn't go.Xu Kaiyuan was making random guesses in his mind, but he didn't notice that Chu Ying was still trying to speak. He followed Xu Jisi a few steps, pretending that he knew very well, and lowered his voice: I know, are you? for sister-in-lawNot sister-in-law.His cold voice was neither too loud nor too soft, and the clear voice seemed to suppress some emotion. The moment the voice fell, Xu Kaiyuan's unfinished words were paused. He seemed to move his lips before he could react, and his expression became stiff after a few seconds. Pronunciation: AhThere was a hint of disbelief in the rising tone.Xu Kaiyuan blinked rapidly, and when he finally reacted, he subconsciously looked at the girl on the other side.The girl seemed to be frozen in place. I don't know if it was his imagination, but her fair face seemed pale for a moment, and then she seemed to notice his gaze. She curled her lips stiffly, and there seemed to be something wrong with her soft voice. But I couldn't hear it.Yes, you misunderstood.Mr. Xu was just kind-hearted and helped me out. It was too late that day. Sending my friend and I home just to be a gentleman is not the kind of relationship you think.You guys chat, I won't interrupt. Goodbye.She spoke very fast, and without waiting for the two of them to react, she hurried home and closed the door.Xu Kaiyuan froze on the spot again, his brain slowly processing the information conveyed in these few sentences.His brother said he was not his sister-in-law.Sister-in-law, no, Chu Ying said he misunderstood.The two parties concerned clarified separately.So he did make a mistakeThen what is the purpose of his brother living in this shabby place?Here comes the funThen his brother helped others like this last timeThey warned him and asked him to apologize, and he was used as a driver to take him home.And you were hugging someone like that just now?Xu Kaiyuan felt that his brain was going into a blur.I had a lot of questions to ask, but I didn't know which one to ask first. Finally, my lips touched my lips and I was about to pronounce a syllable. When I looked up, I saw that the man's face had fallen. Even the curve of the corners of his lips had straightened, and he seemed to be all over. His aura became more than one degree colder.Xu Kaiyuan trembled unconsciously:elder brotherThe man raised his hand and loosened his tie irritably, raised his eyes slightly, and stared at the cold door opposite, with dark emotions in his eyes.After a while, he pinched his finger bones.Under the crisp friction sound between the joints, Xu Kaiyuan intuitively felt that his brother was in a bad mood. The next moment, he saw Xu Jisi's eyes passing over him coldly, and his voice sounded like he was immersed in an ice cellar:No time to entertain, please come back.

Chapter 24 RememberingJust treat it as a favor and accompany me to see it.twenty fourIt feels like I have stayed there for many days, but I still can't feel the smell of human smoke when I enter the house.An indescribable coldness suddenly crawled up her tailbone after closing the lifeless door. The cold electronic sound that sounded when closing the door was like a switch that turned on her emotions. The tense nerves finally relaxed at this moment. Chu Ying didn't even go inside. After two steps, his legs slid along the door, his back leaned against the door, and his whole body slid down uncontrollably.In fact, I have already been mentally prepared for this.But the moment it came out of his mouth, his heart still shrank.The conjectures that had been swirling in her mind for the past two days were like a joke, mocking her overestimation.How dare you have such an idea.Not in itself, is it?It just clarified a fact, so there is nothing to be disappointed about.She seemed to have unknowingly fallen into the misunderstanding she was most afraid of.It was mercy in the past, but what is it now?Chu Ying felt that all the disturbing thoughts made her head become extremely heavy. She let herself hang her head, hugging her knees tightly, staring at the reflective tile floor with some numbness.I do not know how long it has been.The doorbell suddenly rang.Chu Ying stood up as if she had regained consciousness. She even forgot to look at the display screen and subconsciously opened the door first.He was caught off guard and met those familiar eyes.Chu Ying froze, her fingers still clenched on the doorknob, and she instinctively wanted to withdraw her hand and close the door.The man's cold, white and slender fingers reached out and touched him without hesitation.He probably wanted to hold the doorknob, but a few fingers inadvertently touched hers. His fingers were also cold, and she was almost unable to move the moment he touched them.Chu Ying froze for a moment, still trying to pull back her strength, but she didn't expect the man to use too much force. After a few seconds of confrontation, the door only swayed back and forth slightly without any amplitude.The two sides were in a stalemate, and no one said a word for a while.Chu Ying's gaze was dazed for a few seconds, and she finally gave up. She raised her eyes slightly and tried to maintain a normal voice: "Mr. Xu, don't you need to entertain guests?"The man paused, his dark eyelashes drooped slightly, and his tone could not tell whether it was true or false: he was in a hurry and was leaving first.

Chu Ying was silent for two seconds, then slowly loosened her fingers, as if she was aware of her movements, and the man's gentle pressure also stopped.Her ring finger and little finger seemed to be still wet with moisture. Chu Ying retracted her hand and hid it unconsciously behind her back. She said "Oh" and asked stiffly: "What's the matter with you?"Xu Ji thought, why can't he look for it if nothing is wrong, but the girl's mood in his eyes was obviously not right. The black eyes that were always clear and bright seemed to be a lot darker, maybe it was because of his sight. He was even a little droopy, with a look of being very tired but having to cope with it.He paused slightly and frowned: You are very tired.Chu Ying tightened her fingers: No.That's because someone bullied youWhen he came back, he saw the familiar car downstairs. When he was in the elevator, he remembered that it belonged to Xu Kaiyuan, and he felt really nervous for a moment. When he hurried out of the elevator, he happened to see Chu Ying who was in a panic and wanted to escape.Things happened so fast that he really couldn't know what happened to Chu Ying before, but he could also detect some of the girl's emotions that resurfaced after the crisis.He felt that he didn't say a few words, so it wouldn't affect Chu Ying in any way. It was most likely that some of her previously accumulated emotions came back after the accident.Xu Jisi's voice turned cold unconsciously for a moment: Who?In a daze, the man's deep voice seemed to overlap with the distant, slightly immature and cold voice. They were equally sure and struck the heart of the heart.Chu Ying's heart trembled. After a while, she raised her eyelids and opened her lips slowly: No.Xu Jisi frowned even more tightly.Her expression was familiar to him. She always had this look on her face every time she said everything was fine.The man obviously didn't believe it. His narrow eyebrows moved slightly, as if he was thinking of something, and he paused:It was Xu Kaiyuan who scared youChu Ying didn't know in what capacity he was speculating on the cause of her emotions, as if he was not the one who had decisively drawn the line just now.Since we have to put aside the relationship, why do we have to think so much about her?She wanted to laugh a little, but she also wondered for no reason whether her behavior when she speculated about him now was the same as how he speculated about her psychology at the moment.But a sense of fatigue invaded her limbs. The girl lowered her head slightly, and the long hair scattered around her ears obscured half of her sight. Suddenly she didn't have the strength to speak anymore. She shook her head and said in a very soft voice: None of them.After a moment of silence, Xu Jisi obviously realized that she didn't want to talk to him about this. Maybe she thought that the relationship between them was not enough, or there might be some other unspeakable secret. In short, in such an obvious situation, asking again To no avail.A few seconds later, just when Chu Ying wanted to say that she could just go back if nothing happened, Xu Jisi suddenly started talking again:There was a movie recently, do you want to go watch it together?Chu Ying didn't expect that he would change the topic so suddenly. The sudden invitation made her brain freeze for a moment. After she recovered, she could only refuse instinctively. Before she could say a word, she heard him add:"Xuan Ye", the male protagonist is played by Mr. Ling, why don't you support him?Chu Ying paused for a moment. She probably had too many choices about what she had chosen. Ling Tingyang herself didn't talk much about it. Eleven was busy again, so she didn't pay attention to any new movies at all. When I mentioned it, I vaguely remembered that Luo Hui seemed to have mentioned it.Seeing that her expression relaxed, Xu Jisi calmly looked back and continued:Xu Kaiyuan really offended you just now. Just think of me as an apology for him, step back and say, after breaking away from the identity of Party A and Party B, we can be regarded as friends now. You can treat it as a favor and accompany me to see it.It was rare to hear him speak for such a long time, and the word friend was mentioned lightly by him, so calmly that it seemed she felt guilty for rejecting her.Chu Ying was frozen for a moment, then moved her lips for a moment, as if to change the subject:Why do you suddenly want to go to the movies?Xu Jisi's idea of going to the movies really didn't fit in with her knowledge.The man naturally raised his eyebrows slightly: Oh, I invested, let's go and take a look.Chu Ying:You probably don't need anyone to accompany you.Chu Ying still wanted to struggle.You're not blaming me just because of someone else's wordsThe man suddenly glanced at her, his eyes flickering.I didn't even know how to explain it at the moment, as if she was suddenly being held up high, and rejection meant admission. She was so petty, not to mention they said they were just friends. The more coy she was, the more people thought she cared.Chu Ying lightly pinched her arm hidden in her sleeve, trying to calm herself down and stop thinking too much. When she met the man's calm gaze, she gently bit her inner lip and asked slowly:when

It was already midnight when we came out of the cinema. "Hanging Night" is a suspenseful crime film. It seems to be very popular online. It has already passed the National Day, and the night movie is still full.Xu Jisi really seemed to be just going to inspect the project. When he entered the venue, he heard the chatter of people around him and said something thoughtful to Chu Ying without looking away.The light was dim and there were quite a lot of people. When Chu Ying went inside to find a seat, she was almost bumped into by a few young people laughing and playing behind her. Xu Jisi helped her and then walked behind her, his arms intentionally or unintentionally moving away for her. The crowd came up.After sitting down and waiting for a few minutes, the movie started. Chu Ying took a temporary photo and sent it to Luo Hui.In fact, in addition to wanting to support Ling Tingyang at first, she also wanted to learn the details of Ling Tingyang's film dubbing skills. Unexpectedly, the plot was indeed brilliant, and the several reversals in the middle and later stages made her completely obsessed with it, completely forgetting her original plan.There was no glamorous atmosphere in a movie, it seemed like the two of them were just there for support and inspection.After leaving the theater, Xu Jisi asked her if she wanted something to drink.Chu Ying paused and looked up to see Xu Jisi looking at a milk tea shop with a long queue not far away, slightly raising his chin to signal.As if she was a little thirsty, Chu Ying blinked and nodded subconsciously. Before even moving her feet, she saw that the other party was already walking that way naturally.He had long legs and long steps. By the time she came to her senses, the man was far behind in the queue. When he went out, he changed out of his suit and put on only a gray woolen coat. He stood there casually, holding his pockets with one hand. His temperament was somehow different from the people next to him, which attracted passers-by to look at him. .Chu Ying had just regained her composure and was about to follow up when two girls suddenly appeared in her field of vision. The two of them gathered together and whispered. Their eyes looked there from time to time. After a while, they began to fight with each other again. Their laughter could be heard. Within two seconds, they were talking again. As if they had agreed on something, one of them took small steps over there.After walking for two steps, she looked back hesitantly at the girl standing there. The man waved his hand to her, and then gave her a thumbs up. It should be to encourage her, so she took another deep breath. , and walked straight to the end of the line in one go.Chu Ying's footsteps suddenly froze in place, and she watched the girl trot up to him in a daze. She seemed to have the courage to say something, and then handed the phone to him.He seemed to pause for a moment and lowered his head slightly. The girl was a head and a half away from him, and she stood on tiptoes slightly, as if she wanted to hear what he said clearly.Chu Ying's fingers tightened unconsciously, and her heart seemed to be suddenly lifted. The next moment, as if she was aware of something, she saw the man suddenly raise his eyes, his eyes passed through the distant crowd, and his dark eyes fell on her accurately. body, then raised his chin slightly and touched his thin lips slightly.Before she could wake up from this look, she saw that the girl had also turned her head, her eyes wandering as if searching for something, and soon settled on her again, and she blinked.The girl didn't know when she left.Accompanied by the whispers, the two men quietly looked back at her before leaving, and sighed something, but she didn't hear it clearly.It seemed that the only thing left in my mind was the look that the man had just cast.He was still looking at her.Chu Ying put her fingers against her side and didn't know where to put them.I don't know if he didn't wait for her to make a move. The man paused, then lowered his head and took out his mobile phone. His slender fingers jumped on the screen. After a while, Chu Ying felt the mobile phone beside her vibrate slightly.She lowered her head in confusion and saw her phone screen lighting up.Slowly picking up the phone, Chu Ying stared at the received message on the lock screen, blinked slowly, and clicked on the message.The moment I saw the text, the man's cold and teasing voice seemed to ring in my ears.Why don't you come over?I'm lining up for the eldest lady. I can't leave now.

Chapter 25 RememberingChu Ying, do you have a conscience?25MissWhat a young lady.He was teasing her again.Chu Ying really didn't want to move for a moment, but then she thought that he was lining up for her, so she finally moved.With only a few steps to go, Chu Ying turned off her phone and walked slowly to Xu Jisi's side. The team slowly moved forward some distance.There were several long tables on one side. When Chu Ying approached, before she could speak, she saw Xu Jisi gesturing to a nearby seat with his eyes: "Sit down and wait."This seems to be an internet celebrity milk tea shop that has become popular recently. Most of the people it attracts are couples, some hugging each other's waists intimately, and some facing each other with their arms crossed.She seemed to be surrounded by couples coming and going. Chu Ying thought of the episode just now and didn't know what Xu Jisi said. The two girls looked back at her several times.In such an atmosphere, it is easy to be misunderstood, not to mention that if you stand with him, you may be regarded as the center of attention. Chu Ying quickly glanced at the crowd on the left and right and nodded slightly.In fact, it was hard to imagine that someone like Xu Jisi would queue up in such a long line to buy milk tea in person, which made her feel like a proud descendant of heaven.Chu Ying's eyes wandered aimlessly, and her hand unconsciously pressed the power button of her phone back and forth. The screen turned on and off, and finally, after wandering around for some reason, it moved back to that person.I don't know if someone sent him a message. He was typing with his head down. After a while, he seemed to feel tired. He pressed the bottom of the screen and spoke to the person. He could faintly hear words like "I don't have time to be busy". .Although she knew that he might just be looking for an excuse to offend some people, Chu Ying still looked away with an inexplicable guilty conscience.But then he thought again, she was obviously the one who was called out to accompany him, so how could he have anything to do with her.Just as she was thinking this, she accidentally raised her eyes and saw the man put down his mobile phone. His eyes happened to fall on her either intentionally or unintentionally.After looking at each other for a brief moment, Chu Ying was the first to hold on and was about to look away.Unexpectedly, the couple next to them who had been having a bad atmosphere from the beginning finally broke out into a quarrel at this moment.The woman put her hands on her waist and suddenly turned her head without warning.The girl pointed at her, her eyes fixed on Xu Jisi, a trace of envy flashed in her eyes, then circled back to the boy beside her, and her face suddenly fell:Look at other people, they all let their girlfriends rest and wait in line by themselves, but you are not willing to let you come and buy a cup of milk tea with me. Now you are too lazy to even line up with me. Why are you in love if you are so unwilling? I forced you to have sex with this objectThe girl seemed to have a bad temper. She was sputtering and scolding her without controlling her volume. The boy was obviously losing his temper and pulled her arm:If you have something to say, please speak it carefully. Everyone is watching in this large audience.You also know that the embarrassing girl sneered and interrupted him.Chu Ying didn't even know how she had somehow joined the fight between the two and became the so-called girlfriend.However, the dispute here has obviously attracted the attention of the people around her. Yiwu'er Erqi Wuerbayi's eyes swept over her body like a pursuit. It clearly had nothing to do with her, but it made her Embarrassed.They are already sitting far away, why are they still being misunderstood.She shouldn't drink this milk tea.Chu Ying wanted to bury her head in the cracks in the ground, so she could only brainwash herself, pretending not to be aware of those sights, and not daring to come forward to talk. She could only take out her mobile phone and send a message to Xu Jisi:Why don't you wait in line? I don't want to drink that much.As soon as the man's cell phone lit up, he lowered his head, raised his eyebrows when he saw the message, raised his eyes, glanced at her, and replied:I've already finished half of it. Why don't I want to drink it all of a sudden?Chu Ying didn't know how to reply for a moment.Isn't he usually very good at looking at people's eyes? Why is he pretending to be stupid now?Chu Ying pressed her slender fingers a little harder, as if she was letting out a sigh of relief:I just don't want to drink itAfter a pause, I looked at him and called him again: If you want to buy something, just arrange it yourself. I'll leave first.Then she didn't know where the courage came from. She really didn't look at him again, straightened up and walked against the crowd to the other side of the open space.In fact, she didn't know where she was going, she just wanted to escape from that disputed place.When the noisy people around her gradually became quieter and quieter, she also slowed down her pace.Thinking of something again, she looked down at her phone.The man didn't reply.Does he think she is quite strange?Too lazy to keep up.Chu Ying's heart felt heavy.Just thought about it.Footsteps that were faster than hers suddenly sounded behind her, and then slowed down leisurely as they approached.The moon hung high in the sky, and that tall shadow just popped into view, following her closely.Chu Ying blinked and subconsciously speeded up her steps, but she saw that he was also walking faster. She tentatively walked slowly, and the man also slowed down.The two shadows were one behind the other. Even if the man was walking fast, he seemed to be in a leisurely manner, walking at an unhurried pace.It was obviously Xu Jisi.He really caught upChu Ying blinked and suddenly stopped.The man behind him also stopped.She turned her head slowly.A touch of dry warmth suddenly touched her cheek.Her vision suddenly focused, and Chu Ying subconsciously reached out to take the warm object that was attached to her.I squeezed the cup tightly and took a closer look, only to realize that it was the milk tea shop I had just queued up for.She was stunned for a moment: Isn't the queue quite long?There happened to be a girl next to me who just bought it. She was very natural and I bought it from her.He didn't have much change, and he only had a red card in his pocket. After hearing this, the girl wanted to say a few polite words to him, but he was afraid that he would lose sight of her if she was too slow, so he just put the money into her hand, took the milk tea and caught up with her.The girl didn't say anything she wanted to ask for her contact information, but she saw a man with outstanding appearance and elegant temperament chasing a slender figure against the crowd.I don't know if it's the taste you like. Try it and the man will ask.Chu Ying came back to her senses, her expression still a little unnatural: I'm afraid I won't be able to sleep at night after drinking.Xu Jisi raised his eyebrows slightly: Isn't the project at hand finished?Then you have to go to work.Xu Jisi thought for a moment: If I lend you, you won't need it anymore.

Who taught the Xu family to use their privileges in these places.There was a hint of matter-of-factness in her clear voice, as if she was really considering the feasibility of this. Chu Ying panicked and quickly turned her head: It's not necessary, and it's not like she can't fall asleep every time.She lowered her head and gently bit the straw as she walked forward.It tastes really good.Seeing her drinking, Xu Jisi slightly curled his lips. The girl walked slowly in front, not knowing what she was thinking. After a while, seeing that there were fewer and fewer people in front of her, the man raised his eyebrows and asked in a low voice. :Where do you want to go?Chu Ying came to her senses in a daze, her thoughts temporarily confused. She looked at the unfamiliar environment. It was so quiet that she couldn't even hear the sound of cars, and she suddenly stopped walking.Suddenly feeling a little embarrassed, Chu Ying turned around, looked into his downcast and smiling eyes, and tightened her slender fingers on the milk tea cup.She had never been to the park here, so she really didn't know where it was now.After a long while, she whispered: It seems that I went to the wrong place.The girl lowered her head as if she felt guilty, with broken hair falling on her ears. Her long black eyelashes trembled slightly with her gentle words. The tip of her small nose was slightly dyed red due to the cold autumn wind that had been blowing.Xu Jisi couldn't help but chuckle. He opened his slender fingers and quickly rubbed her soft black hair. The tip of his nose could vaguely smell the faint fragrance of her hair:Road crazy, still walking around randomlyIf he didn't follow, he would really lose himself.Invisibly showing her closeness, Chu Ying raised her eyes blankly, and then she felt a numb and itchy sensation on her scalp connected to her tailbone, and then started to feel hot.When she realized something, Chu Ying was momentarily at a loss. Her bright black eyes suddenly widened, and she suddenly took a step back.This seemed to be his first subjective touch without any external stimulation or accident.The movements were very light, so natural that it seemed like they had the right relationship to make such a move, and even a little too gentle to be true.

Really hell.How could this be Xu Jisi.No.Xu Jisi wondered what was going on.Why are you still touching her?Chu Ying was so shocked that she almost knocked over the milk tea in her hand, and the fear of him in her eyes magnified several times, as if a sharp sword was piercing his eyes.Xu Jisi's movements froze.The curve of the corners of his lips also froze for a moment.In the stalemate, neither of them moved first.The faint fragrance of the girl just now still lingers on the tip of her nose.But in his field of vision, the man was now jumping more than half a meter away from him.His dark eyes stared unblinking at the girl who looked away with a guilty conscience.After a long time, Xu Jisicai suppressed any emotion and looked away, and his voice returned to its former coldness:I'll take you back.

Later, she kept half a meter away from him all the way back.They were also in tandem, but the atmosphere was completely different from half an hour ago.Afraid of being too close to him, as soon as he wanted to stop, his steps would stop faster than anyone else, for fear of having any close contact with him again.Chu Ying naturally couldn't see Xu Jisi's gloomy look, but noticed that he didn't say anything else the whole way back, but just as she wanted, Xu Jisi didn't speak, so she could calm down and do it again. Her mind is just a mess.I don't want the silence to continue when I get home.In the elevator, Chu Ying took a sneak peek at his expression, which was as indifferent as ever, and she didn't move her gaze even a little bit as if she didn't notice her movements.Men's emotions are like needles in the sea.Chu Ying thought about it and felt that he had always been like this. Compared to his current indifferent state, it was abnormal to take the initiative to make a kiss like just now.Slowly walking to the door of her house, Chu Ying suppressed the suspicion in her heart and just raised her hand to press the fingerprint lock.The moment the cold electronic sound sounded.A sigh that seemed to suppress some dull emotion or an illusion penetrated into the ear canal.Chu Ying turned back uncertainly.He found that the man was standing behind him with less than half an arm.He is tall, and he always lowers his head when looking at her, and bends slightly when listening to her words. This seems to be a habit that has been engraved in his bones since he was young.At this moment, he was still like that, with his chin slightly closed, his cold eyebrows slightly lowered, and his dark eyes motionless, as if he wanted to see some emotion from her eyes.But Chu Ying was startled when she first turned around, and when she met his gaze again, there seemed to be only confusion in her eyes.youWhy don't you go back?As soon as her lips were half opened, the man lowered his voice and sighed softly, as if he was helpless.Chu Ying, do you have a conscience?

In the early morning, the atmosphere in Ling Ting was very subtle.The milk tea last night still had an effect. She tossed and turned throughout the night and didn't fall asleep much. Later, she took a melatonin pill and gradually started to feel sleepy.I didn't even hear the alarm, and when I woke up I almost fell off the bed when I saw the time.Normally she would put on light makeup when she had time, but today it was obviously too late. Chu Ying got up, washed up, changed clothes casually, and chose to take a taxi to the company.After finally arriving at the company, I found that the atmosphere was eerily quiet. Normally everyone would be chatting lively and gossiping, but today there was only sporadic chatter that was deliberately lowered.It's because we took a day off yesterday and everyone has not recovered from the short vacation.I drank too much the day before yesterday and didn't relax enough yesterday.Chu Ying paused slightly, and while she was distracted in thought, her calf accidentally bumped into a chair nearby.The chair made a sharp and piercing sound as it rubbed against the tile floor, and something fell to the ground as the chair collided with the desk, immediately attracting a lot of attention.Chu Ying took a breath of cold air with some pain. Before she could recover, she raised her eyes and met a familiar sight not far away.Luo Hui was separated from her by a desk, and a complicated look flashed in her eyes. However, it only lasted for a moment, and she quickly rushed over. There was nothing wrong in her tone, only worry:Are you okay, Yingying?Chu Ying paused, still thinking about the strange atmosphere just now, and slowly shook her head.I hesitated for a moment and was about to ask my doubts out loud.However, his eyes inadvertently glanced at several photos that fell to the ground at an unknown time.Chu Ying's eyelids twitched slightly.She paused briefly and was about to squat down to pick it up.The person in front of him seemed to be aware of her sight and movements, and subconsciously reached out to hold her hand.YingyingLuo Hui instinctively spoke out, but then felt that her behavior was too deliberate, and her expression felt regretful for a moment.The ominous premonition became stronger. Chu Ying raised her eyes and saw an uneasy look on Luo Hui's face.Luo Hui's upper body leaned forward slightly, intentionally or unintentionally blocking her sight. Before she made a move, she squatted down and quickly picked up the photo, and then hid it behind her.There is simply no three hundred taels of silver here.Something to do with her.Chu Ying flashed this intuition.Her voice suddenly felt dry, and Chu Ying spoke slowly and softly: Sister

Huihui, let me take a look.There's nothing interesting to see. Luo Hui spoke very fast and was obviously panicked. It's just a little messy and it's not important.If it's not important, why can't I watch it?Her rhetorical question was calm.let me see.she repeated.The girl's always gentle voice contained a hint of persistence, and Luo Hui could see her eyelashes trembling faster than usual, as if she had noticed something and was ready.She stretched out her hand, and her white palm turned quietly in front of her. The bright yellow long sleeves were slightly pulled up due to her movements, revealing a white wrist. She was so delicate that even the wrist bones on one side were particularly clear, and slender blood vessels that were either blue or purple could be seen clearly on her wrists.Luo Hui couldn't bear it.But Chu Ying's attitude was really firm.Even if I don't show it to her now, there are so many people in the company, so it's not necessarily possible to hide it completely.A lot of things flashed through her mind. After all kinds of hesitation, Luo Hui gritted her teeth and took out the photo behind her.The photo was put into the palm of her hand very gently, and Chu Ying heard the comfort in Luo Hui's voice:We know there must be a misunderstanding hereChu Ying slowly lowered her eyelashes and looked at the photo in her hand.My whole body suddenly became tense.They were photos of her and Xu Jisi on various occasions.In the car, in the movie theater, and in the unfamiliar park yesterday.One gets off the bus, the other enters the building, and the other gets on the elevator.Dense, intimate, misplaced.Part of the shot was blurry, but multiple angles were enough to show that it was her and Xu Jisi.Chu Ying's figure seemed to be trembling, but she turned over the pages one by one with an expressionless face. The surroundings were so silent that only the sound of photo paper scraping was heard.Luo Hui in front of her looked worried.She seemed to be aware of the glances quietly coming from all directions.Worrying, curious, complicated. But there are also some who are not friendly, scrutinizing, suspicious, and puzzled.I do not know how long it has been.She finally finished flipping through it and raised her eyelids with a slight tremble.Luo Hui became a little nervous for no reason: Yingying, these are all fake. I don't know who made the prank. It's really too much.it is true.There seemed to be a hint of hoarseness in the girl's voice. It seemed that her throat had never felt so dry before, and it hurt to speak.She continued: There is no misunderstanding.

Chapter 26 Rememberinglie26She thought that one day she would no longer be able to hide it.Perhaps one fine day in the future, the dispute between her and Xu Jisi will be completely resolved, and she can naturally and calmly talk about their past and say that they are actually friends.Or one day Luo Hui might come back to her senses and discover some details and come over to ask her in person, and she wouldn't hide it.The worst idea is that Xu Jisi is a bomb himself.

Maybe one day he suddenly gets sick and casually mentions it, and everyone will know about it.There are many possibilities, but nothing can stop the fire. She and Xu Jisi live so close together, there is no way they can avoid going in and out together.But these should never be exposed like this now, in such a way, even with an unknown humiliating nature.What kind of relationship would be brought to light in such a secretly photographed manner?What do you want to express by sending such photos to her company?Does it imply that there is an inappropriate relationship between her and Xu Jisi?Except for the unknown past experience, they are just Party A and Party B.I want to say that she got this role through her connections.Or do you want her to cause public outrage and criticism because of her ambiguous relationship with Party A?In fact, she has always known that there are people who are dissatisfied with her getting so many resources as a newcomer, but in the end, they are just a few people.Ever since Ling Ting heard about it, she had maintained an open-minded and studious attitude. Most of the people in Ling Ting were very friendly to her, and everyone was happy and happy on weekdays. So much so that when this happened, Chu Ying couldn't even have any doubts in her mind. face.I have no idea who I offended.Luo Hui has always said that she has a good personality, can talk, and is popular. She probably has a kind of temperament that makes people approachable. When chatting with her, she can't help but let go of the conversation, and she also She is indeed a good listener, so even now, many colleagues will talk to her if they really want to talk about something.She thought that she was very happy getting along with everyone in Lingcheng, and everyone's impression of her should be positive.These photos instantly broke the surface of harmony between them.Reality taught her a clear lesson: many things are not as harmonious as they appear.There was a pair or pairs of eyes staring at her in the darkness.This fact made Chu Ying feel cold all over.After she finished speaking, it seemed like even the wind outside the window stopped for a moment.Chu Ying seemed to blink when she saw that Luo Hui had not recovered from her words.Then his eyes widened in disbelief.and youLuo Hui almost blurted out, but her words suddenly came back to her senses in an instant.She obviously remembered the last time Xu Jisi came.Chu Ying held the photo tightly with her fingers and her eyelashes trembled.She felt very guilty for hiding it from Luo Hui last time.This is the reason why she cannot deny the authenticity when facing her and these photos now.It's true that I got in Xu Jisi's car, it's true that I went to the cinema with Xu Jisi, and it's true that we were together in the park.Getting off the bus, entering the building, and getting on the elevator are all real.How could she say without changing her face that this was fake and the person above was not her?Even if she says this, people who don't want to believe it won't believe it either.Although some of the pictures are blurry, people familiar with her can recognize her at a glance, and there is no possibility of AI changing her face.She knew a lot of people were listening.Everyone's eyes were completely blown away when she finished speaking. They were either surprised that she was so frank or shocked that the two of them really had a personal relationship.No one knew whether they had known each other for a long time or were connected because of the project. Everyone had different expressions. Some looked at each other, and each saw complicated emotions in the other's eyes.For most people, they only meet Xu Jisi once or twice.One time it was the official first arrival of that day, and there was a huge battle. Except for some people who were working in the shed at the time who might not have caught up, everyone else basically saw it.Another time, the day before yesterday at the KTV, he suddenly arrived.That day, we got a lot closer to each other, but everyone knew that there was still a big difference in identity. Everyone was drunk that day, and they may have lost some sense of boundaries. Later, when they sobered up, they still felt a little dazed. I really didn't expect Xu Ji. Si can play with them like this.Maybe it's just this once in life.Everyone thinks so.However, the photos I received today really shocked everyone.It's really unimaginable that there are people around me who can have a personal relationship with someone of such status and seem to be particularly close to him.When I recognized someone again, it turned out to be Chu Ying, who was always gentle and gentle and never overly aggressive.The sense of fragmentation and fragmentation of her personality suddenly emerged, and everyone's psychology was very complicated.The point is, the two of them didn't see any overlap at all.When we first met, didn't we introduce each other?Even at the KTV, I didn't see any clues.Could it be that it happened after the day before yesterday?At that time, everyone was so drunk that no one paid attention.Everyone had their own guesses, and their eyes drifted to the girl from time to time. She was slender but stood upright. Chu Ying wore a bright yellow dress today, and her exposed thin shoulders and slender neck were so white that they shone, but they were not as pale as her face at the moment.In the dead silence, Ling Tingyang walked out of the office with a cold face. His eyes passed over everyone, and he obviously knew what happened. Finally, he landed on the figure that was so fragile that it would be broken by the wind, and said calmly. Shouting: Chu Ying, come here.

Ling Tingyang actually didn't have much to tell her. He was half an insider, and he just wanted to pull her away from everyone's scrutiny and speculation.He had a hunch before that the relationship between the two would be discovered sooner or later.Without him, Xu Jisi's every move was too unabashed.In fact, his occasional glances had a trace of possessiveness that perhaps he was not even aware of, just like that day in the shed, under his words, he seemed to be idle, but his eyes casually glanced at him with a hint of possessiveness. The oppression of invasion.It was just like when he suddenly arrived the day before yesterday, and when his glance touched the person beside the girl, his eyes were secretly fierce.He was too proactive, and Chu Ying was too easily influenced.Anyone who is interested can find clues about the aura between them if they think about it for a moment.He didn't know who took the photo. Now that the matter was at this point, the key was to minimize the impact as much as possible.He took all the photos away immediately, but it was inevitable that some would be missed. He didn't expect Chu Ying to see them so soon.Although everyone has been warned not to chat nonsense, gossip is human nature, and an explicit prohibition cannot stop everyone from chatting in private. Even if they say nothing, the look in their eyes will still reveal their attitude.People's words are scary, and he is really worried that Chu Ying will affect his future work status.Ling Tingyang thought about organizational language:I will handle this matter well and will not let it continue to ferment or spread to you. You must adjust your mentality.It seemed that even her brain had become dull, Chu Ying only nodded slowly.Her long eyelashes were like the fluttering wings of a butterfly, and her little face was so pale that there was no trace of anger or grievance. There was an indescribable sense of brokenness.The girl was as quiet and docile as a clear and peaceful lake, but no one knew how much of a ruckus the rocks just dropped actually caused at the bottom of the lake.Ling Tingyang felt as if someone was tugging at her heart.Chu Ying was five years younger than him, and it was he who selected her out of the vast crowd. He has always done everything about her personally, and he has taught her what he has learned throughout his life step by step, and she is so talented that she does not need him to repeat herself. She can do what he basically says once.It was hard to say whether he had ever had any thoughts about her in the past.The girl is beautiful, tall, has outstanding abilities, high emotional intelligence, good personality, and always speaks warmly and softly. They even have common interests and careers, and have the same goals.At work, they hit it off right away, and they often know how the other person wants to feel just by looking at each other. This mental compatibility alone is enough to make her special.After work, Chu Ying probably regarded him as her older brother, and she would not shy away from too many things she encountered in life. Occasionally, when they sat down to eat together, she would also chat with him about interesting things in school.After all, he is just an ordinary normal man. In addition to spending time with her roommates at school, Chu Ying probably spends the most time with him at the company.It's almost inevitable that you'll have a crush on a girl like this.Friends have asked him several times whether it would be better if he took action sooner if he liked it.But he does have concerns.Office romance has never been a nice word, not to mention that she is still a junior who has only been in the industry for two years.He is afraid of causing criticism.But he couldn't give up such a good seedling to others or leave it behind.More importantly, he could actually see that Chu Ying had no feelings for him. To her, he was just a simple boss, or an eldest brother like a father.The emotions that arose in her since Xu Jisi appeared were things she had never felt towards him.He is not the kind of person who sticks to his side just to get some status.It was enough to have such a relationship, so he never expressed his attitude.After all, it was the girl he had been watching. For so many years, he had never seen her in such a broken moment. Ling Tingyang couldn't bear to look at her a second time.Ling Tingyang had many thoughts in her heart. After a long while, she sighed and said in an unbearable tone: Chu Ying.The girl looked up blankly.You should rest at home for a few days. He said.Chu Ying's eyes slowly returned to reality, and she instinctively wanted to refuse.There hasn't been much going on lately, and you just happened to be adjusting at home for a few days. I will do ideological work for other people in the company. You know, they are not bad in nature.Ling Tingyang spoke softly, trying to use soft words so as not to irritate her.The words Chu Ying wanted to refuse came to her lips. When she met Ling Tingyang's worried gaze, she opened her lips, remained silent for two seconds, and nodded very slowly.Her presence in the company will only remind those who see her of the photo, and may also affect the work efficiency of the entire company.Seeing her nod, Ling Tingyang breathed a sigh of relief unnoticeably.At this time, maybe it would be better to let her be quiet. There is no use in talking too much.Ling Tingyang asked her to rest in the office for a while before quietly going out.After going out, he called everyone for an emergency meeting. He repeatedly emphasized not to talk too much. After smashing all the photos, Ling Tingyang called the first few people who came to the company today to chat. Did they see anything strange? people.The company has monitoring systems, but as luck would have it, everyone didn't go to work yesterday, and the monitoring system broke down yesterday.When morning came, the photos were in sets on the table, wrapped in envelopes.I don't even know how the other party knew the password to the main gate.The office door was locked, so the photo was inserted directly through the crack in the door.Ling Tingyang even suspected for a moment that he was someone from within the company, but there was so much to know about this kind of thing. Not only did he have to know the relationship between Chu Ying and Xu Jisi, but he also had to know the specific address of Chu Ying's new home, and even spend money The employees who follow him all the time are so busy, who has such time?Did Chu Ying inadvertently provoke someone?Glancing at the slender figure who had been silent in the office, Ling Tingyang pinched his eyebrows with a headache.

Chu Ying stayed in the office for a long time. The office was Ling Tingyang's territory. No one would come in and out at will. She was able to think a lot quietly.That person was hiding, and she had no clue or any means, so she could only accept it all feebly.It's just ridiculous. She obviously didn't do anything shameful, but now she can only hide with a guilty conscience.No one can ignore the eyes of others.But no matter what they think, how can she explain it?Said that she and Xu Jisi are friendsIt's just a coincidence that we live in the same community, the same building, and the same floorHow do you explain his intimate act of buying her milk tea when we watched a movie together yesterday?Could it be true that he dragged her there and bought it for her on his own initiative?These words sounded ridiculous to her.If the person involved is not herself, she will feel that there is something between the two.Before going home yesterday, his helpless sigh seemed to still be echoing in his ears.It was hard for her to fantasize about anything anymore.His vague approach and specious words were all false, and those ambiguities and illusions were her own random thoughts.Only what he actually said and drew a clear line was true.She remembers it clearly.How could she explain these paradoxes that even she couldn't explain clearly? What's more, when she started to explain the self-evidence, there would only be a steady stream of questions. Not everyone had the same sense of proportion as Ling Tingyang.The point-to-point explanation is just an appetizer for more people that makes them want to keep digging.Ling Tingyang was right, it was best for her to rest at home for a few more days.At the very least, when everyone in the company becomes less enthusiastic, they can look at these things more rationally.When Chu Ying left the office, everyone was planning to go to dinner.Probably because she was warned again by Ling Tingyang, everyone's eyesightened a lot, but some people still greeted her as usual.Chu Ying smiled stiffly.Luo Hui heard from Ling Tingyang that she wanted to go back to rest first, and walked forward with a complicated expression. Seeing that her face was still pale, she gently patted her shoulder: It's such a big deal, don't think too much.Chu Ying raised her eyes blankly, paused, and said in a slightly hoarse voice: Sister Huihui, I didn't hide it from you on purpose.Maybe she didn't owe anyone else, but she definitely owed Luo Hui.Luo Hui was truly worried about her that day.Luo Hui paused and sighed: These are your private matters, and there is no need for you to tell me.In fact, she was a little angry at first, and some unknown words that she had reacted to later became clear at this moment, and her weird emotions at that time were immediately explained.For a moment, I even felt like I was being tricked by her.But soon seeing her pale face, Luo Hui calmed down again.From her understanding, Chu Ying is not that kind of person.She must have something to hide.Let's not talk about the relationship between the two. Whether they are close or distant, if it were her, she would not be able to openly tell someone about her interpersonal relationship when she meets him.It's normal to have a little privacy of your own.It's normal not to want to say it.Luo Hui saw that her eyes were suddenly red at this moment when she saw that she had been maintaining her strong emotions without much ups and downs.Feeling panicked, Luo Hui quickly coaxed: Hey, don't cry.The feeling of guilt spread completely at this moment, Chu Ying suppressed her emotions, and an uncontrollable cry escaped from her voice: I'm sorry, Sister Huihui.She didn't even know how much emotion was contained in her voice.Is there any grievance and helplessness caused by the various looks that people inadvertently cast on her, is there any worry and frustration caused by someone's indifference, or more, those things that are usually hidden in the heart and have never been able to be vented? emotion.It's nothing, Luo Hui comforted, don't care too much about other people's opinions. These people are just gossips. Your relationship with others is your business and none of their business.Chu Ying lowered her voice and nodded, saying I know.We all know these principles, but it is difficult to control our thoughts.When Chu Ying took the subway back, it seemed that their chaotic and muffled discussions were still in her mind.I really can't tell. He looks quiet, but I didn't expect to do something so bold.I don't want to think too much about it, but Chu Ying has indeed always had a lot of resources. She was brought back by Brother Yang without any foundation. It must not be without reason.People are very talented, what can you say. If you are really curious, why don't you just ask her yourself? She is very easy to talk to.Why didn't you ask? Didn't you think much about it when you looked at the photo?Okay, you guys, Brother Yang said no discussion is allowed, why are you still chatting?I'm not telling you, the person who took the photo really has enough time. Isn't it scary to have to keep an eye on people for so long without losing their privacy? Chu Ying is usually a nice person, but who hates her so much?Just like what Ling Tingyang and Luo Hui said, everyone was just gossiping to a large extent. They may not actually want to hurt her, but she really couldn't help but pay attention to these words.When leaving the subway station, she passed by an unmanned vending machine. The messy thoughts lingering in Chu Ying's mind paused for a moment, and she suddenly stood still for a long time.Staring at the drinks and wine in the freezer for a long time, she walked home with a few cans of wine in her arms.

She just fried an egg in the evening. She didn't have much appetite, so she had instant noodles that took five minutes to make for dinner.Then I stayed on the sofa for a long time.I was supposed to take a shower, so the lights in the room and bathroom were turned on.But after sitting for a while, she suddenly felt very tired.There was no light on in the living room, only the light in the room pouring in a corner of light.She suddenly thought about how she was afraid of the dark when she first came to Lizhou.Strange people, a strange place, and a strange home.She will still be in a trance when she returns home. Is this where she will live forever?Later, I don' t know when it started. The light was too bright and I couldn' t sleep. I had to turn off the light.It would be best if there was no light in the entire room.Chu Ying was still free to think wildly.Until the phone suddenly started vibrating.After a while, she picked up the phone belatedly.Clicking on the message, I saw a message from Xu Jisi, asking if she was at home.He probably doesn't know about the photo yet.It might not matter to him at all.Chu Ying stared at it for a long time, then slowly adjusted her posture and rested her chin lightly on her knees, so that her heavy head could be supported.He would ask her if she was at home, and she must not be home either.Otherwise, we will come directly to the door.She thought like this, wrapped her slender arms around her legs, clicked her fingers, and typed slowly, replying to him: Not here.There was silence for a long time, and there was no news for a while.Chu Ying then turned off the screen of her phone again.I don't know that downstairs, leaning against the car, the man with a clear and cold face slowly lowered his head.On the phone, the word "hair is not from" appears in black fonts that are a bit dazzling.The man's slightly curved lips slowly flattened, and he looked up at the brightly lit window with an expressionless expression.lie.